THE
LANGUAGE
OF BEASTS

"*Atmospheric stories that kept me awake, reading in the dark, and getting more and more creeped out. Well worth a read, though expect them to linger in the brain long afterwards!*"

Aliette de Bodard
multi award-winning author of *The House of Shattered Wings*
and *The House of Binding Thorns*

"*With these consistently surprising myths and visions, Mr. Oliver has joined the movement resurrecting a very English form of fantastical short story. In the spirit of Machen and M.R. James he has filled his houses, bars, gardens and churches with phantasmagorical creatures both earthly and spiritual, and has let them loose in the lives of ordinary people. These are tales of old religions and new beliefs, where each of us must find our place between heaven and hell.*"

Christopher Fowler
author of the best-selling *Bryant and May* series

"*I met Jon Oliver as an editor first, and didn't realize what amazing chops he had as a writer. What I love about his stories are how he effortlessly uses the tropes and tools of genre – monsters, angels and demons, myths of all sorts – to tell heartfelt stories about people who feel absolutely real. This is a terrific collection.*"

Daryl Gregory
World Fantasy Award-winning author of
Spoonbenders and *Afterparty*

"The Language of Beasts *is grim and guttural: yet beneath its surface is a whisper of poignant humanity. So listen closely, friends. You won't be disappointed.*"

Helen Marshall

World Fantasy Award-winning author of *Hair Side, Flesh Side* and *The Migration*

"*A good editor doesn't necessarily make a good writer, but thankfully Jonathan Oliver sits more than comfortably in both camps. Using well-crafted prose, a thoughtful approach to genre and a questing imagination, he has invested these stories with wit, wisdom and passion.*"

Gary McMahon

award-winning author of the *Concrete Grove* trilogy

"*Jon Oliver is a prodigy of quiet personal horror. The tension and fear in* The Language of Beasts *sizzles in the background, constantly evoking electric distress.*"

Weston Ochse

Bram Stoker Award-winning author of the *Task Force Ombra* and *Seal Team 666* series

"*A collection of the weird and disturbing, plumbing the depths of human and inhuman nature.*"

Adrian Tchaikovsky

best-selling author of the *Shadows of the Apt* series

"Jonathan Oliver has an eye for the absurdity of life – but also an ear for the rhythms of how people behave, and a heart that ensures you have reason to care. There are dark stories here, but what distinguishes Oliver is how empathetic he is – the situations may be cruel, but the characters are treated with a rare generosity that is always sincere. It sometimes hurts to read tales like this, but it's a good hurt – and once you start, it's very hard to stop. This is an outstanding collection, by degrees wild and uncanny, tender and true."

Robert Shearman
multi-award winning author of *Remember Why You Fear Me*
and *We All Hear Stories in the Dark*

"Jonathan Oliver blends a magical, imaginative brew with ingredients of the spiritual and the everyday."

Stephen Volk
BAFTA Award-winning creator of *Ghostwatch* and author

"The titles of these stories alone are worth entry, but Jonathan Oliver's eye for an attractive word or two goes deeper than that. The Language of Beasts *is the language of beauty. Brutal and muscular, earthy and menacing, but beautiful all the same. Here is a writer with talents beyond his years."*

Conrad Williams
multi-award winning author of *Sonata of the Dead*
and *Dust and Desire*

"In The Language of Beasts *Jonathan Oliver has pulled together his own blend of fantasy, horror, and science fiction elements to create a body of work which is both unique and highly personal. Spiritual concerns are of heightened importance in these tales, as are the pull and gravity of the past and tradition on characters struggling to define themselves. These are stories populated by angels and wanderers, demons and animals, churches and caves and suburban enclaves. Sympathetic magic figures prominently, as does English folk horror. The fact that even the more science fictional pieces reflect the spiritual quest and historical influence evident in the fantasy and horror stories impresses me with the strength and originality of Oliver's voice."*

Steve Rasnic Tem

World Fantasy Award-winning author of *The Man on the Ceiling*,

Deadfall Hotel and *Blood Kin*

"Jonathan Oliver has a fantastic imagination and an ability to write gripping stories that range from the exotic realms of science fiction to closely observed domestic horror. But what impresses me most about these stories is their humanity. This is an author who never loses sight of the human aspect in every situation, no matter how bizarre. His characters are real, breathing, feeling, hurting individuals the reader simply has to care about."

Lisa Tuttle

John W. Campbell Award-winning author of *The Silver Bough*

and *The Somnambulist and the Psychic Thief*

The Language

of Beasts

by

Jonathan Oliver

BLACK
SHUCK
BOOKS

Black Shuck Books

www.blackshuckbooks.co.uk

First published in Great Britain in 2020 by

Black Shuck Books

Kent, UK

Versions of the following stories have previously appeared in print:

'White Horse' in *The Alchemy Book of Urban Mythic* (Alchemy Press, 2013)

'The Day or The Hour' in *Pandemonium: Stories of the Apocalypse* (Jurassic London, 2011)

'Don't You Like the Bird Man?' in *BFS Journal* (Spring 2012)

'Tea and Sympathy' in *Horror Express 3* (April 2013)

'Peter and the Invisible Shark' in *Sharkpunk* (Snowbooks, 2015)

'High Church' in *La Femme Fatale* (NewCon Press, 2014)

'Raise the Beam High' in *A Town Called Pandemonium* (Jurassic London, 2012)

'Star Crossed' in *Shakespeare vs. Cthulhu* (Snowbooks, 2016)

'Control' in *Game Over* (Snowbooks, 2015)

'The Horror Writer' in *Terror Tales of London* (Gray Friar Press, 2013)

'Baby 17' in *BFS Journal* (#11, 2014)

'The River' in *BFS Journal* (Autumn 2013)

'In these Rooms, these Houses' in *Respectable Horror* (Fox Spirit Books, 2017)

Typeset in Adobe Caslon Pro

Cover and interior design © WHITEspace, 2020

www.white-space.uk

Cover and interior art by Simon Parr

www.pyeparr.com

Acknowledgements

The last few years have been somewhat chaotic. I left my role as a fiction editor to have a try at being a non-fiction editor, only to return to the world of fiction, albeit as a freelancer this time. I couldn't have kept writing, or kept going at all, without the help and support of some remarkable people who helped me keep the faith and keep at it. So:

Ali, Lily and Maia, my remarkable sister Anna, Mum and Dad, Chris, Sam and Elaine, Will, Nina and Donna – for love, moral support (and spiritual guidance), for refuge, and beer (and G&T), and much needed time away.

Steve Shaw – for taking on this beast in the first place.

Simon Parr – for the bloody amazing cover.

Sarah Lotz, Rebecca Levene, Gary McMahon, Joan Geddes, David Yates – who down the years have often been the first to read my stories and have provided invaluable advice, encouragement and support.

Writer and publishing pals, Christopher Fowler, James Lovegrove, Steve Rasnic Tem, Adrian Tchaikovsky, Helen Marshall, Malcolm Devlin, Weston Ochse, Lisa Tuttle, Daryl Gregory, Stephen Volk, Alison Littlewood, Conrad Williams, Rio Youers, Rob Shearman, Yoon Ha Lee, Tom Lloyd, Aliette de Bodard, Lavie Tidhar, Gareth L. Powell, Nina Allan, Dave Hutchinson, Derek Künsken, David Moore, Simon Parr, Keith Richardson, Rob Power,

Lydia Gittins, Simon Morden, Simon Bestwick, Jason Arnopp, Megan Kerr, Michael Rowley, Mike Maddox, A.F. Harrold, Rehema Njambi, Johnny Mains and the many many others that have made working in genre fiction such a joy. If I missed you out feel free to track me down at a future convention where I shall provide recompense in the form of beer, or a beverage of your choice.

Jonathan Green, Dickon Springate, Peter Coleborn, Jan Edwards, Kate Coe, Paul Finch, Jared Shurin, Anne Perry, K.A. Laity, Adele Wearing, Ellen Crosháin and Jenny Barber, Ian Whates, Sarah Newton, Guy Adams – those fine editors who agreed to publish many of these stories.

James Tolley, Owen Springer, Peter Mooney, Craig Bardsley and Sam Stinton – fellow nerds and cultists. Praise Cthulhu!

INTRODUCTION
by SARAH LOTZ

I FIRST GOT to know Jonathan Oliver when he invited me to submit a story to an anthology he was putting together. I'd heard of him of course – he's a legend in the genre publishing industry, although he's way too modest to admit it (in fact, if you say this to him he'll shout you down, and as an ex stand-up comedian, he'll make you laugh while doing so). In his career he's launched and nurtured the careers of countless writers, including Yoon Ha Lee, Silvia Moreno-Garcia, Simon Bestwick, Steve Rasnic Tem and Gareth L.Powell, and having been edited by him, I know he's that rarest of things – a great editor.

He's also a great writer.

Like the best stories, none of the pieces in this anthology can be taken at face value. Each one has a delicious undercurrent running beneath it, a subtext that is never heavy-handed and always surprising. It goes without saying that when you're writing a short story, especially in the horror or speculative fiction genres, you have to add another ingredient – believability. The reader has to buy into what you're selling, and Jon excels at this. He's also fearless with his choice of subject matter. In "White Horse" he tackles depression and the hopelessness and guilt felt by those close to someone suffering from it. The powerfully original "The Day or the Hour" dissects issues of faith and what happens when it's tested to the max (it also contains one of my favourite lines in the anthology: 'The trumpets called again and there was a rising stench of fear, of perspiration and piss – the smell of which, perversely, reminded Paul of one of the more spiritual moments of his ministry.') In "Don't You Like the Bird Man?" the cruel legacy of abuse and its far-reaching, insidious consequences are inventively and sensitively explored. In "Tea and Sympathy" a woman finds a unique – and gruesome – way to deal with her grief and loss. Loss of a different kind forms the core of the mind-bending "Turn", as a parent makes the ultimate sacrifice to save his missing child. In "Peter and the Invisible Shark" childhood monsters both real and imagined take the fore, and sharks feature inventively in "The Sea Between the Stars", which skewers superbly the monstrousness of colonialism and genocide (Jon clearly watched *Jaws* as a kid). The best kind of humour – the *dark* kind – also weaves its way through the anthology, especially in the ferociously witty "High Church" with its laugh-out-loud surprise of an ending, and in "The Language of Beasts", which is so well written, witty and visceral you'll never look at a bacon sandwich in quite the same way again. In "These Rooms, These Houses" the mundane and the weird collide, and in "The Horror Writer" – a story that hints at a darker side of inspiration, imagination, writing and publishing – even the relatively innocuous Rupert Bear is given a sinister and unforgettable slant.

In short, the stories are entertaining, heart breaking, funny, crazy, original, and imaginative and if you're reading them for the first time, I envy you. You're in for a treat.

Sarah Lotz
Best-selling author of *The Three, Day Four,*
The White Road **and** *Missing Person.*

WHITE HORSE

-1-

IMOGEN USED TO be frightened of horses.

When she was six, her father's houseboat had been moored beside a field that was home to a vast shire horse. On nights when the river ran slow and calm, Imogen could hear the creature breathing; could feel, through her body, the fall of its hooves onto the soft earth.

Trying to soothe her fears, her father had introduced her to the horse.

"Here, give him an apple. He'll soon be your friend."

But when she held out her trembling hand, and those fat rubbery lips parted to reveal vast chisel-like teeth the colour of old ivory, Imogen had squealed and ducked behind her father.

"Give over. He'll not hurt you."

The horse snorted and stamped, its eyes rolling in anger at being denied the treat, before it thundered away.

Imogen had insisted they move the boat after that.

Sometime later, when the horse and the nightmares it had inspired were a fast-fading memory, her father had taken her down to the coast for the May Day celebrations.

They made their costumes for the event together; Imogen's father displaying a nimbleness with needle and thread that she had never expected. It was the first time in a long time that he had spoken about her mother, how she had once been his Queen of May.

Imogen giggled as her father lathered his face in green make-up. She stood with her arms draped loosely around his neck as he tied ribbons onto her white dress. She thought then that things were perhaps not so bad; that they might be alright after all.

She didn't know what to expect. She certainly hadn't been prepared for the crowds that thronged the town; the clash of colours and the clamour of drums and whistles and pipes. Imogen gripped her father's hand for all she was worth as they danced down towards the sea – he bellowing a song about a maid and a green man.

As they neared the harbour a cheer went up from somewhere behind them, and there was a disturbance as people parted to let something through.

At first all Imogen could see was what looked like the swish of a huge black skirt. There was the tinkling of bells and a sound like two planks of wood being repeatedly slapped together.

The crowd parted before her and the swirling, clacking nightmare thing that had come rushing down the hill to meet Imogen came to a sudden stop.

Atop a rumpled black cloak covered in multi-coloured rags and tiny silver bells sat the grinning wooden skull of a horse. It eyes had been painted a vivid, sparkling blue and its lips were scarlet. The nightmare was taller than any man, and as it leaned over her it opened and closed its jaws – *clack, clack, clack.*

She backed away and reached out for her father, but he wasn't there, and all she could see was the horse and the grinning faces of the crowd.

The wooden horse took a step closer, and then another. A giggling boy darted from the crowd to tear one of the ribbons from Imogen's dress.

"Hobby horse! Hobby horse! Hobby horse!" he shouted as he fled with his prize.

The horse reared, its jaw working maniacally as though it were laughing, and Imogen ran.

She skidded on the cobbles of the vertiginous street as she rushed towards the sea – the *clack, clack, clacking* of the horse sounding as though it were no further away than the nape of her neck.

She was soon beyond the crowd and nearing the docks, the nightmare snapping at her heels as her father ran towards her, waving his arms and shouting at her to get out of the way.

Imogen turned and flung herself away from the swirling skirts of the hobby horse as her father slammed into it, sending it over the edge of the dock and into the sea.

She didn't see the sodden, laughing man swimming away from the sinking effigy. All she saw were those hideous painted jaws, opening and closing as they slowly sank below the surface. Imogen was barely aware of being hoisted onto the shoulders of the crowd and processed through the town beside her father. It was only later that she realised he had known what was coming for her all along, and she would have been angry had it not been for the fact that when it really mattered, he had been there for her.

THE LITTLE RITUALS that Imogen's father performed had always been a part of their life together, so it never occurred to her to think of them as magic. It was only when she casually mentioned to a friend at school that her father protected her from bad dreams by burning herbs as he sang that she found out that's what it was.

"Witchcraft," the school chaplain told her, "is very dangerous indeed, and not to be toyed with. Perhaps I might have a chat with your father?"

But when Imogen had put across the possibility, her father had laughed so hard that he had rocked their boat.

"Witchcraft? He can fuck off. No one's called me a witch before. Imogen, listen, magic is not something to be scared of, or ashamed of. It's what keeps us together. What keeps us safe."

But it didn't always.

Imogen had tried to help her father through depression on countless occasions, but each time was harder than the last, and it wasn't long before the salves and the chants and the prayers were replaced with the bottle.

After she left school, things became worse. There were few jobs available and in the periods when Imogen was employed, she often found that, despite her best attempts, she didn't get along with her colleagues. One job had gone from bad to worse when a particularly nasty woman had snapped "Fucking gypo!" at her when she had dropped a tray of pasties.

That summer – when she needed him the most, when the work had dried up – her father found time for one last spell.

"SOMETIMES, WHEN WE look into the past, we can find the answers we're looking for," he said, as he helped Imogen over the fence and into the field.

"How so?"

"Oh, I don't mean your present past, so to speak. I mean the many pasts stretching out behind you, into the infinite."

Had he not been sober for the best part of a week, Imogen would have thought it was the drink talking, but her father was deadly serious. They had come to Uffington because he said he had something to show her.

Imogen looked out over the Berkshire downs as a light breeze played across the meadow. She thought she could see their boat from here. In the distance she could just make out the cooling towers of Didcot Power Station – giant egg cups, her father had called them.

"You may be suffering now, Imogen. But you've suffered many times in many lives."

"Wow. Thanks. That's reassuring."

"You can learn from the suffering of your past selves, learn to overcome your pain, as those who you *were* did before you."

This was far beyond the simple homely magic that her father usually practiced, but Imogen could see that this was important to him, so she shut up and listened.

Her father began to talk more animatedly now, his breath barely catching up with his words as they climbed the hill.

"You are a princess, Imogen. Or rather you were. I have consulted the cards on this. I've spent many hours in meditation, and it's all pointing to this one past life as the key. You were a princess many centuries ago, part of a tribe that lived here. The earthworks that crown the hill above us were your home. It was a harsh, isolated existence. Though you could see your entire kingdom spread out before you, you were deeply unhappy, because you were forbidden to leave the fort. You would spend many hours watching wild horses galloping up and down the shallow valley at the foot of the hill, wishing that one of them would bear you away. It broke your father's heart to see you so sad, but he could not permit you to leave the security of the fort. Your tribe had many enemies and the daughter of the king was a prize eagerly sought. Your father decided to create for you a gift. Into the chalk of the hillside he carved the likeness of a vast horse to serve as evidence of his love and as the totem of your tribe. All in the plain below could look up and see the white horse – a symbol of strength, and the confirmation of a father's love."

By this time they had reached the crest of the hill and the breeze had become a persistent wind, bearing a winter chill. Imogen zipped up her jacket as her father paused to light a cigarette.

"And now *your* father – that's me by the way, hello – is giving the horse to you. My lady," he said with a sweep of his arm, "your mount awaits you."

At her feet, Imogen could see the chalk lines flowing through the cropped grass. When she tilted her head and took a few steps back, she could finally see the whole picture.

"Well?"

"Thank you, Dad. It's beautiful."

He gathered her up in his arms, enveloping her in the smell of tobacco and warm leather.

"I love you, lass. No matter what; I love you."

THAT NIGHT, THE river ran slow and calm and Imogen woke to the sound of hooves pounding wet earth. Fear creeping through her, she opened the curtains of her cabin window. They had moored beside a field, and galloping through the pasture was a white horse.

Imogen crept from the boat, the dew-wet grass tickling her feet as she approached the beast. The horse had come to a halt by the fence. She held out her hand and it lowered its head to her palm, its breath steaming through her fingers as it nuzzled her. The sudden rasp of the horse's rough tongue against her flesh made her jump, but instead of running into the night, she laughed.

When the horse dipped its head and pawed the ground with a hoof, she understood. Hitching up her nightdress, she climbed over the fence and swung herself atop her mount, as easily and as smoothly as if she had been riding her whole life.

Together they thundered down the ancient roads; the pathways that sung with the bright magic of the moon and knew the footsteps of the living and the dead. Through the dreams of those who had cursed her with cruel words and unkind thoughts they rode, turning them into nightmares from which Imogen's enemies woke gasping – their minds reeling with the image of that terrible elongated skull and those wildly rolling eyes.

Imogen laughed in delight and with each hoofbeat she found herself growing stronger, more herself.

When she awoke – soaked nightdress clinging to her, feet caked in mud, and the sweet smell of horse still in her nostrils – Imogen realised that she was no longer afraid. The white horse – the symbol of her tribe – became for her a symbol of personal strength; an assurance that she was loved.

It wasn't long afterwards that Imogen finally landed a job she liked. Working in care allowed her to make use of the small spells that her father had taught her, though none of her clients would have recognised what she did for them as magic.

Years later, after she had moved out and taken charge of her own life, Imogen would grow to regret that she had not put as much effort into caring for her father as she had those men and women with whom she worked. He still used magic, but now that Imogen was no longer there with him, his spells were less about protecting their own little world than they were about constructing a fantasy into which he lost himself. His drinking had increased, and though Imogen did what she could, it took its toll.

He died penniless, virtually friendless, surrounded by the clutter of arcane knick-knacks. Imogen considered giving him something of a Viking funeral – setting fire to the houseboat before freeing it from its moorings – but in the end she took the option of the impersonal and brief service at the crematorium, followed by tea and cake with family so distant she wasn't even sure of their names.

Even with her father gone, Imogen still dreamed of the white horse. And when she truly needed him, he came to her call.

-2-

THE CAR SHUDDERED as they neared the crest of the steep hill. Steve trembled with barely suppressed rage, shifting back into first gear. Behind them, a queue was forming, and as they were forced onto the verge by a tractor coming in the opposite direction, the driver of the Mini who had been tailgating them most of the way up leaned on his horn.

"Oh, go fuck yourself, you hipster wanker!" Steve yelled, and Imogen laid a hand on his arm, giving him a look that told him to stay in the car.

The old Steve wouldn't have. The old Steve would have dragged the driver of the Mini from his vehicle and beaten him senseless.

Eventually they were on the move. Steve slotted the ancient Nissan into the last available parking space and shot a victorious glance at the Mini driver.

Imogen had hoped that a visit to the White Horse at Uffington would bring a little calm to their lives. But she had forgotten that it was the school holidays, and as it was the first dry day in August for weeks, many other people had clearly had had the same idea.

She glared at a group of rowdy children as they raced to the top of the hill, their hands clutched around rapidly melting ice-cream.

"Little shits," she muttered. "Trampling all over my horse."

Steve laughed. "It's hardly *your* horse, dear."

"No, really Steve it is."

He laughed again, before he saw that she was being serious.

The horse itself had been recently tended to, the grass neatly cut back to the chalk, the borders crisp. Imogen spread a picnic blanket on the ground and gestured for Steve to sit.

He hesitated, a look of doubt crossing his face, but eventually relented. Steve was new to magic. "What is that?" he said. "It smells like bloody Dettol!"

"Herb-infused oil. The aromatics are supposed to help you focus."

"Okay, fine. Let's not be long about this, eh? People are starting to stare."

Imogen breathed the words of the spell. She called on her mount to accept another rider; to carry the man she loved away from the storm.

"Sorry, no. This is no good." Steve got to his feet, reaching for his cigarettes and rubbing the smear of oil from his forehead.

It wasn't just his impatience or embarrassment, Steve was right – Imogen had reached out and found nothing. No, that wasn't quite true. There had been a sense of rejection. And then Imogen realised that the white horse truly was *her*s. No matter how much she loved Steve, he was not of her tribe. This wasn't her gift to give.

"I'm sorry," she said, gathering him to her. "You're right. This was a silly idea. Let's go find a nice pub for lunch instead, yeah?"

"Now that sounds like the sort of magic I like."

IMOGEN HAD MET Steve in a park almost five years after her father had died. She had been sitting on a bench, reading a book in her lunch break. Steve sat down next to her and lit a cigarette.

"Sorry if this seems a bit out of turn, but that's not really the sort of book I'd expect you to be reading," he said.

Imogen thought about being offended, but he had a kind face and there was no malice or mischief in his gaze.

"Oh, really?" she said, "and bearing in mind we've only just met, what kind of a book *would* you expect to see me reading?"

"I'm not sure. It's just that you look too intelligent for, well, *that*."

"I wanted to see what all the fuss was about."

"And can you?"

"Not really."

"Steve, by the way."

"Imogen, by the way."

Steve finished his cigarette.

"Well, that's my break pretty much over, so see you, Steve." Imogen said, getting up.

"Yeah, see you later."

The following day Imogen returned to her usual bench. There was no Steve, but there was a book, wrapped in clear plastic and taped to the wood. *Imogen*, had been written onto the wrapper in marker. Inside the book there was a note:

This is probably more the sort of the thing – followed by Steve's phone number.

He was right; it *was* more her sort of thing. However, Imogen waited until she had finished reading the book before she called him.

She made sure that their first date was in a busy bar. It wasn't that she thought Steve would try anything untoward; it was just that she didn't want to take any risks with a man she had met only once.

"That's not the sort of thing I usually do, you know" he said. "Talking to strange women in parks."

"Strange? Thanks very much."

"No... I mean... Oh, bugger."

"Take a deep breath. In through the nose, out through the mouth. That's it. Now, start again."

After only a handful of dates, Imogen found that she had fallen in love.

Steve was damaged, but then so many people were, and she had a lot of experience in dealing with damaged people. He was kind and quick-witted when brought out of his shell; unpredictable, in a good way. Steve found it hard to hold down any job, mainly due to his severe depression. He also had anger issues, but they rarely manifested against anyone other than himself. The first time they made love, Steve had insisted on keeping his T-shirt on, and Imogen had thought that odd, until his sleeves had ridden up and she had seen the scars.

Steve had been out of work for a year when they started dating, and though he was clearly so unwell, the benefit system was increasingly making life financially difficult for him.

"I can't do this, Imogen," he said, after yet another assessment meeting. "If it's all on the inside, and they can't see it, they just figure it doesn't exist. Maybe I should fucking cut a leg off, or something. Fuck it! I just want someone to take me away from all this bullshit."

THE RITUAL AT the White Horse had failed. Her mount had refused to carry Steve. Imogen realised that she should have known; her link to the horse was just too strong, but she had been so desperate to help the man she loved that she would have tried anything.

Steve tolerated magic but he certainly didn't hold any faith in its results. It was just something Imogen did, as far as he was concerned. Imogen, however, knew how important magic had been, not just in her life, but in the lives of those she worked with. The small enchantments that she wove into her therapy had most certainly benefited her clients, even if they hadn't realised it at the time.

If her white horse would not accept Steve, then she would just have to create a mount for him that would. A fresh ritual was required.

The house they shared looked out upon a steep hillside, an old railway embankment at the top of which stood a row of allotments. Imogen had never been much of a gardener, though she kept the lawn and its borders in decent enough trim, enough not to draw the scorn of the neighbours, anyway. As she looked out on their garden, Imogen realised that what she was about to do might draw more than a few comments.

One afternoon, when Steve was out of the house, battling with ATOS, she experimented on a patch of ground with a trowel. Beneath the grass was chalky soil; it wasn't quite the same brilliant white as the horse at Uffington, but it would have to suffice.

She worked between sessions with her clients while Steve was out of the house, or ensconced in the lounge in front of the TV. Imogen kept the patch of ground where she worked covered by a tarpaulin. This Steve did notice, and when he asked about it she told him that they were having the lawn treated and that the chemicals involved were sensitive to sunlight. It was a bit of a stretch, but he bought it.

It took her two weeks, and at one point she had to go out and buy some turf to cover up her mistakes, but eventually her gift to Steve was ready. As she looked down upon her work, she felt an affinity with the ancient artist who had made the horse at Uffington, though she doubted he had used weed killer. Imogen had focused all of her love for Steve into this horse, and all her hopes for everything they could be together.

She wanted the reveal to be perfect, so that night she cooked them a special meal. The art of cooking was something of a ritual in itself and as she fried the steaks she recalled her father reciting a beautiful poem over a thick ragout. He had done it to make her laugh, but there had been a purpose, a power, to his words.

She was almost tempted to hurry Steve as he ate. The sun was setting and it was vital that the light be just right. When Steve reached for the bottle, she stilled his hand. "There's something outside I want you to see."

"What?"

"Just put down that down and follow me, okay?"

The evening was full of the scents of cut grass and turned earth. Above them, at the top of the embankment, people quietly toiled on their own patches of land. The edge of the sun had not yet touched the roof of their house and it bathed the garden in a soft, amber glow. Ignoring the midges dancing around her arms, Imogen gestured to the tarpaulin.

"Grab that top edge and help me roll this up – gently though."

When Steve saw what was beneath the sheet, he frowned.

"What did you do? Why have you torn up the lawn?"

"No, no… you're not seeing it properly. Come and stand with me at the bottom of the hill and then you will."

She took his hand as they stood together.

"Oh…oh, it's a…" he said

"Yes?"

"A horse."

She could have leapt for joy. "Steve, it's *your* horse. It's your mount – a symbol of my love and a sign of your inner-strength."

"I don't understand."

"Meditate on this with me, and tonight he will come for you and bear you upon his back. And things will get better, Steve. They did for me."

"Sorry, but have you lost your mind? And how much, how fucking much, do you think this is going to cost to put right? We have *no* money, Imogen. I tolerate a lot of your airy-fairy bullshit because I love you, but with this you've gone too far."

Steve marched back into the house, slamming the kitchen door so hard that a crack shot up the pane of glass in its frame.

Imogen looked at her horse, which really didn't look all that much like a horse, and wept.

-3-

THAT NIGHT, THE horse came not for Steve, but her.

Imogen was awoken by a sound like someone snapping bundles of dried twigs. Moonlight shone through the thin curtains, and when she drew them aside, the moon was perfectly framed, sitting dead centre in the upper pane. Its light highlighted what was happening in the garden with startling clarity.

The horse that Imogen had made was pulling itself up out of the earth, its bones crackling like ice as they formed themselves from the inadequate ground. It rose on legs that seemed too thin to support it, and perhaps they were, because it screeched as it tottered forward. Its head was little more than a distorted, grinning skull and Imogen gasped as it opened and closed its mouth – *clack clack clack*.

She turned to look at the bed, but Steve was fast asleep, and she didn't want to wake him – not to this.

Imogen hastily put on her dressing gown and hurried to meet the horse.

When Imogen opened the back door, she saw that the horse had given itself a more substantial form in the time it had taken her to descend the stairs. Earth had given it bones, but the discarded tarpaulin had given it flesh; its tail was the broken end of a broom and its eyes were two dented tin plant pots. The pantomime horse that lurched towards her should have been comical, but when it lowered its head, seeking her hand, Imogen flinched back with a gasp. It whickered at her terror. Close to, she could hear it breathing – a hollow wheeze that sounded like the wind whistling through a vast cave. She looked to either side, fearful that the racket the beast was making would wake her neighbours, but both houses remained shrouded in darkness.

The horse had her against the wall now, its tarpaulin skin snapping in a sharp wind that seemed to have risen from nowhere. Even with her heart in her mouth, and panic surging through her, Imogen managed to hold out a steady hand. With a screech that she felt deep in the pit of her stomach, the horse reared back; its hooves struck sparks from the ground as it landed. Imogen realised that this thing she had made was far too dangerous to leave in the world. There was no way she was going to allow Steve to ride the horse – the love and hope that she had poured into it had become soured somehow, making it into a nightmarish puppet of a thing. No, this was her creation and so she would be the one to ride it.

As soon as she had this thought, the horse stopped its stamping and snorting and lowered its head once more.

When she straddled its back, Imogen expected the horse to crumble beneath her, so fragile did it seem. Instead, the rough cloth of the tarpaulin moved like flesh as it turned away from the house; behind her she could hear the soft swish of its tail.

Imogen reached down to pat the horse's flank, whispering soothing sounds into one of its cloth ears. As soon as she touched it, the beast was off – clearing the back fence and pounding through the allotments beyond. Though Imogen shook with the thunder of hooves, the horse's passage left no mark upon the earth.

A savage wind caught her dressing gown and whipped it away, leaving her naked and clinging to the horse's neck. Imogen, however, felt no cold, only an exhilarating rush of liberation.

They followed a dual carriageway as it carved its way through the countryside; the cars that passed them no more than gentle whispers and smudges of light. The low moon ushered forth a blanket of frost from the land, revealing the ancient pathways; shadows walked upon them, some distinctly human-shaped, others most definitely not. Waiting for a break in the flow of moonlit figures, Imogen turned her horse onto the midnight road.

All sense of movement abruptly ceased and she urged the horse on with a gentle nudge from her heels. After a brief moment of confusion, she realised that they *were* moving – faster than they had been before, the landscape rising and falling around them like a verdant sea; her mount's hooves a silent blur.

Imogen hadn't been sure of where they were going, but when she saw a vast hill rising in the distance like a whale breaching the surface, she realised that there could only ever have been one destination.

The White Horse blazed from the hillside, its graceful curves alive with the promise of movement and power. The moment she saw it, Imogen couldn't help but think of her father – how his gift had saved her, though he had been unable to save himself. The raggedy, weird thing that lurched beneath her was much like he had been: a creature full of good intentions, but one ultimately broken.

Her mount came to a halt at the head of the valley. The strange conical mound of Dragon Hill rose to their right and, atop it, Imogen thought she saw somebody dancing, but when she looked more closely there was nobody there. A warm breeze brushed against her face; the smell of warm leather and tobacco filled her nostrils for the briefest of moments.

There were some who claimed that the horse carved into the hillside at Uffington wasn't a horse at all, but a dog, or even a dragon. Imogen could see how such interpretations were possible, but only she knew the truth behind the creation of the chalk figure. One thing that she hadn't realised until now, however, was that her horse was a she – more, she was a mother.

From out of the night, galloping along the sacred earth of the secret pathways, came the white horse's children, each bearing a rider of its own. They flowed past and through Imogen, a spectral river returning to its source atop the hill. She could make out none of the riders, so blurred had their features become through death and time, though she could feel their kinship – all the selves that she had been, and would be – deep in her heart.

Just as the moon touched the edge of the earth, the horses stopped their prancing at the brow of the hill and looked down upon Imogen and her horse – waiting.

Imogen dismounted and lead her ragged horse up the hill. As she neared the vast chalk figure, the mount that she had made began to come apart: first its tail tumbled to the ground, next its tin-pot eyes fell at her feet, and soon her horse was nothing more than a ragged bit of tarpaulin, gently flowing over the earth, to settle at the hooves of the White Horse.

There Imogen knelt, the cold of the night finally finding her, her breath misting before her eyes.

"I'm sorry," she said. "I tried, and I'm sorry."

There was a snort – almost a laugh – behind her, and a blast of warm, faintly foetid air on the nape of her neck. On her right shoulder, a rough hand briefly rested, and she knew that touch so well that she couldn't hold back the tears.

"I know," he said. "It's alright."

And he, and the horse, and the horses who had danced in the light of the setting moon, were gone.

-4-

STEVE OPENED THE door at 3.20 am to find Imogen standing on the doorstep, shivering and wrapped in a mud-stained tarpaulin.

"Good God! Where have you been?"

"I'm okay. It's a long story, but I'm okay."

"Should I call the police?"

"No, just give me a moment to get into something warmer and then we'll talk."

And once Imogen was showered and dressed they did.

This time Imogen didn't try and elaborate on Steve's depression with arcane terms, or well-meant spells; she just listened. When he had finished, she took him in her arms.

"I'm here for you."

"Are you sure? No more… weird stuff, magic horses?"

She laughed. "No, just me. I promise."

They talked until the sky turned pale, and when they had finished, they went out into the garden, and there began to turn over the earth with their spades, ready to start again.

THE DAY OR THE HOUR

"YOU! EYES FORWARD!"

The Reverend Paul Smith jumped as a sword was thrust into his hands; the moment he gripped the handle the blade began to burn. He almost fell to his knees when he looked up at the creature that had reprimanded him. It was an angel, though this beautiful, armoured creature was a far cry from the graveside statues of mourning, or the messengers of peace and hope depicted in the stained-glass windows of Paul's church. In this creature's eyes he saw only cold disdain and the arrogance that comes with authority.

All through the lines the angels moved, handing out weapons and bellowing at their human charges. Paul heard fragments of conversations; whispers of "the last battle", excited babblings about "the apocalypse" and "God's plan revealed". Noticing the dog-collar at his throat, the woman to his left gripped his arm; the fervour and excitement Paul saw in her eyes reminded him of some of his more zealous parishioners.

"Father, this is it, isn't it?" she said. "The final battle between good and evil? The chosen have been called to fight the forces of Satan."

"I… were you called?" Paul said. "What's the last thing you remember, before coming here?"

"I was walking Bingo and then, well…"

"You simply found yourself here?"

"Yes."

"'You shall not know the day or the hour…'"

"Sorry?"

"Matthew 25:13."

But the Jesus who had spoken those words – the Jesus that Paul believed in – was surely not a God who would wish such suffering on his chosen. Had they been saved only so they could wage war in His name? Was this really the plan of the God that so loved the world he gave his only son? And just where in the world were they for that matter?

The landscape that surrounded them was like nothing Paul had ever seen. Bordering the desolate plain was a mountain range so vast that its peaks seemed to be in danger of toppling and crushing them all. From high in the dark range tumbled waterfalls that were blown to mist before they could reach the ground. Far above, the sky boiled; ochre clouds shot through with flashes of lightning. On the horizon, darkness spread like a stain.

There was a blare of trumpets from behind them, eliciting a

response from the far side of the plain: an inhuman roar, a bellow of rage and hatred that chilled him to the core. The ground shook, the mountains quailed – the apex of one vast peak finally succumbing to gravity and falling – and creation trembled as the damned gave voice to their fury.

Paul was dismayed to see that Satan's army looked to outnumber God's chosen. Not only that, but the Reverend sensed in those infernal soldiers something that was distinctly lacking in the mass of humanity surrounding him: a hunger for battle, a desire to kill in the name of their dark god. Looking at their opponents, Paul feared that the outcome of the Last Battle had been decided even before the first casualty could be claimed.

Beyond Satan's soldiers, Hell burned like one vast forge. This realm of eternal torment was more terrible than anything Paul had ever imagined – not that he had spent much time contemplating Hell. Some trainee vicars during his years at theological college had seemed more interested in Satan and the notion of divine punishment than in revealing the grace of God. Paul, however, had always thought of Hell as the absence of God, rather than a fiery pit into which the wicked were cast. He just couldn't reconcile the notion of hellfire and eternal torment with the God of love and forgiveness that he knew in his heart.

Now, looking at the dark army before him, Paul realised that his theology had been all wrong. For here the worst visions of Revelation and the most phantasmagorical verses of the Bible were manifest.

Where the ground wasn't burning it was piled high with corpses; hundreds of ziggurats of rotting flesh screaming in pain and sorrow, even beyond death. Atop each mound stood a black-winged creature wielding a sword. From the sky fell a constant rain of naked human bodies, each landing atop a mound, there to be despatched by a demon and added to the pile. Though the bodies at the base of each mound had been smashed and rotted down to little more than rags and bones and human jelly, still they screamed in torment. Even divested of their flesh, they knew pain, their souls subjected to eternal punishment.

Almost against his will, Paul's eyes were drawn past the mountains of human suffering, out over a vast lake of fire, to where the ruler of this realm resided. He desperately wanted to look away but Satan held his gaze, a loathsome fascination compelling him to stare into the heart of darkness.

Paul had been expecting horns, red scaled flesh, cloven hooves and a forked tail. Instead, Satan was nothing. It was like staring into a black hole, a pool of the deepest night that sucked in all light, all emotion, all that was good, and destroyed it completely. The cold hard fact of the Devil wasn't that he was some arch-demon delighting in the suffering of damned souls, but that he was the antithesis of creation: a void whose implacable *indifference* was at the root of all evil.

This was the second time that Paul had encountered true evil; the first had almost destroyed his faith.

THE CALL HAD come on a Saturday night; one of those rare Saturday nights not taken up by a Bible study group, dinner with a parishioner, or one of the many other extra ecclesiastical duties he was required to perform. Paul had been sat with his shoes off, nursing the second whisky of the evening and enjoying a favourite Hitchcock movie when the phone rang. Fumbling to secure the dog-collar he had half taken off, he answered with a gruff, "Yes?"

"Reverend Paul Smith?"

"Yes."

"It's DCI Matthews at Ravensthwaite Police Station. I apologise for disturbing you at this hour, but we have a gentleman in custody who has requested to see a priest."

"What about Father Patrick Chandler? Our Lady Immaculate is considerably closer to the station. For that matter, what about the police chaplain?"

"Our chaplain is currently on leave and the suspect has specifically requested an Anglican priest."

"Okay. Give me half an hour or so."

Paul decided to walk. He was sure that he was safe to drive, even with the two whiskies inside him, but the thought of the indignity he would suffer were he to be breathalysed while in clerical garb compelled him to make the sensible choice. By the time he reached the station, he was fairly confident that any alcohol fumes had dissipated and he managed to maintain an air of professionalism despite the lateness of the hour.

"Thank you for coming at such short notice, Father."

"It's all part of the job I'm afraid. Now, what's the suspect's name and the charge?"

"Jeff Barnes. Murder."

Paul knew *of* Jeff, but had only met his wife. Patricia had been a regular member of the congregation, often bringing along her severely disabled adult son, Stuart, to the Sunday morning service. Despite Stuart's condition, Paul had never sensed any bitterness in Patricia, any anger that God could have visited such torment on her child. But it became clear that she had been hiding her suffering all too well when one October afternoon the previous year, she had taken her own life, sitting in a fume-filled car as the engine was left running. For a while Paul had felt angry with himself that he hadn't been able to prevent Patricia's suicide, but everybody in the congregation who had known her assured him there was nothing he could have done. Patricia had never really taken him into her confidence, never given the merest hint of what she was truly going through.

Fearing that he already knew the answer to his question, Paul asked it anyway. "Stuart?"

"The son? I'm afraid so. Mr Barnes bludgeoned him to death before calling us."

"Lord preserve us!"

"Can I give you a moment, Father?"

"No, that's alright, I'm ready."

The interview room stank of cigarette smoke and sweat. The harsh strip-lighting banished all shadows. Unaccountably, Paul suddenly felt even more tired.

Jeff sat at a table against the far wall; the handcuffs that bound him only just allowing him to smoke the stub of a roll-up that was threatening to burn his fingers. When Paul closed the door, he ground out the smoke before looking up.

"Father."

"Jeff. You requested to see me."

"I did, Father. Please, sit."

Paul did so, placing the Bible he had brought with him on the table between them.

He flinched as Jeff looked across at him, the blankness in the man's eyes truly unsettling.

"Shall I tell you what I did, Father?"

"If you think that will help."

"Every day I had to feed him, clean his shitty arse. All the things Pat had always done for him, and she never once complained, you know? She never screamed back when Stuart pounded her with his fists or tore her hair, never blamed him for the destruction and chaos he brought to our home. For all the twenty years she cared for him, she didn't once grumble. And I'm sure that even as her life slipped away, she didn't blame him; not really. But I could see the monster that he was. I could see the glee he felt in the damage he wrought. Did you know that at her funeral, he smiled as her coffin rolled beyond that curtain? All the way home, he was singing to himself and clapping his hands."

Jeff paused to roll another cigarette.

"I understand how difficult it must have been for you both, looking after such a severely disabled son," Paul said.

"No, you don't," Jeff said, before taking a deep drag on the cigarette. "And don't talk to me like he was a human being. He wasn't. As I said, he was a monster. So, I'll tell you what I did."

From the tone of Jeff's voice he could have been talking about the weather, or some other trivial matter. There was no remorse, none of the hysterical regret that Paul had been expecting

"First, I simply stopped looking after him. After all, he'd never done anything for his mother or me. In fact, he'd taken Pat from me. So the solution was simple, when you think about it. I stopped looking after him. I left him to wallow in his own shit and piss, and when he called out in hunger or distress, I just turned the television up a little louder, or went out to the pub. A monster should be made to live like a monster. That's what I was teaching him. Do you understand?"

Paul didn't. What Jeff was describing was the gravest of sins; abuse beyond anything the Reverend had had to deal with in his ministry. But it was his duty, as a minister, to sit and listen, so he gestured for Jeff to continue.

"And after a few weeks of this, after the little shit knew what I really felt about him, I decided to finish it. I didn't want to have to deal with him anymore; this was *my* life he was selfishly destroying. And so, this evening when I heard him calling out, I went to the garage to get the tyre iron."

"Jeff, please…"

"No, vicar. You will sit, and you will listen.

"So, I got the tyre iron, and I went upstairs. And do you know what, Father?"

"Jeff, I—"

"Do you know what? There was so little left of him, he was just so much skin and bone, that for a moment I hesitated. But then he looked up at me with that fucking spastic grin of his, that smile that said, 'Oh, I know what I've done, Daddy, and if you give me the chance, I'll do it to you too.'

"So, I didn't give him the chance. I let him have it until there was nothing left."

When Jeff had finished talking, Paul let out the breath he had been holding. He brushed the tears from his eyes with the back of his hand before picking up the Bible and opening it. He didn't have any specific chapter or verse in mind; he just didn't want to have to look at Jeff anymore.

"Why did you call me here, Jeff?" he finally said. "Would you like me to pray with you? Do you want to repent for what you have done?"

Jeff let out a short bark of a laugh, the first emotion that Paul had seen him express since entering the room.

"Repent? Pray? No, no, Father." Jeff ground out his cigarette on the table. Paul could smell the burning varnish. "I just wanted to see the look on your face when I described what I'd done to that cunt."

The dread that overtook Paul was unlike anything he had ever experienced. Looking up at Jeff, he saw a savage glee in the man's eyes. When he began to laugh, straining against his cuffs as he leaned forward across the table, Paul leaped to his feet and ran to the door, pounding on it with his fists.

"Let me out! Let me out!"

DCI Matthews opened the door and Paul stumbled into the hall.

"I'm sorry, Detective Matthews," he said between gasps for breath, "but there is nothing that I can do."

Paul wasn't able to return to work for a couple of months after that. He descended into a depression he was afraid he would never be able to climb out of. Though he appealed to God for respite, he didn't think He was listening anymore, wasn't sure He even existed. It took him a long time, and the support of friends and family, to re-discover that calm, quiet place at the centre of himself, and there re-encounter the loving presence of his Lord. He never did discover how he was supposed to stand up to the evil men like Jeff were capable of committing, but he did find the strength to carry on, put his trust in God and minister to those who needed him.

THE ANGELS' TRUMPETS called again – instantly hushing the mass of cowed humanity – and Paul finally turned to look on Heaven.

In his ministry, Paul had never really given much thought as to the actual nature of Heaven and what awaited him beyond death, preferring instead to concentrate on the spiritual needs of the living. Part of him felt that the eternal was essentially unknowable and that wherever you went when God called you into his embrace, it would be so unlike anything in human experience that it would be futile to even try to imagine it. Now that he was finally confronted with the reality of God's eternal kingdom, Paul decided that were he pressed to describe it, the phrase he would use would be 'eternal beauty.'

Pasture and gentle woodland rolled away from him; the valleys and hills, the dales and dells folding and flowing into and away from each other – a pastoral idyll painted in impossible vistas. Above paradise, the sky held all the beauty of dawn and dusk, sunrise and sunset – and something of the night – to display a firmament that felt like perpetuity manifest. Every beauteous thing in creation was here, and though such a view should confound the eye and befuddle the mind, instead it spoke only of perfection.

At the centre of this wondrous realm – yet also, somehow, comprising every part of it – sat the celestial throne. Each tier was thronged with angels singing His praises, their faces raised to the light that burned at the apex of the holy seat. Paul could hardly look into its depths before he had to turn away, but before he did, he thought that he saw something at the heart of the light: a figure whose raised arm was greeted by another call of trumpets.

He felt a sharp pain and turned to find that an angel had driven the pommel of its sword into his back.

"I said, eyes forward! The battle is soon to be joined."

As Paul cried out and clutched at his bruised spine, he realised with dawning horror what had been missing from his glimpse of heaven: humanity itself.

The trumpets called again and there was a rising stench of fear, of perspiration and piss – the smell of which, perversely, reminded Paul of one of the more spiritual moments of his ministry.

HE'D BARELY BEEN out of his twenties; a young curate placed at the heart of a broken community. Paul relished the challenge. Not for him the ideal of the quiet country parish with its garden fetes and "More tea vicar?" Here he was truly amongst God's people, ministering to those hungry for the Good News that would lift them out of the despair such faceless urban sprawls fostered.

It was mid-September and the day was overcast and uncomfortably warm, the constant drizzle doing nothing to freshen the atmosphere. Paul had been called by the vicar at six a.m. Elsie Pritchard, who had been a member of the congregation long before the construction of the concrete tower block in which she now lived, was dying. Reverend Stuart asked Paul to call on her with a view to administering the last rites.

Elsie lived on the top floor of the inappropriately named Elysium

Gardens. Paul found the lift doors open, the interior in darkness and stinking of piss, and so took the stairs.

Graffiti crawled up the stairwell, brightly coloured snakes of paint forming themselves into crude depictions of genitalia or gang mottos. Many of the words on the walls expressed the incoherent rage of enforced confinement. The words 'FUCK THIS! FUCK THIS! FUCK THIS!' followed Paul up several flights, and though he disagreed with the criminality of the act that had put them there, he couldn't say he disagreed with the sentiment.

He was winded and sweating by the time he reached the top floor and had to rest a moment to regain his breath. Outside the wind battered the tower, the drizzle having turned into a harsh rain that sounded like it was sand-blasting the walls. Paul closed his eyes against a sudden migraine stab of pain, only to feel the building sway ever so slightly around him.

Muttering a brief prayer, he opened his eyes and knocked on the door of number 68.

"Elsie? Elsie love, it's Paul Smith, the curate from St Matthew's."

There was no response but Paul pushed on the door to find it open. The narrow hallway beyond smelled of over-boiled cabbage and something worse.

"Elsie?"

There was the faintest response from beyond: a hollow croak. Hoping that he wasn't too late, Paul hurried towards the sound.

The bedroom was heavy with the ammonia stench of urine and

the sharp smell of sweat. Elsie was propped up by a mound of pink pillows; the bedspread covering her an equally insipid colour, spotted with stains. Elsie's cheeks were hollow, her lips pale and the few wisps of hair that still clung to her head as fine as candyfloss. Each breath she took rattled in her chest. She was clearly in terrible pain, but the welcome and kindness that Paul saw in her eyes made the breath catch in his throat and threaten to turn into a sob. Composing himself, he realised that he would see a lot of death during his ministry and what he was here to do was a great privilege, an intimate moment of shared faith. He had to be strong for Elsie.

"Father, it was good of you to come." Elsie tried to raise her hands to his, but they were too weak to leave the bedspread.

"Not at all, Elsie. Not at all."

Paul knelt beside the bed and they prayed together as the wind rattled the windows. The low clouds darkened and the rain turned to hail, and Paul had to raise his voice to be heard over the deluge. For a moment, the wind fell and he could hear a neighbour's television, the volume so loud that he was able to identify the show as *Countdown*. In an adjacent flat a row broke out that ended when a woman screamed. Making the sign of the cross, Paul tuned out the sounds of the living and concentrated on the dying woman before him. When he anointed Elsie's forehead with oil her flesh was so cold that he thought that she had already passed. Paul was about to say a final prayer when Elsie opened her eyes and he saw there something of the woman she had been.

"Oh Father," she breathed, a hint of girlish excitement in her voice. "Oh Father, it's the most beautiful, wondrous garden. It goes on forever and my friends and family are all there. It's okay, Father. I'm going to be okay."

And then she was gone. On her last breath, Paul thought he smelt something like a meadow in bloom, and he knew a moment of almost overwhelming peace.

LOOKING AT PARADISE now, nowhere could he see a human being, just the winged servants of the Lord and, of course, God himself. Paul wondered whether Elsie had been granted her vision of the Almighty's kingdom only to be denied entry to the eternal realm. Was she somewhere amongst them now, resurrected and armed for the Last Battle? If so, Paul couldn't help but feel angry at his God for denying an old woman her just reward. Elsie had lived a good, quiet life as a committed Christian and had often spoken of God's plan; he didn't think that this was what she had in mind.

The revelations of this day had made a nonsense of his faith. He had always believed in the ultimate truth revealed in Christ – God made flesh – and had put humanity and what it was to be human at the core of his ministry. But now it was clear that this battle between good and evil had nothing to do with humanity; they were merely pawns employed by forces they couldn't even begin to understand.

This wasn't their war. Paul hadn't given over thirty years of his life to the church just so he could die beneath some abomination's sword. If this was God's plan for those he had chosen to save, he didn't want anything to do with it.

As a phalanx of angels raised their swords, awaiting the signal to advance, Paul turned his back on the conflict, though he had to make a concerted effort to do so. Across the broken plain the forces of Satan were rallying their own troops. The mounds of demon-tormented dead erupted into flame, lighting the battlefield as efficiently as any new dawn. The sound that came from out of the abominations' mouths as Hell prepared to advance threatened to turn Paul's bowels to water. Even so, he found the strength to raise his sword and point it towards his God.

"For all those you have failed!" he shouted. "For the promises you have broken!"

He expected to be cut down at any moment; the feeling brought him peace. He would die knowing he had done the right thing, and if there were nothing beyond this life, he was fine with that too.

The last call went out and the armies began to advance; the accompanying roar deafening in its intensity. Paul began running, not towards the Satanic forces but towards Heaven, screaming his defiance, and anger and shame. He saw movement from the corner of his eye, and turned his head to find himself surrounded by others. By humans. His lone call to arms had been answered and, without intending to, he had formed an army of his own. The vast majority of humanity had chosen to side with the angels, throwing themselves against the forces of Satan without a doubt in their hearts. But some few were with him.

His heart lifted by the fellowship of his rebels, Paul smiled as the light of the Father began to gleam from his blade.

God first; Satan next.

DON'T YOU LIKE
THE BIRD MAN?

THE PHONE WAS ringing. When Kathy looked at her clock and saw that it was close to two am, panic pulled her quickly awake. This could be the call to say that Dad had suffered a heart attack; this could be the call to say that Michael's plane had gone down somewhere over the Atlantic.

Snatching the handset from the cradle, she braced herself for the worst possible news and heard the sound of wings.

"Who is this?"

It sounded like a vast flock of birds taking flight, the rush of wings growing faint until there was only the distant cooing of doves. The line went dead. Kathy dialled and an electronic voice said, "You were called, today, at 1:57 am. The caller withheld their number."

She lay back and listened to her racing heart, feeling shaky, on edge. Sleep eluded her for hours and when it did finally come, the call of birds followed her into her dreams.

THE PLANE DUCKED down out of cloud cover as a jolt of turbulence gave the craft another violent shake. Michael gripped his knees and stared at the seat back in front of him.

"Like riding a bucking bronco down to the ground 'aint it?" the man sitting next to him said, looking exhilarated. Michael said nothing and concentrated on keeping his lunch inside him. He thought of Kathy lying in bed at home and wished he were curled up to her warm back, listening to her sleep.

They touched down at 7:12 pm and, with the increased airport security, Michael didn't arrive at his hotel until after midnight.

A hell of a storm was battering Manhattan and he stood in his room watching the lightning flicker over the city. Michael wondered what the weather was like back home and was going to phone Kathy when he remembered the time difference and decided to let her sleep. He took a whisky from the minibar and went through the illustrations that Derek had sent him as rain lashed the windows.

WHEN MICHAEL HAD created his story of the bird-headed entity stalking the streets of a gas-lit London, Derek has been the first and last artist he had contacted. He had worked with him on a number of other titles and Michael considered him one of the best in the business. There was something about his watercolours that perfectly caught the viciousness and sadness of Michael's tale. The depictions of the brutal murders had a strange melancholy air; every shadowy street promised a phantom. By far his favourite image was the cover of the first issue. Beneath the title, in a barely-lit room strung with entrails and soaked in blood, crouched a figure holding a surgical blade. He had the well-muscled, naked torso of a man and the head of a crow. Michael looked at the picture and considered, not for the first time, that there was something vulnerable about the bird man.

Kathy hadn't thought so. Having read *A Murder of Crows* she declared that it was the nastiest thing he had ever written. "Perfect, wonderful husband, you are a twisted ghoul. Where *do* you get these ideas from? Most of your stories scare me, but this one really upset me."

"Don't you think there's something sad about the bird man? Don't you like him?"

"No. I hate him."

DRY BIRD SHIT crumbled beneath her feet as she climbed the stairs to the loft. The reek of guano became stronger as she opened the hatch and pulled herself into the warm, dusty room. The birds didn't seem to be disturbed by her presence. Remaining in their alcoves, they regarded her with eyes like ebony beads. She lay in a shaft of afternoon sunlight on dirty boards. A feather floated down to her. Catching it, she stroked it against her cheek. Dust motes danced in the light. She listened to the warm, lazy cooing of the nesting doves and closed her eyes.

When she opened them again the shadows were longer and the light was tinted a deep amber. In the centre of the room sat a man. He held a dove and whispered to it as he watched her.

"They don't like to be held," she said, sitting up. "I know because once I tried and it wanted to fly away, and I accidentally hurt it so it couldn't."

"Would you like me to show you how?" He held a hand out to her.

She walked over and he cupped her hands around the bird. The dove twittered nervously. She could feel its rapid heartbeat beneath her palms.

"I don't think he likes it," she said. A tickling sensation climbed her thigh and she looked down to see that the man had put his hands beneath her skirt.

"There now, he likes you. I can tell."

The dove burst free, startling her, and she tried to move away but the man held her close. *He smells like onions*, she thought. The tickling sensation on her thighs had begun to move towards her knickers and the man was breathing heavily. She pushed away from him but he wouldn't let go. She squealed and raked him with her nails, but his grip only tightened. The tickling sensation had turned into pain, and as his fingers sought their way into her there was the sudden sensation of hundreds of wings beating against her back.

"WELL FIRST OF all it's not really a re-telling of the Jack the Ripper story. None of the victims are prostitutes for a start. What was your name again?"

"Tad." Michael repeated this as he signed the dedication on the title page of the graphic novel.

"Well Tad, I think you'll find that the true victim in this story is the bird man himself." The boy in the leather jacket grunted as though he didn't quite believe him and moved aside for the next fan. Derek sat beside Michael, chatting to a girl wearing a heavy metal T-shirt. She was gushing praise and Michael couldn't help but smile at the unconditional love that was coming the artist's way; they never received such adulation in the UK.

It hadn't been a bad day, all in all. At the convention the two of them had picked up several awards for *A Murder of Crows* and now they were at Midtown Comics, drinking complimentary booze and meeting the fans.

"This is for you," said a woman, placing a gift-wrapped box in front of Michael.

"Crikey! Thank you, that's very kind, now let's see what have we here." Inside was a small painted statue of the bird man. In intricate detail it depicted the creature looming over a little girl holding a dove. The bird man's right hand was bunched in the folds of her dress, the left was holding a knife. "That's, its..." Michael stammered.

The woman looked down at the statue sadly and seemed to be about to say something more but left, leaving the books she held unsigned.

Derek leaned over. "This is incredible! We should commission her to make some more. We could market these, the fans would go nuts."

"Artistic integrity over money every time, huh Derek?"

"I'm all about the almighty dollar my friend."

"If I thought that for a second, I wouldn't be working with you."

"So, are you going to take this home as a present for your good lady wife?"

"I don't think Kathy would appreciate it. She's not a big fan of horror as it is and she's taken a peculiar dislike to the antics of the bird man." Michael picked up the statue. "I wonder what made that woman add the little girl? She's not in the story."

"Artistic license I suppose. Now look sharp, the queue is getting longer."

KATHY AWOKE TO a storm of feathers. A hole in her pillow spilled them across her face and the bed. Down stuck to the corners of her mouth, threaded her hair. Feeling grubby and drunk with tiredness she lurched to the bathroom and tried to wash away the night.

In the kitchen she sorted through the post which was mostly for Michael and looked to be mostly from fans. She checked the answer phone to see whether he had called and felt disappointed that he hadn't. This house was too big for her alone. Even though Michael had only been gone a day, she still felt at a loss as to what to do.

That problem was solved a few minutes later when the phone rang.

"Hello Kathy love. It's your mother."

"Hi Mum, how're things?"

"Good. Although your Dad's been swearing at flat pack furniture all day, so the usual mix of chaos and hilarity. Listen, I have some news. I'm afraid that your great uncle Robin has died."

"Uncle Robin? I don't remember him."

"No, well, no one was close to him. Anyway, the main thing is that I need your help. I've agreed to go up to his cottage and start clearing stuff out. I've hired a skip and I thought that with your eye for antiques and collectables you could advise me on what to chuck and what to sell."

"I'd be glad to, Mum. I'll go cabin crazy if I have to stay here on my own for too long. When do you want me?"

"In about an hour?"

IT WAS A hot day and with the windows rolled down, the drive to the cottage blasted away the remnants of Kathy's nightmare. Her mother, Laura, drove faster than Kathy thought was safe, but it was so good to be out of the house that she didn't say anything.

The cottage stood on its own behind a row of pines. Its windows were grimy with neglect and several ancient automobiles stood on the drive, basking in the mid-day sun.

"Did he live here alone?" Kathy asked as Laura tried key after key in the front door.

"Yes, he never married. Like I said, no one was close to him. We hardly ever saw him. Ah, this is the one." The hallway was crowded with stacks of newspapers and magazines. "Well, all of this can go for a start," she said, flicking through an ancient copy of *People's Friend*. "Tell you what, Kathy, take a look at the lounge. I'll check out the kitchen."

In the lounge, bird cages hung from the beams. Each was empty and Kathy wondered what had become of the inhabitants. She could smell them just below the odour of stale smoke that emanated from the yellowed wallpaper. Kathy imagined her uncle sitting in here, smoking roll-ups and trying to hear the television above the screech of budgies. She imagined that he walked with a stoop and had small, intense black eyes. The furniture in here was old, cheap and much repaired. A corner cupboard was full of mostly empty bottles and ugly porcelain figurines. Picking up a statuette of a boy sitting next to a dog, Kathy took it to the kitchen where her mother was crashing around in the pantry. "Find anything?" she called.

"Bugger all I'm afraid, Kath. Anything worth keeping in the lounge?"

"I imagine that this could fetch up to 10p at auction," she said, giving her mother the figurine.

"Yes well, I don't know quite why I imagined some hidden treasure trove. Let's have a quick look through the place and then we'll come back tomorrow and start filling that skip."

Upstairs Kathy found a bathroom with a rusting tub half full of brackish water, a box room containing a few coins of out-of-date currency, and Uncle Robin's bedroom. The bed was old, the headboard wrought iron curlicued into elegant designs. The mattress was disgusting and would have to be burnt but the frame could certainly fetch some money.

"Eureka!" Kathy shouted down the stairs. "We have an antique."

"That?" Laura sounded incredulous as she looked at the bed.

"Yep. That frame is, I think, genuine Victoriana."

Kathy looked out of the window onto an untamed English jungle as her mother examined the find more closely. Sunflowers nodded. Through the trees she could see the outlines of a barn.

"What about that? Is that part of the property?"

"The barn? Well, I suppose it is. Shall we hack our way through the jungle down there and take a peek?"

THEY DIDN'T NEED to look for a key to the padlock because when Kathy gave it a shake it fell apart.

The heat had found its way inside and intensified. The smell that rolled out was a strange mix of animal and machine. In a far corner a ride-on lawn mower had became a home for spiders and rust. Gardening equipment and tools littered the work surfaces and floor.

Stairs lead up to a hatch in the ceiling and part of Kathy wanted to stop her mother as she ascended, because she had begun to realise what they would find there.

It was quiet above. The alcoves were empty but for the occasional clump of feather and bone. The floor was so encrusted with dust and guano that it crunched beneath their feet like snow.

"I'd forgotten that he was such a fan of birds." Laura said. "In fact, I seem to remember that he cared more for birds than people."

There was something on the floor and as Kathy bent down she saw that it was a pair of child's knickers.

She felt the brush of a wing against her cheek and turned, startled, but it was only the touch of her mother.

"Kathy love, what's wrong?"

WHEN THE MUSE hit, Michael was trying to force himself into sleep; trying to shake the jet-lag. He called room service for some coffee. Opening his laptop, he placed the statue of the bird man and child on the bedside table. He had been thinking of how the creature related to the humans in his story and looking at this small statue had provided a spark of something.

The bird man can love but how, and with whom? Michael typed. *And how does he understand children?*

Reading through Michael's notes over breakfast the next day, Derek appeared to be distinctly uncomfortable.

"I know that this is a horror comic, but this is pretty strong stuff."

"Well, the bird man doesn't see it as abuse. The bird man is in *love*. He doesn't understand humans the way we do. To him, he is consummating a passion he thinks is shared. The little girl doesn't fear him. In fact, he's her only friend. The horror of the violation is offset by the tragedy of the bird man's ignorance and that, in the end, is what will kill him."

"Hang on! Hang on! Okay, two things disturb me here. First, the story, although I realise that's kind of the point. Second, the bird man *dies?*"

"We can't keep him alive forever Derek."

"My accountant would like to disagree with you. And why now? I thought that there were other places we wanted to go with this. I thought that there was going to be some sort of redemption arc."

"I've changed my mind. I want to end this on a black note."

"Yeah, pretty bloody black. Where *do* you get your ideas from?"

"I should slap you one for that, but since you ask…" Michael placed the statue on the table.

"Strange the places inspiration can come from isn't it?"

Michael looked at the bird man looming over the little girl.

"Yes, it is."

THERE'S SOMETHING STRUGGLING inside and Kathy looks down. Her belly is taught against her dress. She runs her hand over the smooth bulge and feels it again. It's not the kick of a tiny foot or the nudge of an elbow; it's the beating of wings.

KATHY'S SCREAM ROSE to a high pitch as she struggled awake. Reaching for the bedside table, she found a blank wall and panic almost set in before she remembered that she was sleeping in her parents' guest room and was not back in her own bed.

The nightmare began to lose its hold but the anger and shame was still there. Her discovery in the barn had brought with it a wave of revulsion as the memory had surfaced. Kathy had rushed from the loft to the car, and there she had thrown up.

"That's a dreadful thing to say, Kath!" Laura said later, as they sat in the gaudy café of a service station.

"I know, but it's real. The dream last night and now this. I must have buried it when I was young. Do you not remember *anything?*"

"We only took you to visit Robin once and that was so long ago. I can't really remember much about that day. Kathy, look. Have you been over-doing it at work? Perhaps you and Michael are going through a rough patch?"

"I am not having a breakdown if that's what you think!"

"Kathy, I didn't mean to... please calm down..."

"Let's just go."

Back at her parents' house dinner was eaten in the shadow of an uncomfortable silence. Her father, confused by the sudden gloom, tried to break into it with small talk, but Kathy's mother stared at him until the silence resumed.

After the meal Kathy talked and her parents listened as she told them what she remembered about Uncle Robin. Her mother, flushed with shame, spluttered something about it being ridiculous. It was just a nightmare. But it wasn't – Kathy knew that now.

"Dad, what do you remember?"

"Not much. He was a bit of a strange man, a loner. Never married. I always thought he was gay, actually."

"Do you remember that day, Dad?"

"Your Dad won't remember love. You know what's he's like. He can't remember what day of the week it is sometimes."

"Mum!" Kathy glared at her mother. She wasn't taking this seriously and that hurt almost as much as the memory of what had happened.

"I'm not that useless thank you very much, Laura. I suppose we felt kind of sorry for him, out there all on his own. Felt that someone in the family should at least acknowledge his existence. He probably would have rather been left alone but, you know, being good Christians and all that…"

"What did we do that day?" Kathy pressed

"Had lunch. Talked a bit. Had a drink. Actually, I remember that you got very upset at one point. We had to go home early, you were grizzling so much. Your mother and I were relaxing in the lounge when you ran in. You were screaming something about your uncle's pigeon loft. Seemed you'd almost fallen down the steps. Uncle Robin said that he'd caught you just in time."

"I didn't fall down the steps."

"Well this is ridiculous, Kathy! What do you expect us to do now?" Her mother shouted through her tears. "It was years ago. Robin is dead. We can't just dig him up and have him arrested. Let's just bury this. We're sorry, Kathy, we really are, but we didn't know and there is *nothing* that we can do."

KATHY LAY IN bed, feeling so angry and frightened that she couldn't get back to sleep. Her mother was right. There was nothing that they could do. The anger and pain could only go back inside where it would yell and caper at Kathy from her dreams. There was no redemption, no resolution. Robin had abused her and had died without having faced retribution.

Throwing on a dressing gown, Kathy went down to the kitchen where she poured herself a glass of water. She looked at the window as she drank. Her mother's car sat in front of the garage. Its wheel rims were still covered in mud from their country drive. Kathy closed her eyes against a sudden rush of grief and when she opened them again she saw the car keys sitting on the kitchen table.

If Robin couldn't be punished then she didn't want anything of his left in the world. No one deserved to profit from him.

Taking the keys, Kathy went upstairs to get dressed.

IT WAS ALMOST dawn when she arrived at the cottage; two hours later Kathy watched it burn in the rays of a new sun. The barn added its own smoke to the dark pall. Kathy thought that she saw feathers spiralling through the updrafts but it could have been a trick of the smoke. She had begun to giggle like an errant school child as the flames had started to take, but now she was crying as the cottage roof collapsed into the quickly spreading flames.

* * *

DEREK AND MICHAEL spent the last few days in New York working on the final bird man story. The preliminary sketches that Derek produced didn't satisfy Michael and the artist's patience was sorely tested by his friend's insistence that the panels be darker still until almost nothing could be seen of the bird man. Only the sheen of light on his eyes was visible in the blackness.

"I'm not convinced that this is going to work," Derek told him on the way to the airport. "I'm not sure I can produce exactly what you want."

"Don't worry, Derek. I'll get the text to you over the next month or so and we'll organise to meet up again later in the year. Trust me, this will work. The bird man will find a way."

Michael started to drift off as soon as he got himself settled into his business class seat. He was woken by a rush of cool air and he thought that someone had opened a vent until a black wing slapped his cheek and something ragged and dark began pounding itself against the seat back in front of him. As he made a grab for the bird his hands were torn by sharp talons, but for just a moment he had a hold on the creature's body and could feel a rapid, panicked heart beat. Then the crow barrelled into the window and lay still on his lap, its neck broken.

"Oh my God sir, you're bleeding!"

Michael looked down at his hands. Bloody red lines criss-crossed his palms. A stewardess was leaning over him, looking unsure whether to attend to the bird or Michael first. "We tried to catch it but it just shot straight through the cabin. We've no idea where it came from. We are *so* sorry. On behalf of United, I apologise most sincerely. If there is anything *we* can do…"

"It wasn't your fault. Here, take this," Michael said, handing her the dead bird, "and if you have any whisky going spare that would be just lovely."

After the drink Michael closed his eyes. He opened them again some hours later and was convinced that something vast and dark had been pacing the aircraft, but looking out the window all he could see was a new moon and, far below, a silvered ocean. He thought, wistfully, of Kathy and wished he were home in her arms.

THE ANSWER MACHINE tape spooled back to the beginning. Kathy pulled it out of the machine and threw it in the bin. She had memorised most of the messages anyway.

"*Kathy it's your mother, please contact us. I know you're at home, I've seen you through the window, please get in touch love. We're not angry with you. We just want to know that you're okay.*"

Kathy unplugged the phone and then went around the house closing all the curtains. She climbed into bed and tried to sleep, but it still wouldn't come. She lay, exhausted and tearful, willing the hours away. Eventually she floated through a kind of slumber but her thoughts ran a million miles an hour, and sometimes Kathy wasn't sure whether she was conscious or not.

Cold silence descended and it seemed so loud that it made her sit upright in bed. Someone was standing in the doorway watching her and she only knew he was there from the light of her alarm clock reflected in his eyes. Kathy rolled on her side as he entered the room and lifted the duvet so he could slide in beside her. She sighed as his comforting weight made the mattress dip and stretched out in delight as a wing enfolded her. Kathy stroked the tips of his black feathers as his beak lovingly ruffled her hair.

"Don't you like the bird man?" He asked, pushing himself against her.

"No," Kathy said. "I love him."

TEA AND SYMPATHY

WHEN THE PHONE rang, one rainy Wednesday afternoon, and the man on the other end told Sarah that her husband was dead, she simply refused to believe it. After all, there was no reason for Sean to die. He didn't smoke or drink to excess; he played badminton twice a week and ate well. And Sarah was only thirty-two – who had ever heard of a thirty-two year old widow?

Even so, she was told that somewhere between his desk and the coffee machine, Sean had dropped dead. "Like that," the man on the phone said, and Sarah thought she heard him click his fingers.

AFTER A WEEK of being alone in the house, she finally had to acknowledge that Sean was gone; to where, she had no idea. At the funeral a great aunt had told her that he was in a better place, but then people who were not far from the grave themselves tended to say that. If Sean believed in God or heaven, he'd certainly never discussed it with Sarah. They never talked about death. Why would they? They were both young and had decades of married life ahead of them, or so Sarah had thought.

Now she was a widow, and she had no idea what widows did. Perhaps it had something to do with knitting circles, bake sales or *Countdown*.

Going back to work was the hardest thing to begin with. Sean used to e-mail her regularly throughout the day, just idle conversation or snarky comments about his boss. When twelve o'clock rolled around and the only messages in her in-box were to do with accounting deadlines and the office fantasy football league, Sarah opened a new window and typed, *Hey. What do you fancy for tea?* before she remembered. Part of her was tempted to send the e-mail anyway, but after a moment she deleted it and ran to the toilets to hide her tears.

When she returned home that evening, her declaration of "I'm back" echoed down the empty hallway, swallowed by the unlit house. Later, in bed – still sticking resolutely to her side, despite the fact that she no longer had to share – she looked up at the ceiling and could see the years stretching ahead of her. What was the average age of death for a woman these days? 70? 80? Either way, that was a lot of time to fill. She and Sean had so many plans – three children, an extension to the kitchen, maybe a property abroad. Sarah found herself drifting towards sleep as she recalled the place in Crete they had seen that was just perfect. Beside her, she was vaguely aware of the mattress dipping slightly, and she smiled as she felt Sean's familiar warmth.

And then the light was on and she was sat bolt-upright, staring at the empty side of the bed, her heart racing.

"Hello?" Sarah called, tentatively adding, "Is anybody there?"

Her mother had told her that grief did funny things to a person.

"Ha, bloody ha." Sarah whispered as she turned out the light and wrapped the duvet around her.

SHE WOKE UP with an idea, and it was silly and perhaps had the suggestion of madness about it, but she thought it might just help as she adapted to life without Sean.

She booted up her laptop and accessed Sean's hotmail account. The password wasn't hard to figure out; he'd used the same one for everything: Boba_Fett1

Sarah opened a new e-mail, addressed it to herself at work and began to type.

Hi Babe

Long day at work. Mr Preston called again, complaining that I had messed up his order. I think this is a weekly hobby for him. Can't wait to get home so we can cuddle on the sofa, and maybe something more... :)

I love you

Xxxx

Sarah hit Send and then opened another new e-mail.

Hi Babe

Anything you want me to pick up on my way home tonight?

Love you

Xxxx

Again, Sarah clicked Send.

IN THE OFFICE, her heart skipped a beat when she saw the two new messages from Sean. She opened the first and as she began to read, the smile slipped from her face. It was exactly the kind of thing Sean would have written, but she knew full well that he hadn't written it. She was talking to herself, doing an impression in the vain attempt to cheer herself up

She deleted the second message unread.

A colleague passing by her desk, noticing her distress, stopped and said, "Is there anything that I can do?"

"Yes. Bring my husband back!" Sarah shouted, before being overcome by emotion.

HR sent her home after that, to "give her space", but space was exactly what she didn't need; the emptiness of the house was almost as depressing as the fake e-mails.

Sarah turned the television on for want of anything better to do. An orange puppet with green eyebrows filled the screen and bellowed, "It's four o'clock! It's Friday! It's time for the Friday Frenzy!"

It was Friday? Sarah honestly hadn't realised.

Every Friday night they had done exactly the same thing. Sean had taken to calling it "their little ritual." Now that he was dead, there seemed little point, but perhaps it would give her something to do, give her more of a sense of him and help her to enjoy a memory rather than wallowing in grief.

At six-thirty Sarah called the Garden of Delights and ordered a quarter crispy duck with pancakes, sweet and sour pork balls, prawns in black bean sauce, special fried rice and prawn crackers. In all the time they had been together, the order had never varied. When the food arrived, she set out two plates and opened a bottle of wine. She selected a DVD – an old favourite, Hammer's *Brides of Dracula* – and put it in the player before settling down to eat.

She managed barely two bites of duck and only a little of the prawn dish before the sight of the congealing food on Sean's plate turned her stomach and she had to run for the bathroom. When she returned to the lounge, the sight of Peter Cushing fighting off a bevy of vampire wantons reminded her so fiercely of her husband that she had to sit down rather suddenly.

That night she didn't bother going to bed. Instead she slept where she sat, the TV turned down low, the noise a poor substitute for his company.

THE SNAP OF the letterbox awoke her as a free newspaper hit the mat. She looked over at the clock; it was almost midday and Sarah immediately felt guilty for sleeping so long. She picked up the paper and went to the kitchen to make herself a coffee. Leafing through the local news items, an advertisement caught her eye:

Bereaved? At the end of your tether and in search of comfort, hope and answers? Join us every Sunday at 10.30am for fellowship, spiritual enrichment and contact with the dearly departed – Our Lady's Reformed Spiritualist Church, Stokes Community Hall, 67 Bath Street.

Grief would be so much easier to bear, Sarah thought, if she could ask Sean why he had died. Oh, she knew what the doctors had told her, but there had to be more to it than a congenital heart defect.

Perhaps someone at Our Lady's Reformed Spiritualist Church would offer her the answer and solace she sought. At the very least, it would get her out of this empty house and give her an opportunity to meet new people. Maybe one of them would be able to explain this seemingly endless grief.

67 BATH STREET was sandwiched between a sex shop and a dry-cleaners and to call it a Community Hall was to give it an aspiration that it failed to live up to. Sarah was greeted at the door by an elderly gentleman in an ill-fitting suit who took her hand in his own and pressed it weakly.

"It's so nice to see a new face," he said, "please be welcome and at peace."

Inside, the hall was stiflingly warm. Four wall-mounted, ancient-looking three bar heaters lightly toasted the congregation, which was mainly composed of old ladies, one of whom was crouched arthritically over an electronic keyboard, playing a hymn accompanied by a samba beat. At the far end of the hall stood a pulpit draped in a purple cloth with a picture of a dove sewn onto it.

Sarah took a seat in the front row next to a lady with a blue-rinse and thick horn rimmed spectacles. She looked at Sarah, smiled and lightly patted her hand.

The woman at the keyboard finished her piece, rose and shuffled to the pulpit.

"Beloved," she said, "Let us sing hymn number 242."

As she slowly shuffled back it was obvious that she was in pain and Sarah desperately wanted to go and help her, but she remained seated and waited patiently along with the congregation.

Once the hymn was sung, the woman donned a white cassock and took to the pulpit.

"Hello, beloved."

The murmured response of "Hello Edith" was accompanied by hacking coughs and phlegmy wheezing.

"Oh but it's been a busy week in the spirit world, my loves, it really has. Dorothy, your Frank has been telling me of all the lovely things on the other side and how he's so at peace since he passed on." The woman beside Sarah nodded and dabbed at her eyes with a hanky. "And Mavis, your Tommy is saying not to worry yourself about Ada. She's up there with him right now, looking down at you and smiling. Her sins have been absolved and whatever she did in the past, it doesn't matter now, my love."

Sarah was beginning to feel rather foolish. Sitting in a dingy hall, surrounded by weeping old dears didn't seem like such a good way to spend a Sunday morning after all.

"And it's so nice, brothers and sisters, so very very special to welcome a new member into our fellowship. What's your name, my lovely?"

Edith didn't look directly at Sarah, rather she seemed to be staring a point above her left shoulder.

"Don't be shy, love."

"Sarah. Sarah Rothwell."

"Sarah, lovely Sarah. You've come to the right place, my love. And he's here by my side right now, and he's smiling and he's so happy, Sarah."

Sarah looked but Edith was the only person on the stage.

"And... yes, thank you, my love. His name is... Am I right in thinking that it begins with an F?"

"No."

"No, my lovely, but it sounds a bit like an F doesn't it? Maybe an..." Edith was looking closely at Sarah's lips now. "Yes, S. I'm right, aren't I?"

"Yes."

There was a smattering of applause at this revelation and Edith looked up at the congregation proudly.

"That's right, my love. And he suffered for such a very long time, didn't he?"

"No."

But Edith clearly wasn't listening. "Yes, yes he did. But he wants you to know that he's not suffering anymore, my lovely. Your father is amongst friends now, and he's at peace and so very happy."

Sarah got up so abruptly that she pushed her chair into the knees of the woman behind her. As she strode towards the doors she heard Edith scuttling to her keyboard and the opening chords of 'Abide with Me' started up.

The gentleman who had greeted Sarah earlier was stood by the door, and as she made to pass him, he grabbed her arm.

"Sarah, don't go."

"Get the fuck off me. You're all nothing but parasites."

"It's me. Sean."

"What?"

"You brought me back, Sarah. Okay, granted, this isn't my body, but... look, I can see that you're about to freak out, so let me convince you. Something that only you and I would know, okay?"

Sarah nodded, her mouth dry with fear.

"On our first date you wore a white top. At the restaurant you managed to spill red wine on it and years later you told me you thought you'd blown your chances there and then."

"It's... it's you?"

"Yes, it's me. Now, you'll understandably have a lot of questions and I promise you that I'll answer them later, but for now there's something I must do, if you'll humour me for a few more minutes. Okay?"

He held out his hand and when she took it, his grip was nothing like the weak handshake she had received on arrival. The man before her must have been in his mid-eighties at least, but behind his eyes she thought she could sense someone much younger.

Sean lead her back to the congregation and they sat a few rows from the stage. At her pulpit, Edith was continuing to converse with the dearly departed.

"Now Laura, my lovely. Even though you didn't see Jim go, he wants me to assure you that it was peaceful and he was thinking of nothing but you right until his last breath."

"*Bullshit!*" Sean coughed into his fist. "I know for a fact that's not true," he whispered to Sarah. "Dirty old bugger died under a prostitute in Magaluf. He certainly wasn't thinking of Laura when he popped off, so to speak."

Edith looked over to where they were sitting, frowned, and then carried on regardless.

"Now. Yes... yes, my lovely, thank you... Now I've got a lovely gentlemen here and his name is Peter."

There was a gasp from somewhere in the congregation.

"That's right, Nell. It's your Peter. And he may have had some difficulties in life, but he were a good man at heart and he's so at peace now in the lovely eternal garden."

"Lies!" Sean surged to his feet and then winced at a loud click from his right knee.

"I'm sorry, what?" Edith said, her hand going to the silver cross at her throat.

"It's all bullshit, Edith, and you know it. Peter was far from a good man. He swindled, connived and cheated his way through life, not caring how many people he ruined in the process. And as for him being at peace, I can assure you that he most certainly is not. Nell, you just pray that you don't see him again once you pass over yourself. You don't want to go where he's ended up."

"I... I..." Edith held onto the pulpit for support, her face turning a similar purple to the cloth that covered it.

"What's the matter, Edith? Your spirit guides not telling you what to say?" Sean turned his back on the medium and faced the congregation. "This woman, ladies and gentlemen, is a fraud. She's not in touch with the dearly departed and as one of the dearly departed myself, I should know. She's a leech. As for the monthly 'optional donations' to the church that are required of you all. Well... how about that nice new car Edith is driving? Where do you think that came from?"

And with that Sean grabbed Sarah's hand and marched out of the church.

Outside, he put a hand to his chest as he struggled to catch his breath.

"Sorry about that… I just, had to do it. Now…"

Sean grasped his left arm, bared his teeth in a grimace and fell at Sarah's feet. He did not get back up.

Sarah looked down at the corpse of the elderly gentleman, and ran.

SARAH STIRRED A teaspoon of brown sugar into her tea, but found she couldn't drink it. Her stomach still churned with anxiety at what had happened at the church. What had she been thinking? She had been raised an Anglican, but had only ever gone to church once a year, at Christmas. There was something comforting about the good old C of E, but were she asked whether she believed in 'all of that', she'd have to admit that she probably didn't. So what she had been doing putting her faith in a bunch of crazy, old, grief-raddled dears, grasping at hope as their time ran out, was beyond her. In the café, the sound of the living, the banality of overheard conversations, was something of a comfort.

"This seat taken?"

An elderly gentlemen in a mauve suit with a rather ostentatious scarf at his throat indicated the brown plastic chair opposite. Sarah nodded and went back to stirring her tea.

"Anyway, I'm sorry about that," the man said. "That old codger was rather more frail than I had anticipated. Turns out all that excitement wasn't good for his ticker."

Fear stopped the spoon in her hand and made Sarah look up.

"Sorry? What?"

"It's me, Sean."

"Oh god, no…"

"Yes, I realise that it's a lot to take in, but just hear me out. After all, it was you who brought me back."

"I did?"

"With those rituals that you performed – the e-mails from 'me', our Friday night take-away and a movie; all that coupled with your intense grief gave me an in."

The elderly gentleman leaned over and laid his hand on hers. Sarah looked down at the bony claw and when the man spoke again there was a strong waft of stale pipe tobacco.

"The thing is, I'm only able to inhabit bodies that are close to death themselves. Some of the elderly put up little resistance to being taken over, but my time can be rather limited. Sorry, I know that it's probably not what you were hoping for. But I'm here now, so what say we make the best of it, Kittenkat?"

The use of Sean's petname for her made her forget the OAP for a moment and she found her grief taking over.

"I've missed you so much and people try to help, but they don't, you know?" she said in a rush. "Nothing they say, nothing they do, really actually helps. And nobody knows what to say to a young widow, do they? Nobody knows how you're supposed to deal with that sort of tragedy, so everything they say is so empty. And the house is empty, and it seems too big. And every morning I get up and I think, *I wonder whether Sean has put the kettle on*, and I listen for you moving about in the kitchen, listening for the radio, and every single time the silence hurts just as much as it ever did."

Several people looked over as Sarah broke down. Sean looked at them and smiled. "It was her Nan," he said, "they were very close."

When Sarah had regained her composure, she found the man holding out a tissue to her and the smile he gave her – that look of love and sympathy and just the most bottomless patience – convinced her that she was looking at Sean.

"Look," he said. "It's all been a bit much and that's entirely understandable. How about I give you the day to settle your mind and we meet up tomorrow evening?"

"Okay. Where do you want to meet?"

"Ours. I know the address after all. See you at seven?"

Sarah nodded as she wiped away her tears.

THE FOLLOWING EVENING, Sarah waited for the man in the mauve suit but when there was a knock on the door at exactly seven o' clock, she opened it to a gentleman whose steel grey hair and sharp features reminded her of one of her uncles.

"What happened?" she said.

"Would you believe hit by a car? If I'd paid more attention when crossing the road that old boy would have had maybe three more months more in him, but he didn't see the oncoming vehicle. Something wrong with his eyes, I think. But I have to say that I'm somewhat more pleased with this new model. What do you think?" Sean said, holding his arms out. "A more mature George Clooney, perhaps?"

His description was a bit of a stretch but Sarah had to admit that he had something of a mature charm.

"Come in, Mr Clooney," she said, waving him into the hall.

For dinner she made Sean his favourite – spaghetti Bolognese – but when she looked up from her plate, she saw him frowning at his.

"Is something the matter?"

"I'm sorry, it's just this old body. I'm sure it's delicious but it tastes completely different to how I remember it. And did you put chilli in this?"

"Yes. I always did. *Do*, I mean."

"Well, it would appear that this one is not a fan of spicy food. But, no matter. The important thing is that we're together."

"But for how long?"

"Let's not think about that for the moment. Let's just be thankful for this remarkable thing that we have."

"What happened, Sean?"

"What do you mean?"

"The day you died. What happened?"

"My heart gave out. That was that."

"What was your last thought? Was it of me?"

"To be honest, I didn't have time for much of a last thought. It was over pretty damn quickly." Sarah burst into tears. "Hey, it's okay. I'm back now."

She looked at the man who was and wasn't her husband and wished that it could really be him; *all* of him. Even so, she had been blessed with a miracle of sorts and she should at least try and make this work.

After dinner they sat in companionable silence. Sean finished the last of his whisky and put down the glass with a satisfied sigh.

"Well thank fuck that still tastes the same, eh? Anyway, bedtime methinks."

"Oh, sure. I've made up the bed in the spare room. There's a clean towel and I managed to find you a toothbrush."

"What? Jesus, Sarah! Am I a guest in my own home? And, anyway, when I said bedtime, I didn't mean that it was time for sleeping."

"Oh. *Oh.* I see. I..."

"Let's at least try. I'm not entirely sure how long I've got in this one and the next old codger may not be quite so fit."

Sarah still couldn't help comparing the man who sat in the armchair opposite her to her uncle; the same uncle who had grabbed her arse during the disco at his own daughter's wedding. But this was her husband, she reminded herself; the man she loved.

"You look gorgeous, you know," he said, when they finally made it to the bedroom.

Sean had been a slim man of around six-foot-two with a well-defined upper body and a toned waist, so when he removed his shirt and Sarah saw the wrinkled flesh and the over-hanging belly, she was somewhat taken aback. She tried not to look at the tangle of grey above his flaccid cock as he removed his underpants. Even so, when Sean opened his arms, she went to him.

They started with a kiss. His mouth didn't fit hers quite as well as Sean's had and when her tongue brushed against the hard plastic of his dentures, she had to suppress a shudder. His hands ran down her body, his rough palms finding her breasts and his twig-like fingers brushing her nipples. When he touched her between her legs, Sarah had to will herself to relax. Only when Sean dropped to his knees and buried his face in her sex, did she finally allow herself to let go.

She remembered their honeymoon and how they had made love every single morning before making their way down to the secluded beach below their apartment. Every time Sean had looked at her, every time he had said her name, she was filled with a love so intense that she thought it would burn a hole right through her. Sean had been her first and only boyfriend and she had never wanted another man. They were perfect, made for each other – that's what everybody said.

"Fuck it! Goddamn it!"

"What? What is it?" she said, as Sean got to his feet.

"I took four Viagra before I came over and not a fucking sausage. I mean, look at it!"

Sarah tried not to.

"Listen, it doesn't matter."

"It does to me. Fucking thing, why won't you fucking work? I go and choose what appears to be a fully functioning body only to find that the old bastard is impotent."

"Sean, calm down. We can just hold each other."

"But I want to do more. I want to be everything a husband is to his wife."

"It's enough just to have you back."

Despite Sean's protests, he came to her and they lay together. Sarah listened to the slight wheeze deep in his chest as he breathed and when he began to snore, she extracted herself from his slack embrace and went to sleep in the spare room. Not that she got much sleep. Sean had her waking every half hour or so with his seemingly endless trips to the bathroom.

In the morning he looked frail, his skin bleached by the sunlight flooding the kitchen.

"I feel terrible," he said.

"Do you want anything to eat?"

"I couldn't possibly."

He lived for only a couple more weeks after that. The old man Sean had possessed had no family and very few friends, so Sarah was the only one who witnessed his passing. As his breathing became shallow and his grip on her hand weakened, he managed a final smile.

"Don't be frightened," he said. "I'll come back to you."

Another few weeks passed, in which Sarah went to work as normal, returning to an empty home every night, starting to feel the loneliness and grief wash over her like a black tide once more. She was beginning to think she had imagined it all – she wouldn't have been the first widow driven to distraction by the loss of a spouse – when there was a knock on the door one Sunday morning.

"It can take a while," said the skeletally thin man who towered over her, "to find an elderly gent with very few connections. Sorry it took so long."

They had another month together. This time they managed to make love, though the experience of Sean's thin limbs folding themselves around her like the legs of a giant spider made Sarah reluctant to repeat the experience. Instead, they spent their time doing pretty much what they had done prior to Sean's untimely demise – watching movies together on the couch, going out for the occasional meal or taking long walks by the river.

There was one rather mortifying moment when they bumped into one of Sarah's work colleagues on one of their strolls.

"Oh… hi, Alice." Sarah said, her eyes looking anywhere but at her friend's face.

"Sarah, it's so good to see you out and about. And this is?"

"Gerald," Sean said, "Sarah's grandfather."

From the glance Alice gave to Sean's hand resting on her hip, Sarah could tell that she didn't entirely believe him.

"So what?" Sarah said, as they walked away. "Let her think I'm into older men."

Just as she was beginning to feel comfortable with Sean, just as their relationship was falling into a pleasant routine, he died again.

This time he didn't go peacefully. His last days were spent in agony; the room reeking of sweat and vomit. Sarah didn't dare take him to the hospital for fear of the questions they might ask. So for five sleepless nights she sat by his side and watched him fight death. And when he breathed his last, she didn't weep tears of sadness, but relief.

Over the next twelve months, Sean died five more times before Sarah decided she couldn't take it anymore. She was too young to be dealing with old age and infirmity on such an intimate, regular basis. Most normal couples had decades of relatively comfortable marriage before the issue of mortality came into their relationship. Living with the knowledge that Sean's next death could be days, hours, or even minutes away – one old gent had barely had time to knock on the door before the paramedics carted him away – was making her feel elderly herself.

Sarah was finally done with saying goodbye and when Sean began to sicken once more she said, "This can't go on. This isn't a marriage. No matter how badly I wanted you back, I never wanted this."

Sean smiled and weakly grasped her hand. She looked down at the liver spots, the wrinkles and the brittle nails, and covered his hand with hers.

"I'm sorry, my love."

"No. No, you're right, Sarah. You deserve better than this. I'm holding you back."

"I'm starting to forget what Sean was like, what *you* were like, you know?"

And there was no screaming, or crying, no drawn out death rattles; he breathed his last and was gone.

FOR A WHILE, she didn't miss him at all. The house was finally hers again. She no longer had to flit between the roles of nursemaid and frustrated lover; no longer had to mask the stench of death with the sickly smell of air-freshener. Sarah even enrolled in a few night classes at the local college and began to make new friends. But then she began to find reminders of Sean wherever she looked: young couples walking hand-in-hand by the marina; the waft of a familiar aftershave in a crowded bar; his favourite film on the television. And just like that, just when she thought she had forgotten it, the grief was back.

Sarah found herself envying her married friends. She'd see their houses, their children, their holidays abroad and she'd burn with a bitter sense of injustice that Sean had been denied such things. The dates well-meaning friends set up for her with single men just never worked out. No matter how nice the man, how considerate of her feelings, they hadn't been made for Sarah in the same way Sean had. Just because he was gone, it didn't make him any less her soul mate.

The first time that Sean had returned, he'd told Sarah that she had brought him back. And so, after a week of sleepless nights in which her grief had whispered to her from the dark – dragging her deeper into anger and despair – she decided that she would try again. This time she would have what she wanted, both of them would have the life they deserved.

THE YOUNG MAN wasn't a bad fit at all. He had Sean's build, the same hairstyle and he was sweet, in a quiet sort of way. She'd felt rather shameless, fishing for a suitable candidate on the internet. Most men she'd encountered on dating websites seemed rather desperate, and some clearly wanted to date her only so they could do unspeakable things to her, but this one was a keeper – a loner, but perfectly good natured.

They'd been out for a few drinks and a meal and when Sarah had suggested she accompany him back to the house, for a moment he'd looked frightened. She thought she had blown it, but when she gently took his hand, he went with her.

She left him sitting in the dining room while she made tea. The clear liquid she poured into his cup had also been sourced from the internet, after several weeks of fairly detailed research. It would bring him to the verge of death and with the vial of liquid in her right pocket, Sarah would bring him back, once it was all over.

Back in the dining room she sat opposite him and draped a scarf over the table lamp.

"It makes the whole thing rather more intimate, don't you think?" she said, and he smiled and drank his tea.

As his eyes began to droop Sarah leaned over and took both her hands in his.

She took a deep breath, felt herself open up, felt her sadness and anger reach into the darkness beyond.

The young man's eyes flickered opened briefly and when they did Sarah leaned forward and said, "Is there anybody there?"

PETER AND THE INVISIBLE SHARK

Within the heart of the dark, sleeps the shark.

Peter stopped typing. Outside, something had just swished past the window. He was sure of it. He turned in his chair and looked into the night, at the street below, but of course there was nothing. At least not the thing he was imagining – *that* he would hold within these words

The glint in the trees is the light on the eye of the shark.

He'd met with his illustrator a few weeks before and Jane had laughed when he'd told her the title of their new book.

"I like it. Perhaps we can go for a Doctor Seuss thing with the illustrations."

"I was thinking Edward Gorey. It has to be scary."

"But funny, too?"

"Yes… yes, I suppose it had better be funny."

But in the writing this book hadn't made him laugh out loud like some of the others. The story was perhaps a little too close – the shark a touch too near.

Again, Peter's fingers stuttered to a stop. He watched as the shadow moved across the wall above his laptop, from left to right; a sinuous, yet muscular shape.

Outside it was quieter than before; not even a whisper of traffic from the nearby ring road. Peter's chest tightened as he thought about all those miles of air above him; here he sat, on the ocean floor, the pressure of an entire world pushing down.

I hear him
I hear the shark, within the night, amongst the trees.

Peter typed as quickly as possible, keeping the circling shark within the story, holding it to the page.

WHEN HE GAVE it more thought than he was comfortable with, Peter had to admit that it was a silly thing to be haunted by – a shark. And not even a real shark. Instead, it was the model of a shark he had encountered in an aquarium as a young boy.

It hadn't been during the school holidays, so why he and his father – not his mother, he wasn't sure where she had been – had undertaken the trip, he couldn't recall. There were so few visitors to the aquarium that day, it felt as though they had the whole place to themselves.

Peter's father stopped in front of a large tank to watch a turtle swimming up and down the glass, rising and falling. For a time he followed it, his head rising and falling, until his eyes became unfocused and he seemed to be looking far beyond the glass. When his father was like this there was nothing that he could do.

Peter let go of his hand.

At the far side of the room was an archway, beyond which ripples of green light played across the dark walls. Whale song echoed from within the cavern, calling to him. When he stepped beyond the arch, for a moment he really felt as though he was standing at the bottom of the ocean, and he held his breath.

Vast forms hung beneath the ceiling, dappled with the constantly shifting aquamarine light, which made it difficult to tell where the floor ended and the walls began. The clicks and squeals of a school of dolphins drew his gaze to the far corner, where they were frozen in flight, their toothy smiles forever open. In the centre of the room hung the great blue whale, its sides encrusted with barnacles, its tail upraised as though it were about to come down and propel the behemoth across the aquarium. Arresting as these forms were, however, it was one in particular that made Peter let go of his breath in a shocked gasp.

The shark hung just above the entrance to the next room, daring him to approach. Even though he could see that it was attached to the ceiling via two metal rods, the creature was no less terrifying – or maybe it was its unreality that made it worse, somehow. Whereas the whale boomed and the dolphins clicked, from the shark there was a strange, watery *shushing* noise.

Peter walked back to where his father stood watching the turtle, and took his hand. Even though his presence offered little comfort or reassurance, there was no way that Peter was going to walk beneath the shark on his own.

His father didn't look up as the shadow of the shark passed over them. Again there was that strange noise – *shush, shush, shush* – as though the shark were trying to calm Peter, to reassure him, before it attacked.

THAT NIGHT, AS he slept, Peter returned to the aquarium.

This time there was no whale or dolphins in the submarine grotto, though their calls haunted the space. Peter could see the metal rods that had secured them to the ceiling, their ends ragged and torn.

The shark, however, was still there – the Great White with its rows of sharp, incurving teeth and its alien eyes. Soon, the strange *shushing* sound was the only noise in the room, and then that too fell silent.

It's just a model. Just a big toy.

But Peter couldn't move, could barely breathe – a warm, wet trickle ran down his leg.

Two bangs in quick succession shocked him out of his torpor. The shark had broken free of its restraints and drifted silently towards the floor. There was no sign of life in its pure, black eyes but, with a flick of its tail, it surged towards him.

Peter ran, charging past the tanks of neon fish and slowly undulating sea anemones, bursting through the gift shop, overturning racks of cards and stumbling over stuffed toys in his hurry to get away. The shark made a further chaos of the shop as it barrelled through after him. *Maybe*, Peter thought, *I'll be safe outside.* But as he hurried out through the doors, the shark was close behind. With a sound of glass shattering and metal tearing, it threw itself into the night.

Peter didn't look back, he just ran.

He couldn't remember the aquarium being close to their house – in fact he knew that it was at least an hour's drive away – but all of a sudden he found himself on his street. Hearing nothing behind him, he chanced a look back.

There was no shark.

At least until that soft, watery sound made him look up.

There was a shadow on the moon and Peter watched as it grew, the shark descending out of the night sky like some strange alien craft.

It stopped before him, hanging only a few metres above the road. The shark drifted slowly forward and nudged Peter with its nose, pushing him back towards his house.

He didn't want the shark in his house. He didn't think that there would be anything his mother or father could do to stop it.

He stumbled away and ran for his front door, slamming it in the creature's face before lunging for the stairs. Again, there was the sound of breaking glass and tearing metal as the shark invaded their home. Peter ran for the only sanctuary he knew – his bedroom. There, he did what he always did when there was something to be afraid of; he dived under the covers and cowered in their womb-like warmth.

Peter sheltered within his duvet cocoon for what felt like an age, before he finally risked a peek above his blanket, only to find himself looking directly down the gullet of the shark.

It was dark within the shark.

THE DREAMS HAD persisted into his late teens and each time they came, it always ended with Peter screaming himself awake, drenched in a cold sweat. Once, when he was fourteen, he'd asked his father to check his wardrobe for him, convinced – even in the light of a bright morning – that the shark was hiding amongst his clothes. Of course, there was nothing to be found amongst his shirts and trousers, but Peter had slept in the living room for a week before daring to return to his bedroom.

Eventually, he found refuge in writing. Encouraged by one of his teachers, Peter discovered that making light of the things that scared him diminished them, made them more manageable. In his early twenties, Peter discovered an aptitude and then a passion for poetry, leading him to regularly perform his comic verse at poetry slams and open-mic nights.

On his twenty-first birthday, Peter's father had come to see him perform. Peter hadn't told him where he was going to be that night, but just before he took to the stage, he saw his father sitting down at a table towards the back of the bar. Afterwards, Peter had brought him a drink, perhaps in the expectation that he would tell him how proud he was. Instead, he messily downed the whisky before saying with contempt, "You've made a joke of me!"

Peter replied without thinking. "No, Dad. You did that yourself."

ON THE BUS home after the gig, the shark returned.

Peter tried to convince himself that someone had spiked his orange juice. But he had watched the barman pour the drink from a freshly uncapped bottle, and though there were certainly some strange characters on the poetry scene, he didn't think any of them would have stooped so low as to spike his drink.

No, the fact of the matter was that after the gig he had got onto the bus stone cold sober, the argument with his father still making his guts churn, and fifteen or so minutes later, sitting on the top deck, Peter had looked out of the window to see the shark drifting silently alongside the vehicle, almost touching the glass.

He was the only one on the top deck, so there was nobody he could ask, "Do you see that?" He wondered whether it was some sort of prank, whether the creature outside was some kind of remote-controlled helium balloon.

But there was no mistaking it; this was *his* shark.

This time, however, the creature elicited little terror, more a sense of curiosity.

The shark was damaged. Its flank had been slashed open, revealing the fibre glass structure within; one of its glass eyes had been cracked, and several of its teeth were missing.

Peter knelt on the seat and opened the window. As soon as he did so the strange watery *shushing* noise filled the bus. The shark butted up against the glass a couple of times, making a hollow plastic sound each time it struck.

Putting his arm through the window and leaning out as far as he was able, Peter tried to reach the shark. His fingertips had just barely managed to brush its fin when the creature drifted away. It turned on the spot and ghosted towards the park. He watched it thread its way through the trees, occasionally bumping against a branch, before the bus turned a corner and the shark was lost from view.

IT WAS ONLY when he woke up screaming in the bed he shared with his fiancée early one morning, several years later, that he finally told someone else about the shark.

The dream had been particularly horrific. Lying in their bed, Peter had watched as the shark ate his legs. It had taken its time over its feast and, in any case, Peter couldn't move. He could only watch as his feet disappeared between those vast jaws. The blood washed up against him and Natasha; a warm tide that lifted his fiancée's hair and fanned it out over her pillow.

The shark moved further up his body, almost lazily snapping a femur in two as it slowly bit down. Peter found that if he concentrated he could move a little. He reached out a hand to push the creature away, but his hand met not with living flesh, but slick, cold fibreglass.

He hadn't understood that he was within a dream, convinced that this time the shark really would consume him. When the scream that had been trapped in his chest finally emerged and shattered the nightmare, Natasha held him as the terror faded.

"I don't think it's odd at all," she said a short time later, as they sat in the kitchen in their dressing gowns, sipping tea. "Lots of people are scared of sharks."

"Shark. Singular. Not sharks generally, but a specific shark. The model of a shark in an aquarium."

And Peter told Natasha about his childhood trip and the encounter that had filled him with a lifetime of fear.

"Maybe you should get an outside perspective." Natasha said. "It may be worth your while going to see a councillor. It certainly helped me when I went through that dark patch last year. A good therapist can help you unpack things, see them for what they are."

Peter agreed to give it a go, but after three sessions of being told that he harboured a lot of anger towards his father, he decided that that was quite enough of that bullshit.

"He's just making stuff up, Natasha!" Peter said. "I never even think about my father these days. It's like he's not even real."

"Okay," Natasha sighed. "How about, in that case, you write about the shark?"

"Because my books with Jane are supposed to be fun. Sometimes dark, yes, but always silly and fantastical."

"So make this thing that has a hold on you silly and fantastical. Peter, I'm sure that with Jane's help you can untooth the bastard, and produce a fun story into the bargain."

Though Peter loved Natasha, and though he had listened to what she, and, to a lesser extent, his therapist, had said, he chose to ignore their advice and push the shark to the back of his mind.

SIX MONTHS LATER, during a flight to Chicago that he and Jane were taking to promote their latest book in the US, Peter looked out of the window and saw a dark speck moving against a brilliant white cloud. The speck quickly grew as it flew towards the aircraft and Peter hurdled over Jane in his panic, lurching into the aisle and shouting, "It's going to hit!"

The thing that struck the plane, however, was not a missile or another aircraft, but the shark. It pressed its eye up against the window before darting away, disappearing back into the cloud that was now pregnant with the promise of thunder.

After the air stewards had calmed the other passengers and assured them that nothing had struck the aircraft, Peter was put under restraint. The only thing that alleviated what had turned into an awful flight was the presence of Jane, who remained by his side throughout the ordeal even though he could read an expression on her face that said, *I think that my co-author is having a massive nervous breakdown.*

The slew of questions Peter faced once they reached the United States, and the hours spent in small brightly lit rooms drinking indescribable coffee, finally convinced him of the wisdom of Natasha's words; he'd write about the shark.

It was only when they finally got to their hotel that Peter found out that his father had died while they had been somewhere over the Atlantic.

You cannot see
You cannot hear
But I tell you that he is near
He's in your room
Beneath your bed

Peter re-read the last two lines again before deleting them. This book was supposed to be fun and writing those words had made him feel queasy.

He had drawn the curtains several hours ago, but that had only brought the shadow into sharper definition, outlined on the cloth now by the light of the full moon.

Natasha had long since gone to bed. He wanted to wake her, just so that he had someone *normal* to talk to, someone who would tell him that the shark was most definitely not drawing near. But he was so close to finishing the book, once the words were written perhaps the haunting would be over.

Even so, when he had hit Save and closed down the laptop there was that sound

shush shush shush

and when he climbed into bed it followed him down into sleep.

PETER AND JANE wouldn't normally have gone to see one of their books being printed, but this was part of the publicity programme, tied in with a wider campaign to raise awareness of the book industry amongst children.

The event was almost a wash-out, literally. That winter had seen the worst flooding in the UK for almost two-hundred years. Many of the roads surrounding the print works were under water and the car that delivered them had driven down a narrow tarmac causeway which appeared to be in imminent danger of disappearing. Both of them were keen to get the visit over with as quickly as possible to avoid being stranded.

A handful of school children had been bussed in for the event and Peter and Jane had even been asked by some of them to sign books;

the majority, however, looked as bored and anxious as Peter felt, distinctly underwhelmed by what they no-doubt thought of as the outdated technology that surrounded them.

"How have things been?" Jane asked when they had retreated to the relative quiet of one of the offices, though even here the boom and rattle of the machinery forced her to raise her voice. "Natasha told me that you've been through a rough patch lately, but you seem pretty good to me."

"Actually, you know what? I am."

Peter was telling the truth. After he and Jane had signed off the proofs of the book almost a month ago, he finally felt that he could breathe again; it no longer felt like he was at the bottom of the ocean, under the shadow – and at the mercy – of those creatures that roved the depths above. He was even starting to look forward to the school tour. And, despite his earlier misgivings about writing the book, he was pleased with what they had produced, especially Jane's illustrations. Her shark was so unlike his own that it had dispelled much of his anxiety concerning their latest collaboration.

The printing press finally wound down. Outside, Peter watched the racing clouds begin to fragment; weak, milky sunlight fighting through. In a flooded field he saw a fin emerge from the water. But that was okay, Peter was pretty sure it was the last he would see of his nightmare.

The door to the office opened and the print manager entered.

"Are you two ready to see the finished product?"

"Yes," Peter said. "Yes, we are."

JAMES LIKED STORIES, but he wasn't sure that he liked this one. The man reading to them seemed nice enough, but from the tone of his voice he was enjoying reading the story about as much as James was enjoying listening to it. The pictures projected onto the wall behind the man made things worse. The drawings showed a shark and there was something sad and angry about it that James really didn't like.

He closed his eyes but that didn't stop him from hearing the words, and when the man shouted,

"You cannot see

You cannot hear

But I tell you that he is near,"

James opened his eyes to see the man pointing. None of the other children turned – they seemed to be enjoying the story far more than James – but James couldn't help but follow the direction of the man's finger.

And it was there, outside, hovering beside the bike sheds. It had emerged from the man's words, swum out from the pictures, and now it was watching James, the rain pattering on its blue-grey fibreglass flanks.

HIGH CHURCH

MADELEINE WAS CONSIDERING a second gin and tonic when a man in a garish Christmas jumper sat himself on the stool beside her. The plastic reindeer's nose on his chest lit up and the relevant ditty issued from somewhere within the cable knit.

"That's unusual," she said.

"Yes, isn't it? I'm Richard. Can I buy you a drink?"

"I wouldn't say no to another G&T."

When the barman placed the drinks before them, Richard fanned his face theatrically and said, "Rather warm in here, isn't it? Think I'll just take this off."

"Now that its desired effect has been achieved, you mean?"

He blushed. "Something like that."

Madeleine waited until he'd struggled out of his novelty jumper before she put down her drink.

"You know," she said, "you're right. It is a bit muggy in here."

And she removed her own jumper, folding it neatly on the bar beside her.

She looked up to see Richard's drink hovering before his lips, his eyes fixed on the dog collar now revealed at her neck.

"Cheers," Madeleine said, clinking her glass against Richard's, his drink slopping over his frozen hand.

"So," she continued, "are you looking forward to Christmas?"

"Erm... yes, that is..."

"Perhaps we'll see you in church?"

"Is that...?" Richard patted his pocket and retrieved a mobile phone. "Yes... I think it was. Sorry, I just have to..."

He hurried away from the bar, his phone glued to his ear, his face burning.

Madeleine raised her drink to his back and smiled.

Being a single woman could be tricky at times, but being a single woman vicar presented its own set of challenges.

"Can I get you another, vicar?" The barman said as he whisked away her empty glass.

"No, I think that's enough sinning for one evening and, besides, work in the morning and all that."

"Work? It's Sunday tomorrow is it?"

"Oh, ha ha."

Outside the pub she waited a good five minutes before a break in the traffic allowed her to cross the road. It took all of her Christian resolve not to raise her middle finger at the Mini which came dangerously close to clipping her.

The dark bulk of the vicarage loomed as Madeleine made her way down the rutted drive. She'd heard of newly appointed clergy who had been placed in quaint country cottages with ivy climbing the walls and thatch covering the eaves. She even knew of one vicar whose job came with a five-bedroom Georgian terrace complete with underground garage and live-in housekeeper. Though Madeleine loved her parish dearly, in terms of housing she hadn't been quite as lucky as some of her fellow ministers.

The vicarage may have been built in the brutalist style – Madeleine wasn't sure, not being *au fait* with architectural terms. Either way, it had probably seemed like a good idea in the sixties, but now it just screamed *eyesore*. She had requested some modernisation from the parish office, but was, for now, stuck with living in the past with temperamental central-heating and rising damp.

That evening, after trying to hear the radio over the knocking of water pipes, she was about to turn in for the night when the phone rang.

"Madeleine? It's Peter Barkely at All Saints. Listen, I wouldn't usually ask this, only I can't find any other clergy to cover for me. Anyway, long story short, Grahame Staines is on his way out."

"Grahame Staines?"

"Ah, yes. Sorry, I forget how new you are. Grahame was the last but one incumbent of St Mark's. He'd still be there, haunting the place, if the parish hadn't removed him on grounds of ill health. Anyway, his carer just called to say that he's not going to last the night, so I need you to be there to attend to him."

"And you can't because...?"

"I'm in Antigua until next week."

"Lovely. I'm sure that it's very nice this time of year."

"Oh, it's not a holiday. No, it's a conference on pastoral care."

"In Antigua?"

"Yes… anyway, would you be a love and do this one favour for me?"

Be a love? Who does he bloody think… Christian thoughts, Madeleine. Christian thoughts.

"Of course. Let me know the address and I'll head over now."

"Thank you so much. I owe you one."

"Just get me on that conference next year, eh?"

LAKE VIEW HOUSE looked out not upon a lake but a landfill site on one side and a busy road on the other; not a place one would choose to die in. The high-rise should have been pulled down years ago but, for reasons Madeleine didn't entirely understand, had recently achieved listed status.

Inside, the lifts were out – "Of course, why wouldn't they be?" Madeleine mumbled to herself – and Peter had told her that Grahame Staines lived on the fourteenth floor.

She started up the poorly lit stairwell – Bible in her right hand, small leather satchel in her left – fervently hoping that the Reverend Peter Barkely was having a lovely time in Antigua, and not at all wishing a bizarre accident involving the pointy end of a cocktail umbrella befall him.

By the eighth floor she was seriously out of breath, and so not at all prepared for the sight that came lumbering down the stairs towards her.

The Rottweiler stopped. Its tongue lolled and its tail wagged, and for a moment Madeleine thought that she was going to be okay. But when she held out her hand and said, "Hey there. And what's your name?" a growl issued from deep in the dog's throat, sending a jolt of fear lancing through her.

Madeleine knew that if she turned and fled the dog would be on her before she could reach the next landing, and trying to edge past the beast and continue on her way was clearly not an option. Realising that she may well die before she could get to the dying, she did the only thing she could. The Bible was a family heirloom, originally belonging to her great-grandmother on her mother's side. Its pages were edged with gold leaf and the cover was red aromatic leather stretched over wooden boards. When the book connected with the dog's jaw there was a sickening *crack* that at first made Madeleine worry about the integrity of the Bible, and then made her hope that she hadn't injured the dog too badly.

The Rottweiler dropped, the stink of dog briefly filling her nostrils as it tumbled past her, its flank connecting with a meaty thud against the landing railing below.

Madeleine stood frozen to the spot, wracked with guilt at the thought that she may have killed the dog. But then its hind legs twitched, its eyes opened, and it growled.

A frenzied barking followed her as she fled, and Madeleine was terrified that the dog would be on her in seconds before a cry of "Rommel, you cunt! Get the fuck in here" silenced the animal. There was the scuffle of claws on concrete, a door slamming, and then silence. She breathed a sigh of relief.

Outside 14b she tried to regain some of her former composure, wiping her brow with her stole and straightening her jacket. When she knocked, the door was answered by a young man with a stethoscope around his neck and a name badge that read *Stu*.

"Oh, hi. I'm Madeleine Drew." Stu didn't respond and seemed to be considering whether to close the door in her face, perhaps thinking that she was trying to sell something. "You know, the vicar?"

"Oh, right! Right, sorry." Stu laughed. "I wasn't expecting..."

"A woman?"

"I was going to say someone so young."

"Well, thank you, Stu. Is Grahame...?"

"Still with us? Just. Follow me."

This wasn't the first death bed that Madeleine had attended, but it was perhaps the most Spartan. There was nothing in the room beyond the bed on which the elderly priest lay and a cabinet, on top of which stood a lamp and a glass of water. Madeleine thought that in one's last moments, a person would want to be surrounded by family, or at least the mementos of familial love – pictures and the like – but the room was virtually bare.

As his carer had said, Grahame Staines clearly didn't have long. Each uneven breath rattled as it was dragged in and out, and the shadows were deeply pooled in the hollows of his face.

"Would you like me to leave you alone with him?" Stu said, nervously fingering his stethoscope.

"No, that's fine, Stu. You can stay."

Madeleine placed her Bible on the bedside cabinet and took a small vial of oil from her satchel.

"Grahame, as you are coming to this part of your journey, may I pray with you for God's blessing?"

The rattling wheeze stopped abruptly and Madeleine thought that he had gone before she had even begun, but then the priest's eyes briefly fluttered open and the wheezing began again.

"I'd just go ahead if I were you, vicar," Stu said.

Madeleine dipped her index finger into the oil and then made the sign of the cross on Grahame's forehead.

"Grahame, receive the sign of the cross, the mark of your baptism, the sign of your salvation. May God who is faithful bless you and—"

A clawed hand shot up from the bed and clamped painfully around her wrist. The elderly priest's eyes snapped open, and this time they stayed open.

"A… ah…" he gasped, his head straining above the pillow.

Ignoring the trickle of oil running beneath the sleeve of her shirt, Madeleine leaned in close.

"Yes, Grahame? Is there something you would like to say?"

"*A woman!*" he shouted directly into her face.

Stu hurried to the bedside and tried to gently remove the priest's hand from Madeleine's wrist, but she was held fast.

"Now, Mr Staines. We gain nothing from being agitated, do we?" Stu said.

"*They sent... a woman?!*"

The water glass on the bedside table jumped into the air and exploded; Madeleine was only vaguely aware of the shards peppering her face. All of her awareness was on the pain of the priest's fingers digging into her. It was as though his grip were sinking deep into her flesh. She thought that she smelled incense burning, though she hadn't brought any with her.

"L-lord... now let your servant depart in peace, a-according to your..."

But she got no further, for a great darkness rose up from the bed and took her.

PETER BARKELY BLEW out the candle and, at the same time, the chanting ceased.

He released his grip on the hands he had been holding and uncrossed his legs. As he got to his feet, a sudden cramp gripped his right calf and he hissed in pain.

"You know," he said to those sat within the circle, "all things considered, I really would much rather be in Antigua."

MADELEINE CAME TO, jerking back into consciousness so forcefully that she dropped the glass of whisky she had been holding. She watched it roll across the carpet of her study and fetch up against the foot of her desk.

She had no memory of returning to the vicarage. The last thing she could recall was praying over the elderly priest. And now, here she was.

Somehow she'd made her way home, somehow she'd poured herself a whisky – a spirit she didn't drink or keep in the house. Madeleine saw the empty Londis bag in the bin and realised that somehow she had also been shopping. She dialled Peter Barkely's mobile, but there was no reply. She would have called Stu or even Graeme Staines himself, but she hadn't been given either number, so there was no way to check just what had happened.

After a couple of hours spent trawling the internet for the symptoms of a brain tumour, Madeleine realised that she was only making herself more anxious. No doubt exhaustion, job stress and the two gin and tonics she'd consumed earlier had all added to... whatever had happened. For now, she decided to go to bed and call her GP first thing in the morning.

THE FOLLOWING TWO days passed without incident. Madeleine didn't suffer from another 'episode', as Doctor Ewing had called it, and life at the vicarage continued much as it had before. On Friday the local paper ran an obituary of Grahame Staines. The accompanying photo showed a severe looking man with a shock of jet-black hair and a piercing gaze. He had apparently been the vicar of St Mark's for six decades – a parish record – and tended to his flock with 'utmost diligence, dedication and fiercely held convictions'. "Sounds like a right barrel of laughs," Madeleine muttered as she threw the paper in the bin.

Six decades, though, that *was* impressive. The Reverend Staines must have made quite the mark.

On Sunday she rose early and walked down to the church, breathing deeply of the spring air and admiring the daisies scattered across the vicarage's lawn. Ahead of her, St Mark's was wreathed in a light mist, the headstones in the graveyard seeming to hover before the dark granite of the church.

Madeleine thought that she saw someone pacing her down the hill – perhaps Gavin Nesbitt, the organist, who usually liked to arrive good and early – but when she turned there was nobody there. Ducking beneath the lichgate, she remembered fragments from the dream she had experienced – something about earth raining down on her upturned face.

Shaking her head clear of the night's phantoms, she used the massive iron key to unlock the double doors of the church porch. She had barely stepped across the threshold when the darkness rose to take her again.

"...A LOVELY SERVICE, vicar. Just lovely. And, pardon my French, but I'm glad that you finally had the balls to say it. Something *does* need to be done about those scroungers and immigrants – expecting free handouts as they pop out yet more children they can't look after. Anyway, keep up the good work."

Madeleine found herself outside her own church, shaking hands with the departing congregation, the sound of the organ echoing through the porch behind her.

Another hand grasped hers. It was Ivy Butler, one of the more senior members of her flock. "Good for you, Madeleine. You know, your sermon reminded me of the good old days of Grahame Staines."

Good Lord, what had she said?

Not all of the people filing past offered their hands, and from the expression on some of the faces a good many would not be returning to St Mark's next Sunday.

Am I going mad?

"Not mad, no."

The voice sounded like it came from directly behind her, a chill breeze insinuating itself into her ear.

"Madeleine," said Patricia Stevens, a young mother who she had shared a bottle of Shiraz with on many an occasion, "I don't know what happened in there, but get help."

"Yes... yes, I will."

Ignoring the rest of the congregation, Madeleine fled back up the hill to the vicarage, where she shut herself in the study.

The whisky glass was still where she had left it, on the floor against her desk, and she had to fight the urge to pick it up and fill it. Instead, she closed her eyes.

"Lord, be with me during this time. Let me get to the heart of the problem and know that you are by my side at all times."

No sooner had she spoken the words than the phone rang. It was Paul Green, her curate.

"Madeleine, I must say that I was rather shocked by the content of your sermon."

She wanted to say that she was under a lot of stress, she wanted to tell him that she was seriously worried she may have a brain tumour, but when she opened her mouth, the words that came were not her own.

"It is time, Paul, that we stopped stepping so daintily around the truth. It is time that this modern church of ours stops dressing up scripture to appease the liberal agenda. It is not my job to tell people what they want to hear."

There was a long silence, during which Madeleine railed against the words she had unwittingly spoken, but she was trapped within her own skull, her silent screams echoing in her ears.

"I think, in that case, Madeleine, I'm going to have to reconsider my position at St. Mark's."

"Yes, I rather think you should."

And before she could command it to do otherwise, her hand had returned the phone to its cradle, ending the call.

For a moment, all she could do was sit and stare at the phone, her body rigid with shock. Whatever she had said during the sermon, they hadn't been *her* words. And now she had dismissed her curate entirely against her will. It was as though she had been taken over by something, as though she had been...

...no. She didn't want to start using *that* word. This was the modern church; this was *her* church.

"No! This church is mine"

This time the voice that came from her lips was most certainly not her own; the vehemence behind the words, the spiteful tone, could not be mistaken.

"Reverend Staines?"

"Ah... at last you understand."

"Hang on... hang on just a moment." *No no no! This cannot be happening.* "When I prayed over you the other night, when you passed on, did you..."

"Enter you? Yes." And the filthy laugh that came from her lips chilled her to the bone.

"What do you want with me?"

"With you? Nothing. What I want is my church back. What I want is to return my flock to the true path."

"Sorry, *your* church? I hate to break this to you Grahame, but you died. St Marks is *my* church."

"The priesthood is no place for a woman!"

There was a knock on the study door and Madeleine realised that, in her haste, she must have left the front door of the vicarage wide open. Had whoever was standing on the other side heard her conversation? If so, what would they think when the door opened and they found Madeleine alone?

"Come in," she said.

The man who walked into the room was wearing a grey suit, blue shirt and a dog collar. Madeleine didn't recognise the vicar, but she was glad of the clerical company – if anybody could understand her predicament, it would be another priest.

"Can I help you?" she said.

"Madeleine? I'm Paul Barkely. We spoke on the phone the other day."

"Oh... yes. Actually, your timing is perfect. You see, ever since I went to see Reverend Staines, I... wait a moment, aren't you supposed to be in Antigua?"

Peter Barkely walked slowly towards her, his eyes studying her face intently – perhaps he was looking for signs of madness?

"Reverend Staines, are you in there?" he said.

"What? You can't be—" but before Madeleine could finish the sentence her words were stolen from her, and the strange male voice emerged once again.

"Yes, I'm here, Barkely. However, I don't yet seem to have full mastery. This one still has... opinions, and some semblance of control."

Peter Barkely sat down and removed his dog collar before undoing the top button of his shirt. Madeleine could just make out the blue-black stain of a tattoo scrolling up the base of his throat.

"Bugger," he said. "I told them. I said the chant wasn't pitched right. Though, to be fair, the book that you gave us wasn't exactly clear on the details of the ritual."

Madeleine found herself pouring a whisky for the rogue priest and as she handed it to him, he ran his fingers lightly over her hand. "Ah, but such smooth skin, Reverent Staines."

"Shut up! Quite why a woman had to be the vessel—"

Peter Barkely held up his hand, cutting him short.

"You've got your church back, haven't you?"

"But I don't have full control!"

"You will, soon. The new ritual will see to that tonight. In the meantime," Peter Barkely stood, knocking back the whisky and re-securing his dog collar, "hang in there."

MADELEINE CAME TO as the last rays of the sun dipped below the roof of St Mark's. On the desk, the flashing light of the answer machine told her that she had twenty-five new messages. She wanted to call everybody back, tell them that she was still here, that what had happened was not her fault, but she realised that she did not have the time do so. Peter Barkely had said that the ritual would be completed tonight.

There was only one thing for it. Madeleine would go over to All Saints and put a stop to this right now while she still had at least some control.

Taking down the parish directory from the shelf above her desk, she looked for the listing for Peter Barkely's church. There was an All Fathers, but no All Saints. A quick Google search confirmed her fears: whoever Peter Barkely was, he was not a minister in the Church of England. She was, however, surprised to find that a search on the Reverend Grahame Staines threw up a fair amount of information. He was the author of three books – all self-published: *The Hard Truth: Christ's Words as He Actually Meant Them; Marriage: The Tenets of an Institution,* and *Sons of Christ – Daughters of Servitude.* His views were often regarded as 'inflammatory' and 'reactionary' and one theologian even described him as a 'good old-fashioned, hellfire and fury tub thumper; a dying breed and a remnant of an archaic and patriarchal institution'. An enterprising parishioner had even seen fit to transcribe several of his sermons, in which he spent much of his time 'shocked': at the moral laxity of the young, at working mothers, at immigrants and, in particular, homosexuals.

Madeleine looked up as something black and ragged passed by the window. She could feel a presence at her back, a hand resting on her shoulder that felt like it was made of sticks. She blinked and the last of the daylight was gone, the North Star now shining like a promise at the apex of the church spire. She had a sense that silence had just returned to the room, that she had finished a conversation, though she could recall nothing of what had been spoken.

"Right, Reverend Grahame Staines," she said, getting to her feet, pushing the dark whispering to the back of her mind, "that's quite enough of that."

PUTTING ON MAKE-up was something of a challenge with the revenant of a recently deceased Anglican priest standing at one's shoulder. On several occasions Madeleine had felt the Reverend Staines trying to regain control, but she had focused her will and pushed him away. Unfortunately this hadn't stopped him talking to her, or scowling at her in the mirror.

"And here we see the moral laxity of the modern church," he railed. *"Here we see a priest, a woman priest no less, applying paint to her face so that she looks like nothing more than a common whore."*

"What? I'm hardly tarting myself up, Grahame. Anyway, Margaret Thatcher wore make-up. Are you about to tell me that she was a whore, too?"

The dead vicar had nothing to say to that. Instead, he slammed the front door in her face as she made to leave the vicarage.

Ignoring the outburst, Madeleine opened the door again and made her way across the road, all the while aware of a dark muttering in the back of her mind.

The pub was clearly the place to be on a Sunday night. Disco lights sprayed whirling rainbows against windows fogged by condensation. Pop music thudded through the walls, so loud that Madeleine could feel the vibration of it against her skin.

"Madeleine," one of the door staff acknowledged her with a nod as she entered the pub.

Inside, it was busier than she had ever seen it. The tiny dance floor was packed and the queues at the bar were three deep as people drank as though tomorrow wasn't a Monday. Tinsel brushed her head as she ducked past a low beam to find a place from which she could order a drink.

"You would bring me here? No wonder the reputation of the church is in the pits!"

"You're telling me that you lived opposite a pub and never popped in for a swift pint? No wonder you're such a joyless wa—"

"Madeleine, what can I get you?" The barman stood before her, ignoring the shouts of frustration from some of the other booze-hungry punters.

"Glass of red wine, please, Ted. Bit mad tonight isn't it?"

"Well, Christmas and all that."

"Ah yes. At least the meaning of Christ's birth hasn't been lost on this lot, eh?"

"Well, it's clearly been lost on you!" The dead priest tried to drive the words beyond her lips, but Madeleine covered his utterance with a fit of coughing.

"Nasty cold you've got there, vicar. You should be tucked up in bed."

"Yes, I should be. There's just something I need to do first."

Securing herself a seat, Madeleine scanned the room, looking for a likely candidate – but many of the men here were either far too young or far too drunk.

When a well-groomed gentleman leant against the bar next to her to order a drink, Reverend Staines took control of Madeleine's legs and she had very nearly marched all the way to the door before she managed an abrupt about-face. She noticed then that she was beginning to draw looks, and not of the sort that she intended. On the dance floor in the corner, a woman threw her arms into the air, turning round and round in the circle of men who had gathered to watch her. The scene was obscured by a blast of dry ice and, as it rolled towards her, Madeleine could smell incense. The room darkened and the music slowed, becoming a low sonorous chant. At the bar, a man was using a puddle of spilled beer to sketch strange symbols onto the dark wood.

"The ritual is coming to a head. This will all be over soon, Madeleine. All you have to do is just let go."

Madeleine focused her will and fought her way back into her body just in time to catch the wine glass before it hit the floor. She straightened up to see the door in front of her opening and a familiar face stepping into the fug of perspiration and alcohol.

It was Richard, the man from the other night; he of the novelty jumper and the poor chat-up technique. She grabbed his arm, hoping that the sudden grave-like stench that assaulted them wasn't coming from her.

The colour drained from Richard's face when he recognized her.

"Vicar? I—"

"Richard, I don't have much time to explain but I need you to do something for me."

"Erm, listen. I'm supposed to be meeting—"

"It's for charity and it will only take a second."

Richard smiled, letting his guard down a little. "Yeah, okay."

"Kiss me, Richard."

Madeleine closed her eyes and leaned in close. She allowed the Reverend Staines almost all the way in then; she could feel his foul presence pouring into her like ice-cold water. Her legs were his legs, her arms were his arms, and her lips were his lips.

And so, Madeleine used the last of her will to push those lips up against Richard's in a warm, moist kiss, hoping that the Reverend Grahame Staines could feel everything.

There was a bellow of appalled rage that seemed to go on forever, and then nothing.

"THIS IS THE word of the Lord," she said, closing the Bible before returning it to its stand. As she quickly shuffled through her sermon notes, she saw Peter Barkely enter the church and quietly slip into a far pew. There was a look of anticipation on his face, a sick kind of hope.

She adjusted the radio mic clipped to her stole and cleared her throat.

"'You shall love your neighbour as yourself.' It's simple, isn't it? But so many of us seem to forget. And here, we must also remember that neighbour means everyone. *Everyone.*"

Madeleine glanced up and the look of shock and disappointment on Peter Barkely's face filled her with a triumphant joy. Getting up so abruptly that he almost tipped over the pew, he stormed from the church.

She smiled and it took all of her will, all of her Christian resolve, not to call out after him, "And don't let the church door hit your arse on the way out!"

RAISE THE
BEAM HIGH

SOMEONE HAD FINALLY cleared the lot beside Theodore Wright's grain warehouse. For as long as most could remember it had been a tangle of weeds, mesquite trees and broken bits of carriages; a place stray dogs went to sleep when the sun got too fierce. Come sun-up on Wednesday it was all gone, the ground clear and even. Not one stone reared its head above the neatly-raked earth. No one had seen it happen – though Theodore, working late in his warehouse, had said there had been a strange noise, as of a sudden gale rising up – and, come Thursday, pretty much everybody had forgotten that this patch of ground had once been a place of nature run rampant.

On Friday a procession of carriages brought a whole load of pine timbers which were placed carefully, some would say reverentially, in the centre of the lot. Some folk asked the strangers unloading the materials what they were planning, what was to be constructed here. The only answer they got was, "Ask Mr. Chauncy Montclair."

But nobody knew a Mr. Montclair and someone with such a fancy name would surely have attracted a great deal of attention in a town like Pandemonium.

STRAWBERRY UNDID THE top two buttons of her blouse and ran a comb through her hair one last time. She sprayed perfume onto her décolletage before giving the room a quick spritz, though no amount of eau-de-toilette would mask the true odour of this place – the sour musk that rose from every soft furnishing and clung to every curtain.

She looked over at the clock on the mantelpiece and her heart skipped a beat: there were only two minutes to go until her appointment. The gentleman has asked for her specially; Strawberry had never been requested before. She wasn't one of Waterloo Jones' youngest girls and it wasn't like she was known for a certain thing, like Chantal and her beads. So quite why a gentleman would choose her from all the other perfectly nice girls on offer, she had no idea. Not that she was about to look a gift horse in the mouth. Tonight could well bring her more money than she was accustomed to taking in a week.

There was a knock on the door and Waterloo entered, followed by a well-dressed man. He wore a sharply-cut charcoal black suit over a crisp white shirt and mustard-yellow waistcoat. At his throat a green cravat was held in place by a silver tie-pin. On his feet, rather than boots and spurs – which was what most of her customers wore – were a pair of black leather shoes, so polished that their shine dazzled her.

The gentleman removed his bowler hat and held out his hand.

Strawberry had to stifle a giggle as she took it. She wasn't used to such niceties, though she managed to regain her composure when she noticed the stern look that the Madame gave her. Her customer, in marked contrast, had one of the kindest faces she had ever seen. His eyes were a brilliant emerald green and his skin was smooth and youthful, yet to be marked by the passage of time or experience. Beneath his nose was a neatly trimmed and waxed moustache.

Again, Strawberry wondered why someone of such obvious means would request an evening in her company.

"Take your time now, duckie," Waterloo said. "No need to rush. You just enjoy yourself. If you need me for anything you'll find a handbell on the bedside table."

Which Strawberry hoped he wouldn't be inclined to use. She didn't intend to share her gentleman caller with anyone.

"Thank you, Miss Jones. That will be all."

Once the door was closed, he stood looking at Strawberry for a while, his hat in his hands. She understood: for some the first time could be nerve-wracking. So she waited patiently for him to speak while rising to her feet and giving him her best 'come-to-bed' eyes.

"Good evening," he said, and once again she had to stifle a giggle. "I am Mr. Chauncy Montclair."

"Well now, Chauncy. That is a pretty name. I'm Strawberry."

"No, you're not. And, please, don't touch my face."

Strawberry's hand stopped an inch from caressing his cheek; she could feel the heat rising from his skin.

"Whatever you like," she said.

Her hand moved down to his crotch and though she caressed him and breathed gently into his ear, he refused to grow for her.

"Neither," he said, gently removing her hand, "am I here for that."

"But you asked for me specially. Come on, tell me what it is that Strawberry can do for you."

"To begin, you can sit down and stop calling yourself Strawberry."

"But—"

"Your name is Claire Fairfax." And at that Strawberry did sit down, because nobody had called her that for quite some time.

"Who are you?"

"I told you. I'm Mr. Chauncy Montclair."

"And you don't want to... do the usual, do you? Well, Mr. Montclair, I don't know what impression they gave you about me, but I'm not that girl. I'd say that Chantal is probably more to your taste."

"This isn't about physical pleasure."

Claire sighed. "I don't know whether you've noticed, honey, but this is a cat house."

"Of that, I am well aware."

"Well, for the love of all that is good and holy, won't you just tell me what you want?"

"What brought you to this place, Claire?"

"We all have to make a living."

"Mouths to feed?"

"No… not any more. It's just me."

"What happened?"

Claire blinked as the grief that she had kept hidden for so long threatened to overwhelm her. She looked up into the stranger's kind eyes and saw something there that made her want to tell her story. Never before had she found the words to describe what had happened to her children.

"Paul and Annie got sick didn't they?" Chauncy said. "So sick that you didn't know what to do. Like any good mother, you were desperate for them to get better. But nothing you did seemed to help. Then…"

"…then there was this man, this peddler, going door to door. He said that he had all manner of cures for all manner of ailments. And he seemed so kind, so good. He reminded me of my Stanley. You've got to understand, I was at my wit's end. I didn't know what to do, so—"

"You brought a bottle of medicine."

She nodded. "The peddler said they'd be right as rain in a few days – just a few spoonfuls before bed and the fever would be gone. It wasn't cheap. But Stanley had left me a little something, and, I thought, if this wasn't the right time to use it…"

Chauncy held out a handkerchief and Claire took it, dabbing at her eyes and blowing her nose before continuing with her story.

"I did as he said: two spoonfuls each before bedtime. Three hours later I was woken by their screams. I've never heard such agony, never want to hear the sound of children in so much pain again. Come dawn, they were both dead.

"I was the only one who attended their funeral. You see, everybody thought I'd killed them. They saw a mother without a husband, struggling to make ends meet and... well, folk can be so judgemental can't they? And in a way, I felt that I *had* killed them. I'd brought the medicine after all."

"You were only trying to help."

"It doesn't matter. I had failed as a mother. A widow, with two dead children – I had nothing to live for. I lost my position at the mill and... and I needed money. When people around town started calling me a whore, I thought, if the shoe fits..."

"Thank you, Claire," Chauncy said, rising to his feet and donning his hat.

"Wait, is that it? Didn't you want anything more?"

"You have been most obliging; I have what I came for."

He closed the door quietly behind him. Claire Fairfax sat staring blankly at it for a moment, before bursting into tears.

HE KNELT AMONGST the rocks and the scrub, looking into the night. The thin sliver of moon above provided little illumination, but it was enough. Chauncy knew that the stranger was there as he told him Claire Fairfax's story.

THE FIRST TIME he'd met the stranger had been the evening Pa had dragged him out into the scrub and left him there. He had been covered in bruises from his daddy's belt. The old man had stood over him as he snivelled into the dust and said, "You stay here and think about what you've done, and don't you dare move 'till sun-up. Jesus wept, son! You're a man in your twenties. Why don't you start acting like one?"

He had just about sobbed himself dry when he heard a whisper that he couldn't put down to the sighing of the wind.

"Is anybody there?" he said.

There had been a charge in the air, like the harbinger of a storm, and there was a taste on his lips that reminded him of the tang of blood.

"Why are you crying?"

The voice seemed to come from in front of him, though it was so faint it was hard to be sure.

"Who are you?"

"A traveller, and a friend. Why are you crying?"

Though the voice sounded like it had come a great distance, there was in it a reassuring kindness. He had never before been spoken to with such consideration. He had been told not to trust strangers, but he found himself trusting this one. He wanted to tell him everything.

"I kicked over a pail of milk and Pa took his belt to me and this time he thrashed me for longer than usual and then he dragged me out here and I don't even know where here is and..." He ran out of breath. When he sucked in the next lungful it was to start crying again.

"Your father beats you?" This time the voice sounded closer. "A big man like you?"

"All the time. Even when it isn't my fault. Sometimes he doesn't need a reason and sometimes Mama beats me too."

"Would you like to tell me more about it?"

And like a dam breaching, every injustice, every hurt that had been visited upon him, came flooding out. When he was finished there was silence and he thought for a moment that the stranger was gone. But then he spoke and this time he thought he could make out a figure kneeling in the dirt; it looked like it could be blown apart by a strong breeze.

"Thank you for your story. If you ever have any more to tell, you know where to find me."

And then the stranger was gone.

After that, every time something bad happened to him – which was often; he lived amongst cruel people – he would wait until nightfall before walking into the desert, and there tell it to the darkness.

One evening, as he had been relating the incident of the man who had spilled his drink in the Silver Dollar and called him a retard, there was a sharp intake of breath and the stranger said, "Enough."

"I'm sorry."

"Don't be. You have given me much and now I have something to offer in return. Pandemonium is home to many, yes?"

"I suppose."

"There will be many stories. I want you to collect them for me."

"How am I supposed to do that? You've heard what I've told you. I'm hardly a well-respected man."

"You are Mr. Chauncy Montclair."

"What? Wait. No, I'm not, I'm—"

"You are Mr. Chauncy Montclair. You are a cultured man of means and people trust and respect you, even though they do not know you.

"Chauncy, stand up."

When he got to his feet there was a sickening lurch, as though he had just been turned upside down. The stars wheeled above him and the moon skittered across the sky. He felt his gorge rise and, for one terrifying second, he thought he was going to fall into that vast nothingness.

And then, just as suddenly, he found himself facing back the way he had come.

"Go and collect their tales, Chauncy. Bring them to me."

YOU COULD LOOK a steer right in the eye just before you brought the hammer down and it wouldn't look away, wouldn't even flinch. It would stare at death in the same impassive, vaguely imbecilic way that it would look at the grass at its feet or a crow on a fence post, or pretty much anything really.

"Stupid son of a bitch."

Thwack!

The steer dropped. Phil grabbed it and Eddie helped him heft it onto a hook to be bled. The next steer was secured into the stock and Spector gripped the head of the sledgehammer in his left hand.

"Least you could do is show a little emotion," he said as the animal turned its empty gaze up at him.

Thwack!

Spector had never met a beast as stupid and docile as Rep's beef cattle. Maybe he put something in their feed.

"And down she goes! Right boys, that's lunch. I'll see you in an hour."

Spector stripped off his apron and gloves and stepped out into the blistering heat of the yard.

Usually when he stepped out, he'd be immediately surrounded by clouds of flies, or a posse of stray dogs, drawn by the stench that permanently clung to him. Today, however, he was greeted only by a gentle breeze.

Somebody was sitting on his favourite bench. The stranger didn't look like he worked round here; he was far too well dressed.

"I brought you lunch, Spector," the stranger said without looking up. "Saves you the bother of going to the cookhouse." He gestured at the picnic basket beside him.

"Do I know you?"

"No, I don't think so. But I'd like to talk to you a moment, if I may."

To hell with it, Spector thought, the stranger had brought him lunch, hadn't he? He'd earned the use of his ear, at least for a little while. If he wasted his time he'd simply pop him in the jaw and walk away. Spector Philby didn't take shit from nobody.

Spector sat beside the gentleman and took a sandwich out of the basket.

"Corned beef?"

"With a touch of mustard," the gentleman said. "Just—"

"—the way I like it. Who the hell *are* you?"

"My name is Chauncy Montclair, and I'd like to talk with you a while."

There was a companionable silence then as Chauncy stared into the middle distance and Spector ate.

"Was the first one easy?" Chauncy said.

"The first cow? Well now, there's a trick to it. The first one, I must admit, wasn't easy. I didn't hit it right and it kicked like a mule. Near ripped the stock out of its mountings and it took three blows before I finally killed it. But once you know where to hit them, it gets real easy."

"I'm not talking about cattle, Spector."

A morsel of sandwich seemed to be lodged halfway down his throat and Spector had to cough a few times before he could speak.

"Are you one of Rep's men?"

"No, Spector, I'm not. Now, what was his name?"

"Oh, God… oh, God. No. I'm ready for this. Instead of hanging me you can shoot me right here. I don't want to hang."

"Calm down, Spector. I'm not going to shoot you. I just want you to tell me about it."

Generally speaking, Spector wasn't one to open up, even when deep in his cups. There was something behind, or in, the gentleman's eyes however that compelled him to talk.

"This is going back a few years now, to the time when silver mining still meant something around here. Before Rep and his beef. I worked underground with my daddy and my brother – God rest their souls – and we made a decent enough living.

"Anyway, there was a strange fellow who worked with us down there, name of Jebediah. He was a simple type, some would say touched, but those of us who worked alongside him knew there was something strange going on there. The kid just wasn't right. Once I caught him touching himself in an abandoned tunnel, singing to himself as he tugged away, this strange far-away look in his eyes. And he didn't even stop when he noticed me standing there."

"Tell me about that first collapse, and what came after."

"Sure, sorry. Jeb was working on a seam one day when it crumbled unexpectedly. There was a cave-in. Seven men dead, but Jeb wasn't among them. In fact, there wasn't a single scratch on him when we pulled him from the rubble."

"Two weeks later it happened again?"

"It was even worse this time. Twelve dead. Biggest disaster in the history of the mine, and there was Jebediah, standing among all those bodies. Smiling away like he was pleased as punch."

"That must have been pretty hard on everybody."

"Sure was. Some of the men refused to work alongside him after that. Said that Jeb had been touched by the devil. Said somebody should do something about him."

"And so you did."

"It's not difficult to hide a body in a mine. There are plenty of abandoned tunnels and deep holes. Accidents happen. Jeb was a trusting boy. I told him that we were going to play a game."

"Hide and seek?"

"What else? I told Jeb that I was going to hide first and that he should kneel facing the wall and count to a hundred. He started counting and I took up my pick-axe. He didn't make it past four."

"And how did it feel?"

"When his skull cracked open... I can't... Mister, it was a rush. That's the best way I can describe the feeling. It's completely different to killing a cow. It's like the difference between a pork chop and a fillet steak. Killing cows all day is never going to give me the same satisfaction."

"Were there many more?"

"When the mine closed, it got harder to hide the bodies. I haven't killed a man since, though I've come close on a couple of occasions."

"Well, Spector, I appreciate your honesty."

The gentleman got to his feet and tipped his hat, as though to bid him good day.

"Hang on. Who are you, anyway?"

"I told you. I'm Mr. Chauncy Montclair."

And with that, Chauncy walked away.

WHEN CHAUNCY FINISHED telling Spector's story, the stranger sighed with pleasure.

The moon was full, the stars brilliant and sharp. For the first time Chauncy could make out the complete silhouette of the man. He looked to be a little wider and taller than Chauncy, and his head appeared strangely elongated.

"I think I like those kinds of stories the best, Chauncy."

Most of the tales he told featured suffering of some kind or other. Perhaps it was because those struggling under the burden of guilt or pain were more willing to share. Chauncy had told the stranger more pleasant tales, but these never seemed to please him in the same way.

"There's something on your mind, Chauncy. I know you."

"You once talked about taking me with you when you leave. Once I'm done being Chauncy. You remember that?"

The stranger approached him, and Chauncy felt a sudden rush of fear. This was the closest he'd ever been. When he placed his hand on Chauncy's shoulder, he didn't feel it. When Chauncy looked down, he could see through the stranger's fingers. But when he spoke, his voice was strong and clear.

"First, we're going to need a place to store all those stories."

"Store them? What do you mean?"

"Chauncy, you're going to raise a barn."

WHY ANYBODY WOULD want to build here, on the tiny lot beside Theodore Wright's warehouse, was beyond Stephen Sinclair. Theodore certainly didn't need the extra storage space – his business had been in decline for a number of years – and the small patch of land was hardly a prime piece of real estate. Rather more intriguing, however, was the matter of why anybody would employ a workforce composed of such disparate souls.

Stephen adjusted his spectacles, took the cheroot out of his mouth and leaned further over the porch rail.

"Is that... is that Strawberry? Now why on earth would anybody use a whore to lug around two-by-fours?"

"Beats me," Ezekiel said. "I wouldn't trust none of them folk with the business end of a hammer."

As well as Strawberry, Stephen could see Spector from the abattoir; David Hoghton, who lived – most of the time – in the gutter outside of the Silver Dollar; Terrence Brown, who was once nearly hanged for stealing horses, and a whole host of characters from Pandemonium's back alleys and tar-paper shacks.

Moving among the workers was a gentleman dressed in an expensive-looking suit, wearing a bowler hat. He issued instructions to his workforce as he surveyed the site, but he didn't once stoop to help lift a beam or pick up a hammer.

"That must be the enigmatic Mr. Chauncy Montclair we've been hearing so much about," Ezekiel said.

"You would have thought that a man who dresses like that could afford better people."

"He must have his reasons, Stephen."

"Really, Ezekiel? Because I sure would like to know what they are."

THEY GATHERED BEFORE sunrise. Not one of them had been told to come, but when they had risen that day they had done so with the full knowledge of the task that lay before them.

They weren't exactly surprised to see Mr. Chauncy Montclair – something this out of the ordinary just had to have something to do with the stranger – but they were rather surprised to find themselves in such unusual company. Even so, they took to the job quickly and efficiently.

Spector had once seen a group of Mennonites raise a barn, but he knew next to nothing about the process himself. His hands, however, seemed to know what to do, and he was soon bracing uprights and hammering pegs like he had been born to it.

Claire, likewise, moved across the site with confidence. She was surprised at her own strength as she helped to raise roof beams, needing little assistance in handling the timbers. For the first time in a long time, she felt pride in her work.

By mid-day the skeleton of the barn was complete. It clearly wasn't going to be the grandest structure ever raised – it would hold little more than a couple of carriages, or house a modest stable – but its compact beauty was aesthetically pleasing.

Claire worked on the roof and when the barn was near finished, her hammer was momentarily stilled as she sensed a presence below. She couldn't put it into words and wasn't sure whether anybody else felt it, but she could sense that with each beam secured, each roof slat nailed into place, something was drawing closer.

Work on the barn was completed around seven that evening. The light of the sun was just beginning to leave the heavens and a full moon had risen, sitting bloated on the horizon. To Claire, the stars had never looked so sharp; it was as though they had been drawn closer to earth with the onset of night. She noticed the guy from the abattoir – he had lain with her many times, but she had never got his name – looking up at the barn with delight on his face. Which was a little disconcerting, as his was not a face usually given to such expression.

"It's beautiful," he said.

They all had to agree. True, it was just a barn, but it was the most *complete* barn any of them had seen, and they had made it with their own hands.

Chauncy Montclair stood by the open double doors and gestured inside.

"Shall we?"

As one they moved within, and as soon as Claire stepped over the threshold she knew that she had been right: something was here. In the far left corner of the barn there were more shadows than there should rightly be. Chauncy Montclair went straight over and someone stepped forward to greet him. In the uncertain light it was hard to make out any particular features but the stranger looked to be a man, a little taller and wider than Chauncy.

Chauncy conferred quietly with him for a while, before returning to stand with his work crew, gazing expectantly at the new arrival.

"Thank you for raising this barn," the dark stranger said. Claire jumped at the sound of his voice. "Thank you for building this vessel. Your tales have brought me far and they will send me further still."

The stranger opened his arms and Claire found herself telling her story again, realizing as she did so that everybody around her were telling stories of their own.

Every emotion felt, every word said in anger, pain, or regret, or joy, flowed from them and into the stranger.

With every story told, the darkness began to peel away from the stranger, drifting like black leaves to the dirt floor. It became clear then that though the stranger had taken the form of a man, that wasn't truly what he was. Light began to pour from him. At first it was just a hazy glow, like the sunshine on a late summer afternoon, but that glow grew in intensity until everybody in the barn had to close their eyes against it.

One by one they finished their stories, until the only voice left was Chauncy's. The raw pain that filled his words made him almost unintelligible. When at last his story came to an end, the light in the barn was so intense Claire could see it even with her eyes closed. The stranger departed then, exploding into a thousand shards of light that swirled around the barn like a flock of starlings before fading away.

As they blinked the purple blotches from their vision, they heard Chauncy throwing himself against the far wall, so hard it seemed he was trying to break through. His bowler hat had fallen from his head and at his throat his cravat has become unfastened. He looked much less like a gentleman now and Claire wondered why she had ever trusted him.

He was screaming as he threw himself at the wall, again and again.

"No! No! You promised to take me with you."

MAKING HIS WAY home after a quick drink in the Silver Dollar, Stephen Sinclair decided to take a detour. He had been thinking about Chauncy Montclair and his strange crew all day, and he wanted to see whether they had managed to raise their barn.

When he turned the corner he thought, at first, that a fire had broken out. But the light pouring from the barn had nothing to do with flames. Stephen could hear a multitude of voices: a confused babble that rose to a frantic pitch as the light intensified. And then there was only the one voice. As soon as that fell silent, the whole of the barn was consumed by a blazing nimbus that threw the shadows of the surrounding buildings far across the street.

Stephen ducked and covered his head with his hands, expecting to be showered with a hail of burning timbers, but instead there was only silence. When he looked up, the street was once more in darkness. He scanned the night sky, but all he saw was the fast fading streak of a shooting star.

Stephen turned and ran back to the Silver Dollar.

CLAIRE FAIRFAX WAS one of the first to leave. Nobody had made a move towards Chauncy. They left him where he lay, sobbing in a heap. Outside she thought she saw Stephen Sinclair hurrying away in the direction of the Silver Dollar. She considered joining him; she could do with a drink. But she was done with noise and light for now, so she headed away from town. She paused briefly to pick a bunch of wild flowers, growing through a crack in the mud beside the general store. They were a little dry, the blossoms a little faded, but they were better than nothing.

The cemetery had grown since Claire had last been there. The rows and rows of new headstones testimony to the fact that life was hard and short in Pandemonium. She had trouble finding what she was looking for at first, and panic began to grip her as she stumbled amongst the monuments and mounds of earth. But then, there they were.

Claire hadn't been able to afford stone markers. The weathered wooden crosses stood side by side. The names were difficult to make out, but all the same she knew what was written there.

Peter Fairfax 1846-1850

Annie Fairfax 1847-1850

She lay the flowers on their graves and knelt down in the dust.

"I'm sorry," she said. "Mama's sorry."

And she was Mama; she *had been* a mother. What she was not was a whore. Not anymore. The stranger had taken Strawberry away and she was never coming back.

Claire Fairfax didn't know what awaited her back in Pandemonium, and that uncertainty scared her to the bone, but she took courage that whatever she faced there now, she would face on her own terms.

WHAT WAS COMING had been a long time in the making, and Spector was almost frantic in his haste to get it over with. He ran from the barn, not looking back. By the time he reached the foothills, his lungs were burning, his legs were aching all to hell.

When Spector reached the boarded-up mine he took a moment to catch his breath, and as he dragged in great, cool lungfuls, he thought he heard voices within; the distant *chink chink* of pick-axes hitting stone.

"Don't you worry, I'm coming. Spector's coming," he said and he set to tearing away the boards.

He stumbled through the darkness, barely aware of where he was going, his way feebly lit by the light of a flickering lantern. But their voices led him to them, calling to him. It was finally time for Spector to tell their stories. He owed them that.

Spector had hauled silver out of this mine. Now he staggered from the entrance and into the night with his arms full of bones. Spector had given Chauncy Montclair his story, and now he was going to take these remains down to the sheriff and tell him exactly what he had done.

CHAUNCY MONTCLAIR WOKE as the crowing of a distant rooster announced the dawn. Pale light filtered through the boards of the barn, dust dancing in the beams. Though they had raised this barn little more than a day ago, it already felt like it had been standing for decades. He had hoped the stranger would be there when he came to, but the place was empty. Emptier than any barn had a right to be.

Chauncy didn't know what to do. His whole life had been one long story of suffering, humiliation and pain. And now the stranger had taken all that with him. Chauncy didn't rightly know who he was anymore. All he had left was this name.

Chauncy Montclair straightened his cravat, donned his hat and brushed the dust from his shoes. He left the barn and didn't look back, walking quickly through Pandemonium, into the desert beyond.

Though he passed several people on the way, not one saw him go.

REEL
PEOPLE

THE BULLET MEANT for Paul had been intercepted by the lens of his camera. Burning earth rained down and machine gun fire strafed the trees. He did not run for cover. Instead, he scrabbled in his backpack for a new lens and, once it was fitted, continued to turn the crank. Or course, much of the footage he was shooting wouldn't make it onto cinema screens. Nobody wanted to see soldiers dancing as bullets riddled them. What they wanted were stirring five minute vignettes showing Our Brave Boys Doing Their Bit. But Paul was determined to capture the truth. The studio could always tell their stories in the edit.

Private Montclair wandered into shot. As usual the Frenchman's helmet was not on his head, but dangling from a strap on his backpack. His gun was held loosely in his hands, vaguely pointing at the enemy. It was typical of him. No matter where Paul placed the camera, Montclair would eventually find his way into frame. The soldier meandered between the trees, as though out for a walk on a summer's day. A shell exploded barely five metres from where he stood, showering him in mud. Montclair turned to look directly at the camera, grinning.

"Cut!"

DESPITE THE WRY indifference with which Montclair treated every situation – even the deaths of his comrades – he and Paul soon became close friends, the bond between them rapidly cemented in the last days of the war.

When the guns in Argonne finally fell silent, they had looked out at the devastation and the Frenchman said, "I think, my friend, that you have shot perhaps the greatest war picture the world will ever see."

Paul laughed, but then he saw that Montclair was being serious. For him, his involvement in the Great War was just another exciting story to tell everybody back home.

"You won't forget me, will you my friend?"

Paul promised that he wouldn't.

THERE WERE THOSE that would never forget Chauncy Montclair, though in the months that followed, few would know him under that name.

In Hanover an actress fell so deeply in love with him that she begged for his hand in marriage. Though he had lived for so long, this was the first time someone had fallen for him; he found that he felt nothing. No, that wasn't strictly true. There was a certain unpleasant curiosity, almost a feeling of alarm that saw him leaving the city and changing his name once again.

In the Pyrenees, he became embroiled in a knife fight with a farmer who was under the impression that he was owed a considerable amount of money. The farmer wasn't the best knifeman he had ever encountered, though he managed to lay open the back of his left hand with one lucky swipe. He returned with a thrust that wasn't intended to kill, but the farmer had unexpectedly stepped forward, and the blade finished him. This was far from the first time he had seen death, but it was the first time that he had killed. He felt very little.

Again, it was time to move on, to change.

He soon grew bored of all that he witnessed; the end of the war bringing ennui. He remembered a place in which it was almost impossible to become bored; a town with more stories than could be found in even the largest city. It was the town where he had been born; the town where someone – *something* – had reached out of the darkness and created him.

Chauncy Montclair decided that it was finally time to return to Pandemonium.

PAUL RETURNED TO an America he didn't recognise. The hero's welcome he and his comrades received felt insincere and stagey; that they were expected to fit back into the life they had left was an audacious, and somewhat insulting, imposition. Even so, Hollywood's celluloid mills were turning at an ever increasing whirl and Paul was quickly pulled back into the machinery of the system.

He soon found, however, that he was no longer as willing to turn out the crowd-pleasing flicks starring plucky dogs and sassy kids as he had once been. For a time the studio tolerated him – he always shot under budget and on time – but one day he turned up for work to find only the Executive Producer on set.

"Frankly, Paul," he said, lighting a cigar and leaning back in the director's chair, "we're more than a little worried."

"With what? We're on schedule aren't we?"

"That's not the problem. We've seen the footage and, well, if you want to go down that expressionist route, quite honestly you can fuck off to some kraut studio that will put up with your BS. This is not what we are paying you for."

That night, deep into his third whisky, Paul decided that he would indeed – as had been so eloquently put to him – fuck off. He didn't need the studio system to make his movies. Hollywood wasn't the be-all and end-all of the film industry. He'd find somewhere where his talent was appreciated. But where?

The following morning, the answer was brought to him in a letter.

My friend, Chauncy Montclair wrote, *I am an American! Yes, I am living in the Land of Opportunity. And just as I'm sure you have never forgotten your old friend, I have never forgotten you, though it has taken*

me a long time to track you down. Now that I finally have you, however,
I must congratulate you on The Night Symphony. *It is an incredible*
film and we were sold out for every performance here at the Western Pearl
Picture House in Pandemonium.

It is an extraordinary town. Though I have been here for only two
years, it feels very much like home. And I'm sure you could capture its
unique character on film. Why not visit? It would be good to reminisce
about old times. And perhaps some of the magic of Pandemonium will find
its way into your camera?

When Paul finally found Pandemonium on the map, his mind
was made up. Sitting not far from New Mexico it would be the
perfect place to shoot the Great American Western that he had
always believed was within him. Paul was sick of Californian
cowboys rescuing screaming dames from the threat of the ubiquitous
redskin. He wanted to make a *real* Western, featuring real people,
and Pandemonium looked like it might be the perfect place to film
it.

It was time to leave the land of dreams behind.

THE WESTERN PEARL Picture House was a wedding cake of a
building, standing proud of the surrounding brownstones with its
fronting covered in intricate scrollwork and curlicues. When the cab
pulled up to the picture house, Paul was a little disappointed that
Chauncy wasn't there to greet him. He pulled on the handles of the
tall glass doors and they opened soundlessly and smoothly, admitting

him entry into a lavishly decorated foyer. Marble pillars entwined with golden vines supported a mirrored ceiling. The concessions stand stood in its own soft pool of light, its treasures gleaming enticingly.

"Hello?" Paul called. "Chauncy?" But he was answered only by the quiet music that issued from hidden speakers.

He presumed that the doors before him lead to the auditorium and when he pushed through them he was greeted by a familiar flickering darkness.

Paul didn't recognise the film playing, though it was difficult to tell exactly what was going on from the off-centre and out-of-focus picture. There wasn't any musical accompaniment. He couldn't even hear the whirr of the projector. As he scanned the rows of seats, Paul thought he saw something vast swim up from the centre of the screen, but when he turned back all he could see was a formless blur.

Every seat appeared to be empty and he was just turning to leave when he saw a wisp of smoke rising from the third row.

"Chauncy?"

A dark shape rose and turned silently towards him. A jolt of fear shot through Paul before the shape held out its arms and greeted him with that familiar voice.

"Paul! You made it at last. I had heard the line was flooded."

He gasped when his friend stepped into the glow of the house lights. The war had taken its toll on many of the men Paul had served with but, as far as he could tell, it had left Chauncy entirely unscathed. He still had the same youthful – almost adolescent – face that he remembered. He was wearing a suit that looked to be made from the same red velvet covering the cinema's seats. His hair was slick with pomade and his neat little moustache had been fiercely waxed. Paul had never been a hugger, but even so he allowed himself to be embraced by his old friend.

"My God, Chauncy, look at you! And this place! How on earth did you ever afford it?"

"Ah, well, an uncle I never knew I had died, leaving me a small fortune. When I came to Pandemonium, I saw a town hungry for stories. So I had this place built. All that was here before was some ramshackle old barn that had apparently stood for generations. Can you believe that there were objections when I had it torn down?"

"Well, you have a beautiful picture house, you must be very proud."

"Oh I am, Paul, I am. Now come to my office so that we can chat about our film over a drink or two."

WITH CHAUNCY ENSCONCED behind his desk in the cramped and dusty room, a glass of whisky in one hand and a cigarette in the other, Paul broached the question that had been bothering him all the way up the stairs.

"You said *our* film, Chauncy. What did you mean *our* film?"

"I have brought you here for an exclusive opportunity."

"No, Chauncy, I came here to visit you and to look into the possibility of shooting a Western in Pandemonium, maybe even capture some preliminary footage."

"What did you tell me in Argonne?"

"That's not a time I'm particularly keen to recall."

"You told me, Paul, that you were there to shoot the *truth*."

"Yeah, and much good it did me. Virtually none of that footage made it onto the screen."

"Well I want you to shoot the truth now, here, in Pandemonium, and I can promise you that your film will make it to the screen. We shall have a lavish premiere at the Western Pearl."

"I don't know, Chauncy. I don't make documentaries any more. I make films like *Five Bullets, Six Broads* and *Konga – The Mangrilla*."

"One of the many reasons you left Hollywood, no? Here you will shoot a film more worthy of your talents. And if you shoot this picture for me, I promise that I will entirely fund this Western you're so keen to make. No studio interference."

"You can't be serious."

"I don't know whether you've noticed, Paul, but I'm rich. I can do anything. Now, do we have a deal?"

Chauncy put down his cigarette and held out his hand.

Chauncy Montclair had the two qualities essential in any Executive Producer, he was persuasive and he had lots of money; these, along with the promise of creative freedom somewhere down the line, made Paul reach across the table and take his friend's hand.

BELOW THEM, BELOW everything, something pushed against the other side of the screen.

"SHOULDN'T WE AT least get my camera? I'm at the Silver Dollar, it won't take a moment."

"The camera isn't important. Right now, Paul, I want you to really *see* Pandemonium."

They left behind the bustling streets at the heart of the city and, for a time, Paul thought they were heading towards the ridge on the edge of town, which some may have called a mountain, if they were feeling charitable. But just as it looked like they were going to reach the city limits, Chauncy turned left and they went over a bridge crossing a deep ravine, heading towards the lights of a less heavily built, but no less busy, area.

"This, my friend, is the Swamp. And doesn't it just smell like home?"

Paul inhaled and, indeed, he caught the authentic odours of France: the smell of cooking andouillettes, so redolent of the farmyard; the rich, buttery scent of the patisserie and, of course, everywhere they went, the pungent clouds of Turkish tobacco so beloved of the French.

"Chauncy, this is wonderful, but shouldn't you be helping to run the cinema?"

"*Bof!* Don't worry my friend, the place virtually runs itself."

Paul had expected Chauncy to take him to a restaurant, or a bar, but instead, several minutes later, he found himself standing in a dank alleyway. Above them an open window belched fragrant steam; from somewhere amongst the piles of refuse, Paul could hear the scrabbling of rats.

"This is crazy. Come on, Chauncy, why don't you let me buy you a drink? What are we even doing here?"

Chauncy gestured him to silence and leaned out into the street. He looked both ways before backing into the shadows, shaking his head.

Maybe, Paul thought, the war had affected Chauncy more than he had suspected. Maybe the easy-going manner he had seen in the trenches had been a front. Whatever the case, every time he tried to speak, his friend shushed him.

After half an hour of this, just as Paul was readying himself to storm past Chauncy and head back to his hotel, he was pushed back down the dark passage.

"They are coming! Now, don't make a sound. Stand there and *watch*."

Voices raised in anger approached them. It sounded like two men fighting and, indeed, as Paul watched from the shadows, a couple of burly drunks barrelled into the alley.

"You stinking, no good, motherfucking, cheap-ass frog!" said a man in a white suit as he pushed a shorter gentlemen to the floor. "That potion you sold me was nothing more than pond water!"

Beside him, Paul felt Chauncy tense – whether from fear or excitement, he couldn't tell.

The man on the ground barely had time to utter "Monsieur", and bring up his hands, before the man in white raised a pistol and put two bullets in his head. Paul jumped with each retort of the gun.

The murderer stood over the body only for as long as it took the smoke to clear before fleeing into the night.

"Jesus wept, Chauncy! We should—"

"No, Paul. We are not finished here. Look at him. Really *look*."

Paul felt Chauncy's hand between his shoulder blades. He was pushed forwards until he stood over the corpse.

He had seen death aplenty during the war, and death more violent and grisly than that which had been laid out before him now, but without the intervening eye of the camera, this seemed far more real. Paul could do nothing but look: at the pale face frozen into an expression of surprise; at the two blackened holes that had split the forehead into three curiously even pieces; at the spreading pool of black blood, in which he could see the moon's reflection, bright as a silver nickel.

All this captured by his eyes, as though burned onto a single frame.

"Now," Chauncy said, "now we run."

BACK AT THE Western Pearl, after Chauncy had finished his call to the police and after he had poured a stiff drink into the glass trembling in Paul's unsteady hands, he explained.

"It's just like you told me in France. This is about the truth. Things like that happen all the time in the Swamp, but most people have no idea, or don't want to know. Tonight I wanted to show you Pandemonium as it actually is."

"And you certainly did that. Jesus. Jesus Christ!"

"People think that we left behind atrocity with the end of the war, and they are wrong. And they must be shown that. But there is more in Pandemonium than that which we have seen tonight. Much more."

Somewhere below them Paul heard the whirr of a projector.

"Paul, together we shall capture something extraordinary. Is that not what you want? We will show people something Hollywood could only dream about."

The whisky had burned its way down Paul's throat and now its warmth was spreading through his belly. He found himself beginning to relax, lulled by the Frenchman's gentle tones.

"Together we shall make history. When we show our film, we will truly wake it up!"

"*It?*"

"What?"

"You said *it*, Chauncy. Did you not mean them*?*"

"Of course I did. Now, let's have another drink, my friend. A toast to our success."

Paul heard laughter and applause. It sounded like it came from somewhere far away.

FOR THE NEXT two days, much to Paul's relief, they got on with the business of filming. Mostly they shot establishing footage: cars on the busy streets, well-dressed ladies and gentlemen promenading along the boardwalks, a shot of the front of the Silver Dollar, and even some interior footage of the women at work in the Calhoun Cannery.

On Sunday, Chauncy kept moving them on after only a few moments, as though dissatisfied with the footage they were getting.

"Why don't we take a break, Chauncy?" Paul said, after his friend had stilled his hand on the crank yet again. "It is the day of rest, after all."

Something seemed to light up his friend's eyes and, for the first time in hours, Chauncy looked truly animated.

"Yes. Yes, of course. You're right!"

But instead of returning to the cinema, Chauncy had them standing outside Greyfriar's Methodist Church. From within, Paul could hear voices raised in song.

"Really, a church?" Paul said. "Chauncy, is this one of those hard truths that you wanted me to capture?"

"Wait, Paul. Just wait!"

"Okay, but do you want me to start shooting now? Get some establishing shots of the exterior maybe?" Again Chauncy shushed him and Paul was reminded of his behaviour in the Swamp.

Within the white-washed church, behind the stained glass windows, the organ fell silent. In front of them, the doors opened and the parishioners began to emerge, blinking in the midday sun.

"Now, Chauncy?"

"No. Wait."

It could have been a starling, or a swift; it was hard to identify the avian blur that thudded into the stained-glass window above the porch.

A woman lowered her parasol and picked up the stunned bird that had fallen at her feet. She looked up, shielding her eyes with a lace-gloved hand, and that was when the pane of glass fell.

"Watch!" Chauncy hissed, his right hand gripping Paul's shoulder. But Paul didn't have the will to do anything else.

He saw the shard of stained-glass slash open the woman's right eye as it entered her face, slicing down the soft flesh of her cheek, obscenely exposing the side of her jaw, burying itself deep in her throat. The spray of arterial blood arced high in the air; brilliant droplets shining for a moment in front of the jewels of the stained-glass window before falling to the dust of the street. He saw the woman turn, helplessly appealing to her fellow parishioners, even as she covered them with her blood. Paul saw that their mouths were open and screaming, yet the only sound was the beating of his own heart, pounding in time with the blood pumping from the woman's throat. His gaze followed her as she fell, her hands reaching for, but never getting near, the glass protruding from her neck.

Paul saw that her remaining eye was a rich, chestnut brown; that a single spot of scarlet marred the perfection of the white lace covering her left hand.

She saw him watching her, and then she was gone.

THE DOORS TO the auditorium were open when they returned to the Western Pearl; the foyer was littered with the detritus of an audience that must have just departed.

Paul leaned the camera against the side of an aisle and allowed himself to be lead to a seat in the front row. The house lights were up and so he could only faintly make out the words scrolling up the screen. They didn't appear to be a list of credits, rather a slow progression of poetry or verse. From somewhere in the back, he could hear a voice whispering along with the lines.

Chauncy was whispering too and Paul found himself sinking with the weight of his words.

When he closed his eyes, all the horrors that he had witnessed, both in Pandemonium and during his time in France, were played out before him, and though he desperately wanted to awake, there was nothing he could do to stop the show.

THEY DIDN'T TAKE the camera the next time they ventured out; Paul no longer needed it to see. He merely had to turn his gaze as Chauncy directed and everything he witnessed was indelibly burned onto his mind.

Not all they saw in Pandemonium over the next few days ended in violence. The horrors that Chauncy showed him were often more subtle, insidious.

By the waters of a turgid creek, a man and a woman washed a bundle of bones which they then placed, with the utmost care, into a turquoise velvet bag.

Through a window he watched as a woman rode a man, the brand on her bucking behind showing that she was owned.

In the depths of the long-since exhausted silver mine, Paul looked down at a collection of toys amongst the shards of broken whisky bottles.

And from high on the ridge that overlooked the city, the whole of Pandemonium before him, he clapped his hands and shouted, "Action!"

On the main street a car overturned and caught fire. The driver's legs were trapped beneath the vehicle, and the flames were so intense that all the bystanders could do was throw buckets of water over his blackening corpse.

In front of the library, two blocks over, a stranger helping an elderly lady across the street relieved her of her wedding ring as he slipped his hand into hers.

In the road outside the Silver Dollar a group of men were gathered around a youth, cheering as he choked down a bottle of rough liquor, tears pouring down his cheeks, his chest heaving for breath.

All of these sights flooded in through Paul's eyes, filling him, feeding a hunger he never knew he had.

Drunk from the streets of Pandemonium, he did not protest as Chauncy lead him back into the darkness.

THE WESTERN PEARL appeared diminished, streaks of dirt and greasy smudges marring the former perfection of its glass doors. In the foyer, the gilt had begun to flake away from the marble pillars, the carpet was tacky beneath their feet, and there was an unpleasant, organic odour coming from the concessions stand.

None of this would matter for much longer; Chauncy Montclair was almost finished with his illusion.

Paul stumbled against him as he was guided into a seat. His eyes were closed and a line of saliva trickled from the corner of his mouth. Chauncy dabbed a little from Paul's chin before licking it from his finger; there was a faint tingle on his tongue, an almost chemical burn.

He was ready.

Chauncy clicked his fingers and the house lights dimmed. The curtain that had been covering the screen rolled back with the squeal of badly-oiled casters, a shower of dust and the desiccated corpses of moths.

The screen was a pure, uniform black. A warm wind filled the auditorium.

"It's time, Paul," Chauncy Montclair said. "Wake up."

It was just a glimmer at first, a flicker, as Paul twitched and writhed in his seat. But soon he could contain it no longer, and as he opened his eyes and mouth as wide as they would go, three shafts of pure white light burst from him and into the screen. No image played there; the black rectangle swallowed the light and gave nothing in return. When the light died something continued to burn within Paul, and when he fell there was barely enough of him left to disturb the dust on the floor.

Chauncy Montclair didn't even notice Paul's passing. Instead, his gaze was locked onto the void. He stepped up onto the stage and dipped his hand into the blackness.

Behind him, a light fitting fell from the ceiling in a shower of plaster.

"Come on, come on," Chauncy hissed. "I have given you so much, all these stories. Where are you?"

The screen remained blank.

The wind flowing towards him strengthened and a voice spoke, making Chauncy stagger back from the stage.

"Chauncy?"

The figure that stepped from the screen was as brittle as ancient wood, as insubstantial as a charcoal sketch – a drawing on a cave wall brought forth by the flickering light.

Chauncy backed away, feeling behind him with his fingers until he found Paul's camera.

"Why am I here?" The stranger said, passing through the seats that separated them, constantly shifting as he came.

"Because you once promised to take me with you."

"I made no such promise. I used you, Chauncy. But I gave you something unique in return."

"But that was not what I wanted. I never wanted to spend a lifetime – more than a lifetime – pretending, playing one role after another."

"Chauncy… Chauncy, whoever you are now, I cannot take you with me."

"And that's not what I want. Instead, I want to take *you* with *me*."

Chauncy leapt behind the camera and began to turn the crank as quickly as he could. The stranger gave a hollow, echoing cry and rushed forward, but with each turn of the handle, a strand of him peeled away, flowing in through the lens, until he was just a faint smudge, and then not even that.

Chauncy straightened up and smiled. He opened the camera and took out the roll of film before putting it into a can. The metal was warm, almost hot to the touch. "I have you now," he said.

As Chauncy stepped into the street there was a deafening bang and a jagged crack leapt across the front of the Western Pearl. The glass doors exploded in a glittering shower of diamonds. A cloud of dust billowed out of the foyer, bringing with it the stench of decay. Passersby ran screaming in Chauncy's wake, hurrying away from the collapsing picture house. Chauncy didn't once look back. Instead he strode purposefully towards the train station, the can of film tucked snugly under his right arm.

GODDFREY KINGSTON GROWLED and threw the treatment into the metal wastepaper basket before taking another one from the pile on his desk. He was beginning to despair of the dearth of talent in LA. He should have stayed growing oranges with his father. You knew where you were with oranges.

The intercom on his desk buzzed and he reached over to jab the button.

"What?"

"There's a French gentlemen to see you, sir."

"A what?"

"A French gentlemen."

"Why?"

"He says he has a film to show you."

What the hell. He could use a break from reading the slush pile.

"Okay, okay. Show him in."

The door opened and a neat little man let himself into the room, carrying a film can.

"Mr Kingston, thank you for seeing me at such short notice."

"What have you got for me there? A finished flick? I've got to tell you, this isn't our normal way of doing things."

"And I can assure you, sir, that what I have in this can isn't *normal*. What I have here is unique."

"They all say that Mr...?"

"Montclair. Chauncy Montclair. Please, Mr Kingston, just take a look."

Goddfrey sighed, pushed back his chair and fished in a top pocket for a smoke.

"Why, Mr. Chauncy Montclair, should I?"

"Because, when I show you what I have in here, you won't believe your eyes!"

"Look, it's been a slow day, so I'll humour you. Let's take that to the screening room. But don't get your hopes up."

Later, sitting in the warm, flickering darkness beside Chauncy Montclair, Goddfrey had been about to light another cigarette when his hand was stilled by what he saw.

The images came in a flood, a torrent of stories each seemingly unconnected to the one preceding it. As each scene played out, a figure stepped down from the screen to take a seat in the auditorium. Soon the seats surrounding him were full. And when the only thing on the screen was a perfect, depthless darkness, and the only sound was that of the tail of the film spinning loosely in the projector, the heads of the audience turned towards him.

Waiting. Watching.

STAR CROSSED

A BIRD FLYING over Ardenton would not notice anything remarkable about this small Midlands town, yet it is here that we set our scene.

Two will meet, the offspring of two magical families, two lives that will be governed by cosmic forces they can neither understand nor fully control.

Above – far, far above our fictional bird – stars are moving, constellations coming into alignment like courtiers waiting to take their places in an ancient and arcane dance. Beneath the earth, tectonic plates shift infinitesimally, too little to register on any charts – but it is enough.

The conditions will be met. The gates will open, and the actions of our lovers will seek to unleash upon the world forces that could consume it entire.

"I SEE A stranger."

"Tall, dark and handsome no doubt. Really, is that the best you can do?"

"This card suggests a new start: a meeting that will lead to new opportunities. And this…" Jasmine's mother turned over another card. "Is…"

"Is that supposed to be The Hanged Man?"

Penelope turned the card to face her. "Well, obviously… It's, erm… Hand me those instructions again will you?"

"And you've got how many boxes of these, Mum?"

"Around fifteen. I think."

"You think?"

"Okay, I have thirty."

"Great. And how are you going to shift thirty boxes of tarot cards when no one can tell what the pictures on them are supposed to be?"

"Special offer? Buy one get one free?"

"Bloody hell, Mum. Please tell me that you got these on sale or return."

"No… No, I didn't."

Jasmine sighed and looked around the poky little shop. Her mother had once been a highly-valued member of the magical community – a reliable psychic, gifted clairvoyant, and a white witch of considerable power. Now she was reduced to this: selling trinkets and junk to the impressionable and desperate.

"Look, let's put half a carton out on display for now and see how it goes," Penelope said, attempting to sound hopeful. "In the meantime the rest of them are in the kitchen, if you don't mind taking them downstairs."

Jasmine did mind. The basement was at the bottom of three turns of a stone spiral staircase – like something from a medieval dungeon – and it took her a good half hour to lug all the boxes down. The basement had a low ceiling and smelled of mould. On days when it rained heavily there was the disconcerting sound of what seemed like a river's worth of water flowing just beyond the walls.

Jasmine opened the basement door, revealing barely half a metre of free floor space before the towers of boxes and miscellaneous junk that filled the rest of the room.

"Thanks a lot, Mum!" she shouted up the stairs.

A lot of the boxes were either half- or two-thirds full, and Jasmine spent almost an hour redistributing stock, and making room. A stack of cartons towards the rear of the basement budged barely an inch when she tried to move them, the topmost box swaying threateningly towards her.

"Gods! What is in these?" she said, looking for a product description. "*Obsidian skull essential oil vaporisers.* Fantastic!"

Jasmine sighed and wrapped her arms around the stack again. It leaned ominously, looking like it was about to topple, and, reacting on instinct, she thrust out her hands, pushing the boxes away.

The tower fell with the sound of heavy things breaking.

It wasn't just the ornamental skulls within that had broken, however. One of the boxes had fallen against a damp section of wall, shattering the plaster and revealing a space within.

The smell of mould intensified, but there was something else; something more animal.

Jasmine knelt and cautiously peered into the hole.

Inside, resting on an inch of dust was a book wrapped in cloth.

She briefly thought of calling out to her mother to come and see what she had discovered, but something told her that this was just for her.

Jasmine reached for the book, but withdrew her hand the moment she touched the wrapping. It hadn't felt like cotton or hessian, rather something unpleasantly organic.

Stealing herself against disgust, Jasmine snatched up the book, quickly throwing off its noisome shroud.

It looked ancient. Evidently hand-written, the tome was illustrated throughout; some of the pictures made her flesh crawl. Screw the magical knickknacks and mass-produced enchantments her mother pedalled, this was the real thing. The book was likely worth a fortune, and it might well be just what they needed to turn things around.

"THE BOOK HAS been found."

Uncle's voice jolted him out of his contemplations, so suddenly had it been dropped into the silence. In the study, the only light came from a guttering candle on the mantelpiece. They did not require light for their studies. Any strong illumination would only dampen the potency of their manipulations and transgressions.

Arodias stood. "Is it nearby?" he said.

"Yes."

"Then you were right to bring us here. Rest now, Uncle. Your work is done."

The sigh of the old man's final exhalation filled the room as the smell of decay bloomed from his body. Come the morning there would be little of him left; perhaps just a smear of grease on the chair.

Arodias crossed to the mantel and lit another candle. In the spotted and tarnished mirror his gaunt face looked back at him. He looked old. And he *was* old, his life extended well beyond his naturally allotted span of years. But that was okay, Arodias could change.

BY THE TIME term started at the new college, Jasmine had begun to translate the book. At first she thought it was written in Latin, but after a few failed attempts at trying to make sense of the text with the aid of Babelfish, she realised that what she was looking at was archaic English. It was written in such a crabbed hand and expressed in such an esoteric style that it took her a whole afternoon of staring at one page before the words began to give up their meaning.

It wasn't like any book on magic Jasmine had ever read, and her mother had an impressive library, even if she herself now made little use of it. Jasmine was well-acquainted with natural magic, magical thinking and the various branches of sympathetic sorcery, but the arcane text in the ancient book referred to none of these things.

The passages that she had so far been able to decipher described all manner of beings – or were they gods? – but it focused on one in particular.

This creature was a manifestation of the void and it wielded great power. It had once been a pharaoh, but had since returned to the darkness 'betwixt the stars'. The author of the book – this untitled tome that was as much diary as it was a treatise on the supernatural – had been attempting to make contact with this entity, though for what purpose wasn't entirely clear.

"What are you reading?"

The boy sitting opposite her on one of the ratty armchairs that filled the student lounge had fine mousy hair cut in an unfashionable style, and was dressed in a way that said not so much hipster as failed 1950s beat poet.

"Sorry?" Jasmine said.

"What are you reading?" He leaned forward, his gaze on the book rather than her.

"Oh, this? Just a history book. It's a bit boring actually."

"May I?" He thrust out his hand abruptly, making Jasmine flinch.

"I'm sorry. You are…?"

"Oh." The hand was withdrawn, a confused expression on the boy's face as though he had forgotten himself. "I'm Richard. May I?"

The hand was back again.

"Look. The thing is that it's really quite fragile. And it isn't mine, so I really shouldn't. I'm Jasmine, by the way."

"I see," Richard said, got to his feet and left the lounge.

Jasmine blinked and looked back down at the book. She realised it would take time to make friends at the new college, but she hadn't expected to immediately attract the resident weirdo.

NATHANIEL CREED WAS the author of the book, and he had once owned the building in which her mother's shop resided. He had been a famous 17th century magician, or so he claimed, though much of the book seemed to detail his failures, rather than his successes.

"Then maybe you had better find a way!"

Jasmine was snapped out of her studies by her mother's cry of frustration as she slammed down the phone. The silence that followed was worse, and she crept down to the kitchen to find Penelope with her head on the table, quietly crying.

"Mum?"

Penelope looked up and Jasmine's stomach clenched when she saw the despair on her mother's face.

"Oh, Sweetie, I tried, but we're going to lose the shop."

"What? How?"

"The rent's too high, the footfall too low. I tried. Really, I did."

Jasmine put her arms around her mother. "I know you did, Mum. I'm not blaming you. You did your best."

"Thing is, we may lose the house too. All my finances were tied up in the shop, and with that gone…"

Jasmine could have sworn, could have smashed something, but instead she let her mother cry into her shoulder, wishing that Penelope could again be the mother who had once provided such comfort, who had been her faith in a world that had more in it than most could reckon. Some sort of radical change was what her mother needed, and once she would have been able to use magic to enact such change herself. She had long ago lost her self-confidence, and Jasmine didn't know whether Penelope even had it in her anymore to perform the most basic cantrip.

However, there were still those who believed in her mother; colleagues and friends who could be called upon to bring their own talents to bear.

"JASMINE."

"Jasmine?"

"Jasmine Cooper. I'm Penelope Cooper's daughter?"

"Oh, Penelope, bless her. How is she doing these days?"

"Not good, I'm afraid. She's losing her business and it looks like we're going to lose the house."

"Oh, goddess! I'm so sorry. That's terrible. Is there anything that I can do?"

"Actually, that's what I was calling about. You and Mum were once pretty close, and I was wondering whether you could use your power – perhaps call on some of the others, too – to help turn things around for us... Hello?"

"Yes, I'm still here. I'm sorry, Jasmine, I don't quite know what you expect of me."

"A spell or two, perhaps? I don't know... don't you have some kind of magic to help a witch in need?"

"That's really not the way it works, my dear."

"But, Mum told me you used to get up to all sorts. She told me about things you'd seen, the stories of the magic you'd worked—"

"Jasmine, slow down. Your mother always was one for tall tales, I'm afraid, and that's what they mostly were."

"But she said the spells really worked."

"And did you ever witness any that ever did? Magic just isn't like that, Jasmine. It never was. Look, I think that Penelope was trying to impress you, entertain you maybe. I'm sure she meant no harm."

"But... there's really nothing you can do? That any of you can do?"

"I'm so sorry, Jasmine. Naturally, I'll be thinking of you both, praying for you. And do tell Penelope, if she ever wants to give me a call—"

"Fine. Bye."

ARODIAS LOOKED AT the boy in the mirror. It had been a long time since he had worn such a youthful face; decades since he had spoken to anyone outside the circle of his own family, let alone a woman.

There had been women once, before his studies had intervened, before his discoveries had reshaped his world and himself. Once he had been married. Once he had loved and, if he cast his mind back,

Arodias thought that he could just about remember how that had been.

"Hi, I'm Richard," he said to his reflection. "I'm sorry about all that... strangeness before. May we talk?"

JASMINE HAD READ somewhere that one of the best ways of coping with grief – or mental trauma of any kind – was to throw oneself into work, or study.

For all of the disorientation and anxiety she had experienced in her first few weeks of college, she soon found herself settling in. Her Modern English Literature course was well-taught and engaging, and there was a wide variety of societies and clubs on offer.

One afternoon, she was handed a leaflet advertising open auditions for a forthcoming production of *Romeo and Juliet*, and though it had been a while since she had last trod the boards in Drama Club at school, she decided to give it a go.

At first, she had thought of going in for one of the significant, though smaller, female roles – Nurse, or Lady Montague or Capulet – but deciding to throw caution to the wind, Jasmine put her name down for Juliet.

"Okay, people. I need a Romeo and a Juliet, and we're going to go with the balcony scene. Who do we have?"

Jasmine raised her hand and saw only a handful of prospective Romeos do the same. Her heart sank when she saw that one of them was the weirdo who had quizzed her about the book.

"Right, Romeo, we'll start with... you. Yes, you. Chap in the black T-shirt. Richard? And..." The director cast her eye over the clutch of Juliets. Jasmine was just about to lower her hand when she was singled out. "Yes, you my lovely. And you are...?"

"Jasmine."

"Jasmine and Richard, splendid. Let's go from, 'But soft, what light...'"

She wasn't expecting there to be any chemistry between them, but Richard spoke his lines as though he meant them; he was a generous actor, bringing her more fully into her own role, helping Jasmine give a performance that at least felt halfway real. She left the audition feeling quietly confident and was going over her lines again in the cafeteria when Richard sat down opposite her. It may have been the light or the fact that she wasn't as tense as she had been at their first meeting, but he looked younger somehow.

"Hi," he said.

"Hi."

"I thought you did really well today."

"Yeah, you too."

"Look, I just wanted to apologise about all that... *strangeness* before, with the book."

"Oh, don't worry about it. I'd forgotten all about it to be honest."

"It's just that old books are a bit of a hobby of mine."

"What kind of things are you into?"

"Esoteric study and research, mainly. What some may call magic."

"Hah! You should talk to my mother. She used to be into all that stuff. She owns the shop on the High Street – Destiny. Well, she did. It's going to close down."

"I'm sorry to hear that."

"Nothing to be done about it now, I suppose."

"And what was the book you were reading?"

"Just some old diary. I thought…" *that it could help, that there was magic there that I could use* "…it looked interesting, but it's a bit boring to be honest."

"Even so, I'd like to see it, if I may." Richard leaned in a little too close and Jasmine drew back. For a moment there had been a strange, musty smell and an expression crossed his face that made him look old. She blinked and he was leaning back in his chair. "It might be that I could help you understand what is in the book. Some of the more esoteric texts need a little translating. That is, if you would like?"

She thought back to when she had found the book, and the feeling that had come over her that it was somehow meant to be hers.

"That sounds great," Jasmine said, "I'd like that."

"Splendid. Well then, if we two are to be Romeo and Juliet, as I very much hope, then why not bring it along to one of the rehearsals, and we'll see what we can do."

He held out his hand and Jasmine saw that he had the most beautiful, slender fingers

"Thanks, Romeo... God! I mean, Richard. Richard is what I meant, of course. I'm so sorry." Jasmine was sure that her embarrassment had lit her up like a beacon, but Richard smiled.

"No need to be. Soon then, my Juliet."

ARODIAS WAS CONFIDENT the roles would be theirs. After all, on the morning of the auditions, he had taken the precaution of burning certain powders while describing complex geometries over the smoke.

He had always suspected that the book had remained in the home of Nathaniel Creed. No doubt Creed had set up wards to keep it from his sight. In any case, Nathaniel was centuries dead and the book was back in the world. And the girl might be useful, beyond being his route to the text. When he had first seen her, she had been reading Nathaniel's words not just with a glimmer of understanding, but a hunger for more.

Yes, she had something, this Jasmine. He may yet have need of her.

"OH GOD, YOU utter *utter* idiot. 'Thanks, Romeo.' *Romeo!* Oh yeah, well played Jasmine. Top of the class."

She blushed as she remembered the conversation. She'd never spoken like that to a boy before, and he'd hardly been the master of subtlety himself. *My Juliet.* Any other time, she'd have been running for the hills, but there was something about Richard – a certain intensity, an alluring intelligence. She didn't know quite what it was, but she did know that she wanted to see him again.

"'Thanks, Romeo.' Oh god oh god oh god!"

There was a soft knocking on her bedroom door. "Are you okay in there, my love?"

"Fine, Mum. Just struggling with some homework."

"Is there anything that I can do?"

"No, I'm fine really."

"Okay then. Well… I love you, you know?"

"Yeah, I know, Mum."

Jasmine waited until she heard her mother's footsteps descending the stairs before she took Nathaniel Creed's diary from under her bed.

She needed something to focus her mind, to take her away from thoughts of Richard for a while. Perhaps he had been right to be so interested in the book. Word by word, it was starting to speak to her.

"WELL, MY LOVELIES, we have our Romeo and Juliet. Round of applause please." Richard looked at Jasmine and winked. She gave him a tentative thumbs-up.

Just as she'd promised, she had brought the book with her, and it was this that was on her mind that afternoon, rather than the words of the play.

"That was terrific, Jasmine. Very stirring," the director said, after they had read through Juliet's first scene.

"Really? I think I tripped over a couple of the lines."

"No no, that was perfect, really."

Jasmine looked from the glassy sheen in the director's eyes to the disgruntled expressions on some of the other actors' faces, and felt that the cast were not in agreement. But then they were onto Mercutio and Romeo's verbal sparring, and Jasmine's thoughts returned to what she had learned the previous evening.

Nathaniel Creed's philosophy was unlike anything she had encountered in the world of magic. His approach was unusually misanthropic, and concerned itself not so much with discovering the spiritual side of oneself, as denying the individual's place in the universe. Indeed, he referred to the human race as an 'accident'; a by-product of a vast process humanity didn't have the capacity to understand. He wrote about the importance of erasing one's own identity, becoming a nothingness, a gateway through which something could enter.

Jasmine looked up as Richard sat down beside her. On the stage Friar Lawrence was going through his morning ablutions.

"Penny for your thoughts," Richard said.

"Oh, I was just wondering who this Al-Hazred was that the author mentions. Any ideas?"

Richard looked briefly taken aback.

"Are you okay?" Jasmine said.

"Yes, fine. Fine. Just a bit tired. But, yes, that name does ring a bell. Listen, I was thinking that we could take a look at the book together, tomorrow evening, over dinner at my house."

"Your house?"

"Of course. I'll have a meal prepared for us and… Oh, I see. No, nothing like that of course. It's just that we'd have access to my library and—"

"Look, why don't you come over to mine instead? We have a pretty impressive collection of books too, and I'm sure that you and Mum would get on like a house on fire, being into magic and all that."

"'And all that'?"

"Oh, you know what I mean. I also cook a pretty mean curry. And we can learn more about this."

Jasmine gestured with the book and Richard's hand shot out, as though he meant to grab it.

"Sorry," he said. "May I… may I just take a quick look?"

"Romeo and Juliet," the director called, "you're up. Party scene run through, yeah?"

"Of course," Richard said, and managing a weak smile he turned back to Jasmine. "Later then."

"SINCE WHEN DID you start cooking?"

"Since you stopped bothering, Mum."

"Heh. Fair point. Are we expecting guests?"

"Just a boy from college. Richard."

"A boy from college, eh?"

"Don't start. It's not like that." At least, she didn't think it was.

Richard was simply coming over to help her understand Creed's book, and Creed's book would help her with their shitty life; she was sure of it. "Anyway, I think you'll like him. He's into all that weird stuff."

"How flattering, Jasmine. Thank you so much."

Richard was alarmingly punctual. Jasmine had been intending to change before they sat down to eat, but instead she had to answer the door in tracksuit bottoms and an ancient T-shirt. Richard himself was dressed so formally that it looked like he was on his way to a funeral. As he stepped over the threshold, he brought with him a faint odour of mothballs. He hadn't brought any flowers or wine, but then Jasmine didn't think that it would have occurred to him to do so.

"Dinner's almost ready," she said. "Oh, and this is Mum."

"Mrs Cooper. A pleasure to meet you."

Richard held out his hand and Penelope didn't take it.

Well isn't this getting off to a flying start? "Right, well," Jasmine said. "Dinner is pretty much ready, so why don't we go and sit down?"

Penelope kept up the silent treatment all through the meal, glaring at Richard as though daring him to make a wrong move. Jasmine had no idea what had got into her. She had never been this off with any of her other boyfriends; not that Richard was boyfriend material, she reminded herself.

Richard bolted down the meal as though desperate to get it over with.

"Okay, then," Jasmine said as she cleared the plates. "Shall we make a start on those lines then Richard?"

"Lines?" Penelope said.

"Oh, I haven't told you have I? Richard and I have been cast in the college production of *Romeo and Juliet*, as the leads."

Penelope couldn't have looked less delighted if Jasmine had told her she was pregnant.

"So, we're just going to go over our lines. Okay?"

Her mother didn't respond, but she did hold Richard with that same baleful stare as they left the room.

"I'm so sorry about Mum," Jasmine said, once the bedroom door was closed behind them. "She's been going through a lot, you know?"

Richard didn't answer. He was standing at the dresser with his back to her, staring down at the book.

"So, here it is," he said in a reverential voice. "Nathaniel Creed's book. I've heard so much; had no idea it was so close." Richard turned around with the book in his hands. "Where did you find it?"

"It was under a pile of junk in the basement of Mum's shop." Jasmine wasn't sure why she felt the need for the white lie. Perhaps it was the intensity in Richard's eyes as he opened the book. "Where did you hear about the book in the first place?"

"Creed and I..." Richard cleared his throat and started again. "Nathaniel Creed's work is very well known within certain circles."

"Famous wizard. Got it."

"Wizard is far too… *trite* a word for what Creed was. Creed was…" Richard gestured with the book, as he sought the right words. "*This* is not magic."

"It's not?"

"No, the knowledge within this book concerns itself with something far greater. Magic is mere wish fulfilment; ludicrous ritual, offering, at best, a temporary salve to suffering." Jasmine thought of all the junk in her mother's shop and nodded. "But Creed *knew*. To involve oneself with true knowledge, one must entirely forget oneself. Humanity is nothing; less than nothing – a cosmic joke. There are beings out there that have terrible, infinite power. True sorcery, real magic, lies in attracting their attention."

"But Creed never managed it, did he?"

"What do you mean?"

"Well I've been reading the book, and from what I can work out, it's mostly about his failures. He never seemed to do any actual magic. And the book… it ends halfway through a sentence. What do you think happened to him?"

Richard ignored the question and said, "Creed knew more than he would let himself realise. His philosophy was mostly sound, but his ritual technique was all—"

"—wrong. Yes, that's what I thought." Jasmine said, interrupting him. "There's a bit where he really seems to be onto something, though."

Richard looked at her as though seeing her for the first time;

Jasmine thought that if she wasn't careful she could lose herself in those eyes.

"Show me?" Richard said, holding out the book.

He sat beside her on the bed as she carefully turned the brittle pages.

"Here we are. It's like the words of the ritual are mostly right, but the cadence, the rhythm is all wrong."

"Yes," Richard said, leaning in closer. "I must admit that had never occurred to me."

"It's about patterns. See this diagram? He's got the basic idea right, but he's not followed it through."

Jasmine pointed to a picture drawn in dark brown ink. Richard nodded emphatically and put his hand over hers where it rested on the page. She looked up; his face was inches from her own.

"'And palm to palm is holy palmer's kiss'," he said, entwining his fingers with hers.

"Richard?"

"Yes, Jasmine."

"I believe that's my line."

She leaned in and kissed him. For a moment his lips didn't seem to know what to do, but then they found their place. Jasmine moved away and smiled.

"'You kiss by the book'," she said and Richard laughed. "Anyway, shall we carry on?"

"Yes, Jasmine."

AS JASMINE CLOSED the front door behind Richard, Penelope said, "Jasmine? A word."

"Christ! You made me jump. And don't talk to me like that. I'm not five. Anyway, I have things I need to be getting on with."

"Stand right there and bloody well listen!"

Jasmine had never seen her mother so angry, but there was also an edge of fear in her voice.

"Jasmine, I love you. You know that. But I will not have that boy in our house again."

"What? He was polite as could be during dinner. I only wish I could say the same for you. Honestly, Mum, I have no idea what's wrong with you."

"You really don't see it do you?" Penelope took her daughter by the shoulders, and though she tried to pull away, held her firm. "Listen to me. This is important. Richard is... *polluted*. It's been a long time since I've encountered someone with an aura so awry, but trust me when I say he's bad news. Rare as it is, I know genuine evil when I see it."

Jasmine knocked her mother's hands away. "Oh, please! Don't spin me any more of your Harry Potter bullshit."

"I just want you to be safe."

"No, you're just afraid of what will happen when I take control of my life."

Jasmine did something then that she hadn't done since her early teens: she stormed upstairs and slammed her bedroom door behind her. She could still smell Richard – incense and mothballs – and Nathaniel Creed's book lay open on the bed beside where he had sat.

Jasmine looked at the diagram they had been studying, before picking up a notepad and pen and correcting Creed's mistakes. The ritual he had been attempting to realise was all about the sounds and rhythms of words as they were spoken, except that Nathaniel had been no poet, had no feeling for verse or meter, and his attempts to formulate a cant had fallen at every hurdle.

"The problem, Creed," Jasmine said, "is that you lack poetry."

She looked at her version of the diagram, studying its overlapping lines and symbols. "Poetry…"

Jasmine took up the script, flicking through the text, trying to get a feel for any words that would work. She read aloud from the play while she traced the intricacies of the diagram with her right hand.

"Look to behold this night,

The all-seeing sun

Ne'er saw her match since first the world begun."

She shaped the text to her will and as she spoke, she became aware of another will, beginning to impose itself upon the world. It was coming from almost impossibly far away, and it was approaching fast.

"Our solemn hymn to sullen dirges change."

Her body was filled with a pleasant languor, a seductive dream state.

"Tears distilled by moans."

Jasmine closed her eyes, noting, as she did so, the closeness of the darkness beyond her bedroom window. Her right hand spasmed and twitched as it continued to trace the complex geometries of the diagram.

"Thou sober-suited matron all in black

All the world will be in love with night."

Boundless space surrounded her – a formless chaos imbued with life by each word.

"Thus I enforce thy rotten jaws to open."

A wind arose from nowhere; Jasmine faltered and grasped for her next line before the power could elude her.

A voice spoke into the void.

"In fair Verona, where we lay our scene."

Jasmine opened her eyes, to find herself sitting in a plaza in the environs of an extraordinary city.

Every building, every tower, minaret and spire, had been constructed from the same obsidian stone. Above her, a depthless sky was strewn with the jewels of a million unfamiliar constellations. Across from where she sat, a fountain sang with dark wine – its heady perfume undercut with the scent of bitter herbs. Such a vast city should be home to a vast population, yet she appeared to be alone, even though voices and the sound of footsteps surrounded her. She felt the touch of silk and heard feminine laughter as someone unseen brushed past her. From a church across the way, strange music sounded, as of many pipes playing, not always to the same tune.

Jasmine looked down at her hands to find that she still held Nathaniel Creed's book, though of *Romeo and Juliet* there was no sign.

She rose to her feet and, across the way, a section of wall seemed to detach and come towards her. It took Jasmine a moment to realise that it was the figure of a man, cast from the same stone as the city. His clothes had been spun from a midnight thread – or was she seeing the absence of clothes on the absence of a man? – and neither colour nor lightness relieved his darkness.

"Jasmine," he said, and described a courtly bow, his right foot forward, his right arm swept low. He was dressed like a Renaissance prince or nobleman, and his features were youthful, though Jasmine suspected she would never be able to determine his true age. As he rose, she gasped, for the depths she had first seen in Richard's eyes were here limitless.

He saw the book in her hands, and laughed. "You used Nathaniel Creed's words to summon me?"

"I used the ideas behind the words. The words themselves were from a different source, as I'm sure you're aware," she said, gesturing to the city that surrounded them.

The discordant music coming from the church ceased. Above them the stars began to fall. Sickly yellow light bled from the church's windows and the doors opened; within, she could hear the sound of something massive shuffling across a stone floor – it put her in mind of the elephant house at the zoo. She wasn't sure that she wanted to enter the church, or see what would emerge, but the obsidian man held out his hand and there was nothing that she could do but take it.

"My lady?" he said, gesturing to the church, and together they stepped forward.

ARODIAS FELT INVIGORATED, full of a boundless energy and a breathless anticipation such as he hadn't experienced in many a decade. There had been a period in the late eighteenth century when he had lived, for a time, in the catacombs of a deconsecrated and abandoned monastery where – after much meditation and the ingestion of a number of highly toxic fungi – he had encountered a being that had instilled in him a similar feeling. But that had been an inter-planar entity, and Jasmine was a mortal human woman; one who understood the truth, and in whom Arodias sensed a desire to set it free.

When he opened the front door, he felt like announcing to the entire household that he was in love, but no one would answer, not with Uncle gone and the rest of them lost in their own esoteric venturings.

Still, he had to tell someone.

He found Cousin in the dining room. He had clearly been sitting at the large dark-wood table for some time; a mantle of dust rested on his shoulders and a spider had made its home between his left ear and the back of the chair.

Cousin was a long way away, but Arodias brought him back.

"Arodias," he said, "is it time to attempt to open the gates?"

"Not quite, Cousin, but not long now." Arodias leaned forward, and then recoiled when he got a whiff of his relative's fetid odour. "I have met someone. A girl."

Cousin's dry laugh rattled loose two of his teeth. "A girl? Arodias, are you not a bit beyond that, your present form excepted?"

"But this is no schoolboy crush. She was the one who discovered Nathanial Creed's book, and she *understands it*, Cousin. The dark truths and arcane secrets speak to her."

"You know better than to let love interfere with your esoteric commitments."

"But that's just it, Cousin. None of us – not one member of this family, over however many centuries it's been – has been able to open the gates and call *him* into this world. But with Jasmine it feels not just possible, but probable. The stars are right. You feel it, don't you Cousin?"

"Be careful, Arodias."

"You know that *he* is near."

Cousin expelled a breath and leaned forwards, shedding dust and destroying his spider companion's home. His right hand came up with the crackle of dry tendons stretching. There was the sound of ancient bone fracturing, but he showed no pain as his hand made the sign of the Crawling Chaos.

"Yes, Arodias," Cousin said. "He is near."

JASMINE WAS IN love. She had not slept, yet she was wide awake. Penelope noticed her buoyant mood at breakfast and scowled at her daughter when Jasmine asked her to pass the butter.

"Mum, lighten up. Let's forget about last night and start over, okay? Richard means nothing to me. He *is* nothing."

"I'm glad to hear it," Penelope said, but there was wariness in her words, as though she were a little afraid of her daughter.

The world revealed itself anew as Jasmine walked to college that morning; no more real than scenery painted on cloth and poorly hung, and now that she saw this, she felt confident that she could recast the world to her own desires. All she needed was her obsidian man. If she gave him access to their universe, he had promised that there would be a corner of reality that was eternally hers. It didn't matter that everything else would be gone; what mattered was that Jasmine would be able to rectify the mistakes of the past: the divorce that had changed everything; the misfortune that had dogged her and her mother at every turn. And whether any of it were true or not, well, what did that matter? The obsidian man had told her the truth, or at least hinted at it, and though a part of Jasmine had shrunk away in the face of it – wanting to erase the knowledge that been revealed to her – she realised that unless she embraced the chaos, it would destroy her.

And she was in love. The entity that had eluded Nathaniel Creed had noticed her, and taken her by the hand. Unlike Creed, she understood the true power of words, how the sounds and rhythms they made were as important as their meaning. Jasmine wished that she could share this knowledge with her fellow English Literature students, but her new lover had forbidden it.

Richard greeted her effusively at the lunchtime rehearsal, even going so far as to lean in for a kiss, which she didn't reciprocate, much to the amused glances and raised eyebrows of the cast.

Once she was in character, none of that mattered. The college disappeared and they were in Verona.

Jasmine felt every line, every word of the fated tragedy. This would be her ritual. When she kissed Romeo she could taste the grave and that which waited beyond.

"Okay, and let's leave it there," called the director, shattering the illusion, leaving Jasmine blinking in the shaft of sunlight that streamed in through one of the windows.

"Jasmine? That was excellent, but I'm wondering if we're over-playing it a little. I think you can reign in some of that intensity without lessening the performance."

What did she know? Jasmine merely smiled and tilted her head in something that could be read as a nod.

"That was amazing," Richard said, leaning in again for a kiss, which this time she returned. "Did you bring the book?"

"I think that you love Creed's book more than me."

"I can assure you that's not the case." And she was amused to see that he was genuinely mortified. "I just really enjoyed our time together last night, that's all."

"No, I didn't bring the book. But we can return to it soon."

"Listen, I was thinking that after the play, maybe we could go out for dinner some time? Without the book; just the two of us. We don't even have to talk about the occult."

After the play. Jasmine smiled. "After the play, Richard, all manner of things will be possible."

FOR THE FIRST time in several hundred years, Arodias was having doubts.

Jasmine could help him complete the ritual – that he was sure of – but he could not guarantee her safety once the gates opened. His god didn't give a fig for human relationships, let alone love. He may grant Arodias mastery over chaos, but he could also take away the first person he had genuinely cared about in a very long time.

Usually, he would change out of his college clothes at the end of the day – and sometimes he even changed form – but that evening his troubled mind insisted that he seek counsel.

He couldn't find Cousin anywhere, and both Brothers had shut themselves in the scullery, from which blasphemous sounds and peculiar smells emanated. Arodias found Sister in the attic, studying the patterns of spiders as they spun their webs between the roof beams.

"Arodias," she said, without looking up, "you appear to be flustered."

"Where is Cousin?"

"I believe that he has taken himself to Leng."

Then he wouldn't see Cousin for some time, if at all.

"You should be in a much more jubilant mood, Arodias. The stars are right, yet I detect in you a certain melancholy."

"Do you ever have doubts, Sister?"

"Doubts, Arodias?"

"About whether what we're doing is right."

"Come now, you know not to apply morality to these matters."

"The situation has changed. Sister, I'm in love."

Sister did look at him then, and she laughed, the malice in her mirth distorting her already terrible visage.

"Oh, but that is priceless. Just because you have become a teenage boy, Arodias, it doesn't mean that you have to act like one. Does anybody else in the family know?"

"Just Cousin."

"Yes, well, that would explain his sudden departure. Arodias, do I have to remind you what happened the last time you permitted yourself to fall in love?"

Katherine had been a publican's daughter, and normally Arodias wouldn't have given her a second glance, but there was a wickedness in her that appealed to him. At first they had shared only a bed, but over time, and despite himself, Arodias had revealed certain arcane secrets to her, hinting at the dark realities that lay just beneath our own. One evening, after a long and uncomfortable carriage ride back from Bristol, he had found her paging through a tome from his private library – access to which he had strictly forbidden. Arodias hadn't castigated her, or cast her out, but had instead taken the book from her hands and helped Katherine to understand what was written there. He wished he hadn't.

One stiflingly warm night, not long after, as Arodias had tossed and turned in fitful sleep, while beside him Katherine slept as one dead, something had descended from the moon on membranous wings and plucked his lover from their bed. The shadows thrown by the single guttering candle meant that Arodias only caught a hint of this horror's true from, but it had been enough to send him to a sanatorium for a prolonged period.

The thing had stolen his lover and may as well have taken his heart.

"Really, Arodias," Sister said, "you should have left your humanity behind along with the rest of us long ago. Were we wrong to make your our avatar in this world?"

In Jasmine, he had found something of his humanity again. Much to his surprise he found that he cared what happened to her. The hunger in her eyes for forbidden knowledge – the underlying desperation to impose her will upon the world – reminded him all too keenly of Katherine. This time, however, he could make sure that such a terrible fate did not befall his beloved. For her sake he must put aside his diabolical mission. True, it would mean regaining his mortality – oblivion would come for him in the end – but better that than the eternal alien cruelty he saw in Sister's eyes as she waited for his answer.

"No, Sister," Arodias lied, "you were not wrong." He raised his right hand in the sign of the Crawling Chaos. "Thank you for your council. Praise Nyarlathotep."

JASMINE LOST HERSELF in Juliet. She had come to know the play intimately, had memorised not just her own lines, but the words of every character in every scene. She could recite Shakespeare's play backwards if needs be, though she didn't think that it would ultimately add anything to the ritual. Instead, she focused on the words that held weight; the verses that would best give themselves to her purpose.

No, not mine, Jasmine reminded herself. *His.*

Often, after rehearsals, some of the cast would get together for a drink, and although Jasmine was usually invited, she would never join them. She didn't want to think of any of the other cast members outside of their characters; it would diminish their role in the ritual. Richard she did keep onside, allowing him to join her for the occasional coffee, or meet-up for lunch in the canteen. Though he was keen for them to be closer, she had allowed little more than hand-holding and the odd chaste kiss on the cheek.

"Jasmine?" There was a knock on her bedroom door. "Jasmine, my love?"

"I'm studying, Mum. Go away."

The door opened and Jasmine quickly closed Nathaniel Creed's book, shoving it under a stack of papers.

"I just thought that you could use a cup of tea. You've been at it ever since you got home, and you hardly touched your dinner."

"Really, it's fine. I've got a lot to get through."

But to her frustration, Penelope sat on the bed beside her and put her hand on her shoulder.

"Look, I'm glad that you're not seeing Richard outside of college, but that doesn't mean you shouldn't have a social life. You're young, Jasmine, you should be enjoying yourself."

Jasmine brushed her mother's hand from her shoulder and without looking up said, "I have a lot to do. I do not need a cup of tea, and I do not need you constantly disturbing me."

Penelope didn't back away but leaned in closer.

"Something's wrong. Something isn't... *normal* here." She stood and started to pace. "I could burn some sage, a cleansing ritual would perhaps—"

Jasmine snorted a contemptuous laugh and turned to glare at her mother. She didn't say anything, just held her with her eyes until she backed out of the room and quietly closed the door behind her.

Jasmine shook her head; if only her mother realised that she was doing this for them.

She turned back to the desk and closed her eyes. As she'd expected, the obsidian man was just on the other side of the darkness.

He was leaning against the fountain in the middle of the night-black plaza, an amused expression on his face, as though he had been witness to the mother/daughter stand-off. The stars above were closer than before; blazing ethereal torches that Jasmine felt she could reach up and pluck from the heavens.

"I must say," said the obsidian man, filling a wine glass from the black stream pouring from the fountain, "that using the words of the Bard, the energy of performance, to enact the ritual is a stroke of genius. You are far more gifted than Nathaniel Creed was, or Arodias Thorne could ever hope to be.

"Who is Arodias Thorne?" Jasmine said, taking the cup offered to her.

But the obsidian man only replied with a cruel smile.

AS THE FIRST night of the play drew near, so the tension in Jasmine rose. Any fluffed line, any misreading of a stage direction from any of the cast was met with a rolling of her eyes and a sigh of exasperation. During one of the final dress rehearsals she had cut Mercutio short with a cry of, "No, you idiot! The emphasis should be on *Queen*, not *Mab*."

The director had had to pull her aside. "Jasmine, you need to remember who is directing this play, okay? And you need to relax. Take the rest of the evening off. You certainly know your lines well enough, so perhaps it's time to give the others room to deliver theirs, okay?"

Seeing the colour rise in Jasmine's cheeks, and her glare change from one of annoyance to baleful intent, Richard intervened. "Come on Jasmine, this is supposed to be fun. Why don't we step out and grab a coffee?"

She turned on Richard as though to launch herself at him, but the warmth in his eyes and his smile cut through her rage, bringing her back to herself. He really did look every bit the youthful, brash, daring and reckless Romeo.

"I… I'm sorry," she said, letting him take her hand. "Yes, let's get a coffee."

In the café, she tried to talk to Richard about Creed's book, but he showed little interest and instead, asked, "How have things been, *really*? How's your Mum, Jasmine?"

But she shook her head and said, "I don't know."

ON THE OPENING night, Penelope was as excited as her daughter was agitated.

"I'm proud of you, you know?" she said, as she drove them to the college. "And your dad, he—"

"I know, Mum. I know. Please don't cry. You'll only set me off."

Night had fallen in Ardenton. Across the fields, on the edge of town, a low mist had begun to roll in. No moon shone, but the sky was clear and the stars bright and cold. The air seemed to shimmer as Jasmine stepped from the car, and just for a moment she saw those other, alien stars. Her right hand trembled as she remembered the diagrams and strange geometries Creed described in his book.

"First night nerves?" Penelope said. "Don't worry, I'm sure you'll be fantastic. Now, away, I shall see you inside. Break a leg."

The discordant music Jasmine heard as she prepared herself backstage was only the college orchestra warming up. As she applied her make-up in the dressing room mirror there was a shadow standing in the corner that she knew no amount of light would dispel.

She forgot all about the night as the house lights came down, and it was summer in Verona.

The spell was almost broken in the first act when Tybalt tripped over a line and then forgot the next. He must have seen the look of pure murder that Jasmine shot him from the wings because he quickly recovered. Thankfully that was the worst of the missteps and Jasmine began to sense the reality of the play imposing itself upon the fabric of the universe. The audience must have felt it too, because the gasp of horror when Tybalt was run through by Romeo sounded genuine. Even Richard looked shaken, as though he truly had blood on his hands.

The director glanced at Jasmine and smiled nervously as she prepared for her next cue. Whatever happened on the stage it was out of the director's control; this was no longer her play.

Jasmine allowed herself a thought of what might have been as she shared a kiss with Romeo in Friar Lawrence's cell. Richard held her lips for just a moment too long, as if afraid to let the fated tragedy take its course. By the beginning of the last act, the chill of the tomb filled the stage. There was a fetid odour too, and Jasmine heard the skitter of claws on stone. The stars were so close that their song put all thoughts of death from her mind. Soon she would be in control of her world, and if it was just a dream, she would make sure it was the sweetest dream ever dreamt.

The tomb on which she lay felt like cold stone, though she knew it to be wood. She whispered along to the lines of the actors, feeling how each word was another key turned, another gate opened.

She opened her eyes a crack and risked a glance at her mother, and was surprised to see tears streaming down Penelope's face. She wanted to sit up and tell her that everything was going to be okay, but she would know that soon enough.

Romeo leaned in for a final kiss, believing her as one dead, but she opened her eyes and he stumbled over his next line.

"A… a dateless bargain to engrossing death."

"Richard, do you love me?" Jasmine whispered.

He glanced at the audience nervously, before whispering back, "With all my heart."

Before he could pick up the thread of his soliloquy, Jasmine withdrew the knife she had concealed in her robes and buried it up to the hilt in Richard's chest.

ARODIAS CHOKED OUT a gasp and looked down at the knife handle. Blood was pouring from the wound, but before it could reach the boards the flow was reversed, as the thing that had invaded his body began to use him up. Once he would have rejoiced at this touch of true chaos, but now he could only glance over at his lover with a wounded look as the darkness consumed him.

JASMINE WATCHED IN fascinated horror as Richard dropped to his knees. The mortal wound she had struck was now bloodless, but there was no life left in him – at least, no human life.

Blackness clouded Richard's eyes, like ink dropped in water. His mouth stretched in a silent scream, his jaw gaping wide enough to tear his lips into a ragged smile. Richard's head dropped and a stygian torrent poured from his mouth, falling not into a pool, but the form of her obsidian man.

People were running for the exits now but whip-thin tendrils erupted from the torso of the night-black man and brought them to their knees. The darkness that he had brought with him began to fill the theatre, and when Jasmine felt its touch, she looked to Penelope.

Her mother was on her feet. Though black tendrils held her in place, she was straining against them as she fought to get to her daughter. Jasmine knew then that she had made a dreadful mistake. The obsidian man could not give them a world her mother would want to live in. She remembered what Penelope had said about Richard, that he was *polluted*, and now so was she. She looked over at the husk that had contained her lover, and there was no longer anything recognisably human there. The walls were beginning to dissolve as the tide of infinite chaos washed up against them. Those of the audience who were not dead were either catatonic with fear or gripped by hysteria – crying, laughing, singing. One man in the second row was repeatedly pounding his forehead into the seat back before him, chanting, "Iä, Iä, Iä, Iä, Iä, Iä."

"Mum," Jasmine said. "Mum, I'm so sorry."

But Penelope could not respond. It was too late.

The obsidian man strode to the front of the stage and, looking down on the huddle of broken humanity that made up his audience, smiled.

He opened his arms wide as the tide of chaos poured from him, and said, "Never was a story of more woe."

CONTROL

THE SIGN ABOVE his parent's storefront had said Rutherford &
Sons until recently. If you looked carefully, you could see where the
second *s* had been scraped off. His brother's death had been
unexpected and quick: a fight outside a pub, a single punch to the
head. Adrian had been the heir, but now that responsibility fell to
Stephen, and he wasn't sure he wanted it. For people whose business
was inextricably linked to death, Stephen's parents were reluctant to
talk about their son's passing. They hadn't even buried him
themselves.

Stephen wasn't sure what he wanted to do when he left school,
but he had little desire to be at home with the stiffs, making them
presentable before they were boxed up, dealing with grieving
relatives. He wasn't sure that he understood his own grief, let alone
the grief of others. At school, Stephen's bullies rather
unimaginatively referred to him as 'Dracula'. The idea of an
undertaker wanting to drink the blood of the dead was ridiculous.

His home was far from gothic; the apartment above the business tastefully – if boringly – furnished and as modern as any other household he had been in. Despite this, Stephen preferred to spend as little time there as possible.

Between school and home, there was a haven of sorts – as long as his pocketful of 20ps lasted. The Xenos arcade was owned by a middle-aged man with an acne-scarred face who sat glaring at his customers from the safety of the change booth. Behind the glass, bathed in the glow of the cabinets that boomed and bleeped around him, he looked embalmed.

"Any new games, Mr Xenos?" Stephen said, as he scooped up a fistful of change.

Mr Xenos didn't even glance at the boy as he raised a finger and pointed.

Stephen followed the gesture to a cabinet with a picture of a running soldier on the side, his teeth clenched in a snarl as bullets pinged around him. On the front of the cabinet, instead of the usual joystick and button controls, was what looked like a mounted Uzi. Usually any new machine would be surrounded, but it was early yet. Stephen dropped 20p into the slot and pressed the flashing *Start* button. The fake machine gun felt warm, as though the game had only recently been vacated.

A digitized voice yelled, "Attack!" and the first wave of enemy soldiers came at him.

When he pulled the trigger, Stephen was astonished to find the

Uzi juddering as pixel bullets mowed down his assailants. *Just like the real thing*, he thought. The game was satisfyingly realistic; he pulled the trigger and his enemies died in gory explosions of red, accompanied by electronic screams. He snarled, picturing the soldiers as the boys who taunted him at school.

"How do you like that, Larry Crossman? Not so cocky now, are you? And your smarmy friend can eat lead!"

Wave after wave came at him, their fixed grins and manic eyes taunting. The screen flared red and the gun gave a final judder. The words, *Killed in Action – Insert Money to Continue* appeared, and a timer in the top-right hand corner of the screen counted down from thirty.

Stephen's hands were shaking as he scrabbled in his pockets for more change. He dropped the coin twice before getting it into the slot. Just in time. The countdown had three seconds to go.

He destroyed the first wave of enemy soldiers only to find himself moving into the heart of their compound. Words flashed up on the screen, *Grenades x 3 – Press Side Button to Throw*. A red button lit up on the side of the plastic Uzi as soldiers started streaming out of the barracks. Stephen aimed and threw a grenade at one of the buildings, grinning as it exploded in a digital roar, revelling in the thought of obliterating one of his classrooms in much the same manner.

He reached the last of his change long before he reached the end of his rage.

* * *

STEPHEN WASN'T SUPPOSED to take the storefront entrance to their apartment. The service that his parents provided involved a practice of delicate care and respect. The last thing their customers wanted was some strange teenager trudging through their mourning. Today, however, business was quiet, and so he let himself in the front before making his way through the back rooms.

He noticed that one of the viewing rooms was curtained off and, hearing nothing on the other side of the cloth, he decided to take a look.

A dark wood coffin stood in-front of a fake stained-glass window. It was an expensive model, one that wasn't often ordered by their customers. Stephen placed his hand on the lid and wondered who lay within. After the cacophony of the arcade, the silence of the chapel was soothing; the quiet somehow intensified by the presence of the casket and its inhabitant. It wasn't often that Stephen invaded such sacred spaces, but ever since his brother's death, he'd sought these quiet moments.

Stephen closed the viewing room's curtain and went through the door at the end of the corridor. It was here they stored the coffins. Several open caskets stood on end at the rear of the room, their interiors shadowed. He stood before one of them and looked into the darkness. He imagined lights sparkling in the black, the tinkling of electronic music and the crunch of digital explosions. His hands reached out for controls, only for his knuckles to hit the back of the box, sending the casket rocking. His heart in his mouth, Stephen grasped the sides of the box to steady it. He shook his head, wondering what he had been thinking.

When he entered their apartment, his father looked up from his newspaper.

"You're home early," he said.

"I—"

"That's good. I thought it would be nice if we did something together for a change. Don't you think?"

Stephen had to force down a sigh of relief that his father hadn't brought him up on his truancy.

"We don't spend enough time together, and I know things have been difficult since Adrian's death. Why don't we get away from it all for a bit, see a movie?"

There was one film in particular that Stephen very much wanted to see. He had been resigned to going to the cinema on his own, but now his Dad was offering to take him; *his* Dad. Stephen had almost forgotten how much he missed him.

"I'd love that," he said

"Great, let me just tell your Mum we're off out."

THE FILM WAS just as good as Stephen had hoped, though his father fidgeted and sighed throughout. That was okay; he was making the effort and that was what mattered. On their way out, Stephen saw that the cinema had a small arcade, and his father must have seen him looking as he said, "Hang on a moment. Let me see if I have any change."

Most of the games were fairly old, though they did have a few good machines. Stephen chose a cabinet with controls for two players, encouraging his father to join him, but he looked faintly embarrassed and said that he was happy just to watch.

Stephen got further than he ever had on this particular game; flying his ship deep into the canyons of the enemy space station, and timing the notoriously difficult trick-shot just right to blow it to pieces. As the words *Congratulations Player One* lit up the screen to the accompaniment of digital fireworks, his father squeezed his shoulder and said, "I'm proud of you," as though he had achieved some great feat.

On the way home they chatted for the first time in ages, and Stephen felt that perhaps they had finally turned a corner – that there would be life after Adrian.

IN SCHOOL THE next day, Stephen wasn't treated to the usual taunts and jibes. At break time, as he cautiously scouted out the playground, he came to realise that none of his bullies were in. He asked his friend Lucy whether they had bunked off *en masse;* it was entirely likely.

"Oh, you haven't heard?" she said. "They're all sick. Apparently they can't stop shitting and vomiting." She suppressed a giggle. "I think they're going to give us a letter about it to take home to our parents."

A case of the winter vomiting bug had been identified in a small number of pupils, and parents were advised to keep an eye out for similar symptoms in their own children. Stephen felt just fine (though he briefly considered faking it so that he could get a day off school), and only five boys had been affected. He did think it curious that these five were the same who made his life such a misery on a daily basis; the same five he had gleefully imagined mowing down as he played the new shooter at Xenos'.

Four days later, once his bullies had recovered sufficiently to return, they appeared to have no energy with which to taunt him. Instead, they stared at him sullenly from across the classroom; this Stephen could handle, and soon he learned to ignore them entirely. School became tolerable for the first time in an age.

Though a part of him dismissed the thought as wishful thinking, Stephen couldn't help but consider that maybe Xenos' new machine had played a part in their downfall.

DURING HIS LUNCH break, Stephen's attention was caught by a competition in the comic he was reading.

FIVE NEW HANDHELD GAMES TO BE WON!

All he had to do was fill in his name and address and send off the slip of paper and he would be in with a chance. He was old enough to understand, however, that this would be a very small chance indeed. Even so, he thought he knew of a way to skew the odds in his favour.

After school, Stephen took a pocket full of change and his best friend, Richard, down to the arcade. He knew the machine that he wanted was unlikely to be occupied. It was perhaps the oldest game in the place. He had never been able to beat his top score of 89,998. If he could focus, if he could somehow channel his will and better that number, then he thought he could be one of the five blessed winners of the new handheld game he so coveted. With Richard as witness to this feat, his success would be doubly assured.

Richard watched for a while, but soon grew bored.

"Tell me you've almost done it, Steve."

"Not yet, but not far off."

"Yeah, well it's getting late and I was supposed to be home for tea ages ago."

"Come on, Richard! Just a few more minutes and I'll have cracked it."

"I don't know why you're so obsessed with doing this in the first place."

"I just... I just have to."

"Okay, but tell me about it tomorrow. I really have to go."

Stephen would have protested, but he had to focus. He was almost on the maximum difficulty. The arcade was almost empty, though Stephen was dimly aware of raucous laughter coming from the change booth. There was the smell of cigarette smoke and the pop and hiss of beer cans being opened.

89,003. Almost there.

Stephen's eyes blurred as he tried to follow the frantic contortions of the snake on the screen.

89,421.

"Hey you!"

89,682.

"Hey you, lad!"

Stephen ignored the shout, focusing on his reflexes.

"Come on, fuck off now. You're the last one here and I want to shut up shop and get down the pub."

89,972.

"Yeah, fuck off you little runt, otherwise I'll put my boot up your arse."

More raucous laughter.

"Easy, man. That runt is my best customer."

The score counter clicked over to 90,000 just as a hand fell on his shoulder.

"I did it," he turned to gasp at the man standing over him. "I beat it."

"Did you indeed?" the man said and grasped Stephen's cheek in one hand. "That's lovely. Now fuck off. I'm taking Xenos here to get rat-arsed."

"What... what time is it?"

"Well past your bedtime, sonny."

Stephen looked at his watch and saw that it was almost half-past seven. Any sense of victory he had at beating his score was quickly snatched away by a rising sense of panic. He knew what his mother would be thinking: imagining him being rushed into A&E, his broken body far beyond repair, the victim of some terrible, tragic accident.

The streets were curiously quiet. As he raced home he suddenly imagined a bird's-eye view of the town: his small, poorly-rendered form running through the maze of roads and alleyways; shrouded figures drifting in from the outskirts, inexorably closing in. As Stephen passed the pub where his brother had been murdered, the sound of a smashing glass made him flinch from the doorway. He had a dreadful sense of a hand reaching for him, fingertips just inches from his back.

When he reached the door to the shop, he looked behind him but there was nobody there. Stephen padded as quietly as he could up the stairs to the apartment, though he knew there would be no way to avoid the confrontation that surely awaited him.

His father and mother were sitting at the kitchen table. Stephen's father got to his feet as he entered and rushed over to him.

"Do you even know what you're doing to us?" he shouted. "Have you any conception of the hell you are putting us through?"

He looked angry enough to strike him, though he had never yet raised a hand to his son.

"You had me so worried, Stephen," his mother said. "I'm constantly on edge as it is, and something like this... well, it's just too much."

Stephen had never felt so ashamed. He wanted to go to his mother and put his arms around her, but his father blocked his way.

"Where have you been, Stephen?"

"I…"

"Then let me answer for you. You've been down that arcade again, wasting your money."

Winning, Stephen had the sudden urge to shout, but he kept his silence.

"Well, from now on, I forbid you to go there. You'll be home directly after school each day. Do you understand?"

"I'm sorry – Dad, Mum."

"So you should be," his mother said. "You are not to go to that arcade again."

HAD STEPHEN BEEN in the mood for humour, he would have described the atmosphere at home the next day as funereal. He solemnly packed his bag and left with a perfunctory goodbye. As bad as he was feeling, he still remembered to post the competition entry on his way to school.

One afternoon, a week later, there was a package waiting for him on the kitchen table when he got home. His heart leapt as he opened the small box and saw the game inside. He had won. His time at the arcade hadn't been wasted, despite what his parents thought.

The game was fun, but nothing compared to some of Xenos' better machines. It was called *Track Runner* and you controlled a little man as he raced down an endlessly scrolling course, leaping hurdles and dodging monsters. It didn't take Stephen long to master the game and he found himself wishing it presented more of a challenge, while yearning for the arcade from which he had been banished.

IT WAS ALMOST the middle of the summer term and that meant the dreaded Sports Day would soon be upon them. Stephen had never been amongst the most athletic of pupils and hated the competitive spirit that came with PE lessons. The event was not optional, however, and so he had grudgingly signed himself up for the 100 metre sprint.

"Do you good," his father said. "And, who knows, maybe you'll make us proud."

Stephen thought that there was little chance of that, but the word niggled at him: *proud.*

"Who gives a shit?" Richard said at school. "It's just a bloody game!"

The night before Sports Day, Stephen shut himself in his bedroom and played *Track Runner* for hours. It took almost no effort for him to beat his previous best score. After a while the game became so repetitive that it was easy enough just to keep going. Stephen only stopped when he topped 150,000, finally confident that, in the morning, his victory would be assured.

This confidence was severely dented when he took up his position on the starting line and saw the other competitors. These were boys who actually enjoyed sport, and amongst them was Philip Webb, one of St Sebastian's athletic stars; a boy, it was rumoured, who had already been head-hunted to play in the local football team.

All Stephen's anxiety dissipated at the crack of the starter pistol. He took off, his legs fizzing with uncanny energy; it felt as though he were full of electricity. The ground blurred beneath; the wind whipped through his hair and stole his breath. He looked to either side – he had left the other runners far behind. He broke through the finish line and turned around, delighted to see the expressions of frustration and amazement on his competitor's faces as they fought for second and third place.

His father hurried over, his mother close behind. They expressed delight at his victory, but from the way they looked at him, Stephen thought that they were wondering whether they really knew their son.

"I knew you could do it," his father said, and Stephen didn't believe him.

"Our Stephen," his mother said. "You did it, son."

A part of him felt a little guilty. After all, his win hadn't just been down to him, the game had played its part.

WITHOUT ACCESS TO the arcade, there was little that Stephen could do to change things that summer. The season passed much as it always did – long, dry days at school, yearning for the holidays to finally start, and then, when they did, the interminable, stifling afternoons spent helping his parents run their business. There was also the annual pilgrimage to his aunt's house in Devon. A week spent with a pack of boisterous dogs, and her feral children; a week that would see Stephen yearning for the cool and quiet of the funeral home.

His parents never mentioned the arcade, so Stephen presumed that the ban still stood. He listened with rapt attention and envy as Richard told him about the new games that had come in that summer.

"You should come down, Steve. They can't have banned you permanently, surely?"

Stephen hadn't dared ask. His father had been quieter than usual of late and there was a tension in his mother that he didn't want to test.

One evening, Stephen had been woken by the sound of his father vomiting and his mother crying. The silence that followed was almost worse and, try as he might, he couldn't get back to sleep. In the morning, his exhaustion spilled into dread when he came out of his room and saw his mother sitting at the breakfast table, holding his father's hand; he looked as pale as a corpse.

He cleared his throat when he saw Stephen and nodded at his mother.

"Stephen," she said, "will you sit down love?"

For a moment he thought he had done something wrong, but, looking at his father, he knew that this wasn't about him at all.

"Your Dad isn't very well, Stephen, and he's going to have to go to the hospital for a bit."

"Is he dying?"

"Stephen!"

"It's alright, love," his father said, squeezing her hand. "No, matey. I'm sure I'll be back in no time. They can just look after me better there, and I'll be out from under your Mum's feet so that she can get on with things here."

His mother bit back a sob, turning it into a cough, as though Stephen hadn't noticed.

How odd, he thought, for his parents to lie to him about his father dying when they dealt with death every day.

"I'm going to take your Dad in this afternoon, then you can come with me in the morning to visit him. You'll be alright here on your own for a bit, won't you?"

Stephen threw his arms around his father. He flinched, as though hurt, but then he lowered his head and kissed his son's hair. Stephen breathed in his father's smell – sweat, aftershave, the breath mints he sucked to unsuccessfully disguise the fact that he was a smoker.

His mother broke down then.

"Hey, come on, you two," his father said. "I'm going to be alright. I'll be back before you know it."

When his parents had gone, Stephen went downstairs.

The closed sign was on the door and none of the staff were around, no doubt having been told to knock off early. This time, he didn't go to one of the viewing rooms but headed straight through to the back; the private places of the dead.

A coffin was laid out on two sawhorses, its lid propped against the wall; one of the medium-range caskets – pine with a padded red silk interior. He tried to imagine his father lying there. It felt wrong that an undertaker should be affected by mortality in the same way as those he attended to, as if in dealing with the dead one could avoid joining their ranks.

A long time ago, Stephen had asked his father, "What happens when we die?"

"Well, it depends upon the wishes of the deceased. Mostly, these days, people opt for cremation."

"No, I mean *after.*"

"Nothing, Stephen."

"Is that what you believe?"

"Listen, death will be like when you turn the telly off: the picture shrinks to that one bright dot, and then that fades and is gone. The end."

Why would his father choose to believe such a thing? Why had he chosen this life among the dead if, in the end, he would become one of them?

Stephen could hear the hum coming from the rearmost room before he opened the door. The entire far wall was taken up by the refrigerated body storage units. He knocked on each of the brushed steel doors in turn, until he found one that didn't produce an echo.

Of course, Stephen had been in the presence of the dead many times, but he'd never thought of them as people. He wasn't naive, but seeing his parents around corpses, and seeing them treating the dead as an everyday occurrence, meant that Stephen had lived at a remove from death.

He pulled out the drawer, revealing the sheeted body. He could tell by the shape beneath that it was a man, but when he pulled the covering back, he was surprised to see that it was a relatively young man. Stephen was familiar with the epitaph, *Just Sleeping*, but this really wasn't sleep. It was too quiet, too still, way beyond dreaming. Stephen tried to remember whether he had seen the man on the steel tray around town, perhaps playing with his children in the park, or wheeling a trolley around the supermarket.

"I'm going to be alright," his father had said, and how could Stephen not believe him? After all, there was no way on earth that his Dad would lie down and become *this*.

THE FACT THAT he was in a private room, rather than one of the open wards, spoke of the seriousness of his father's illness. He didn't move or greet them as they entered; he couldn't. He was all but held to the bed by the array of pipes and tubes that threaded his body.

"Hi Dad," Stephen said.

"It's us, love," his mother said, rather too loud, as though she were speaking to someone who was hard of hearing rather than in a coma. "I brought you some grapes and… well, yes." For lack of anywhere to put them she handed them to her son.

Stephen sat down beside the bed, staring at the bag of fruit in his lap, rather than at the ghost of the man. Just the other week he'd been up and about, his usual self. Stephen remembered him speaking to a supplier on the phone, laughing and saying, "Yes, well she's not going to get any less dead is she?"

"When's he going to come home?"

"Be realistic, for God's sake!" Stephen's mother snapped. "When do you bloody think?"

Stephen stared at her until she shifted uncomfortably under his gaze.

"I'm… sorry. It's just hard for me. For all of us. I mean, it's all just so sudden. And after Adrian…"

The deep, almost mannish sound of her weeping alarmed Stephen. She was coming apart and there was nothing that he could do. When her sobs had finally died away, he became aware of the repetitive *beep* of the heart monitor. He looked at the screen – his father's life measured out in peaks and valleys. Occasionally the peaks would be too far apart, the valleys too deep, and then he would hold his breath until the mountains rose again.

Stephen focused on the green dot on the monitor's screen as it etched out a jagged landscape. He imagined himself in a spaceship, flying over the rugged terrain, racing towards an endlessly receding horizon. His heart leapt as his father's skipped a beat, and he surged to his feet.

"I've got to go."

"Sit down, for pity's sake. Think of your father."

"I am, Mum. Really. I've got to do this."

And he hurried away from the hospital, followed by the repetitive beep of the machine.

BEFORE HE HEADED to the arcade, Stephen stopped at home, going through his father's jackets until he found a couple of crumpled pound notes deep in a pocket full of lint.

He all but threw the money at Xenos, and managed to tip most of the 20ps onto the floor as he scooped them up from the change tray.

There was somebody on the game that he wanted.

"I don't suppose I could get on that, could I?" He glanced at the screen. "You're almost out of lives and the next wave is brutal."

"Fuck off," the boy said, without looking round.

"Really, I can't begin to tell you how important it is that I play this game."

"I said, fuck... *shit!* Well I've gone and crashed now anyway. I hope you're fucking happy."

"I'm really sorry. Look, please take some of my change."

"Screw your change, mate." The boy slapped Stephen's outstretched hand, scattering several coins across the arcade before stalking away.

Stephen didn't have time to pick up all of the spilled money, and so he dropped a coin into the slot and pressed the *Start* button.

The alien landscape began to scroll across the screen, his tiny spaceship flying over the peaks and valleys of a monochrome world. Stephen dealt with the first wave easily, flying his ship with expert precision over the lunar landscape, destroying the alien horde. The important thing was to keep going, to keep that digital world moving along as he willed his father to live.

An hour and a half later, Stephen had beaten his top score, and an hour after that he had begun to draw a crowd. His bladder felt full to bursting and his mouth was dry; the fog of cigarette smoke shrouding the arcade scoured his throat. He was getting low on change and as the game became progressively more difficult, he needed to make every coin count.

Stephen's ship crashed and burned and he scrabbled in his pocket as the timer counted down, but his pocket was empty.

He remembered the money he'd inadvertently scattered on the floor, and looked down. Stephen found one coin by his foot, but that was unlikely to be enough. None of the gathered spectators offered him any of their own money; instead, they counted down as Stephen grubbed around on the sticky carpet.

"Nineteen, eighteen, seventeen, sixteen…"

"Shut up and help me!" Stephen snapped.

He looked beneath the game and saw that two coins had rolled under the cabinet. Stephen thrust his hand between game and floor, scraping his knuckles in the process.

"Twelve, eleven, ten…"

He snagged the coins and slotted one into the machine just in time. There was a smattering of insincere applause and cheers. Stephen filtered them out as he focused on the survival of his ship.

Moments later he was obliterated in a cascade of red and yellow pixels and managed to lose his remaining lives in quick succession. His hand shook as he dropped his penultimate coin into the machine. At his back, he sensed some of the crowd beginning to disperse.

"I can do this," he said to himself.

The alien world scrolled past with hypnotic regularity, and Stephen found himself being lulled into a trance-like state. He was running on automatic now, the game almost playing itself. He watched the screen as though he were standing at his own shoulder. The spaceship knew what to do, taking down wave after wave with deadly precision. With a suddenness that snapped him back into his own body, the last of the jagged digital world unravelled and his ship now flew over nothing, suspended dead-centre in the middle of a black screen. Alien ships flickered in and out of existence around him, but when he tried to move to attack them, the controls wouldn't respond. At the top of the screen the score counter was stuck on 99,999,999, flashing red, green, yellow, red, green, yellow.

"What?" Stephen hissed, mashing the buttons and, when that did nothing, grabbing the sides of the cabinet and giving it a shake.

"Hey!" Xenos yelled from his booth. "What the fuck do you think you're doing?"

"I've heard about this," said one of the boys who had stayed to watch. "That's what's called a Kill Screen. You've maxed out the game. You can't push it any further."

"Bring it back!" Stephen shouted, turning to the boy.

"Nothing to do with me mate. You should be proud. You beat the game."

Stephen turned back to the screen, where his ship was replicating itself in a variety of different colours. An awful buzzing sound came from somewhere deep in the cabinet. His sweatshirt bunched around his neck as he was grabbed and pushed away from the game.

"You break my game? You have any idea how much this cost?"

"I... I'm sorry, Mr Xenos. I was just trying—"

"Trying what? To lose me money? Go on, fuck off home. I don't want to see you in here again."

THERE WAS NOBODY home. Stephen sat at the kitchen table and waited. When the door opened and his mother entered, he turned to her in hope, though he had little – after all, that boy had called it the *Kill Screen.*

His mother said nothing, and so he said the words for her, "He's gone."

She nodded. "I'm so sorry, love. He wasn't in any pain."

Stephen held his mother as they wept, wondering what was going to happen next.

***

AFTER THE FUNERAL, after the last of the well-wishers had been given tea and allowed to share in their grief, after the last of the sympathy cards had been received, very little happened.

The rest of the summer holiday stretched on interminably; the days veering between oppressive warmth and thundery showers, days in which Stephen stayed at home as little as possible. Several months after he returned to school, his mother sold the business. She hadn't even asked Stephen whether he wanted to take on his father's mantle; it was clear that he had no taste for the trade. When he left school, he still had very little idea of what he wanted to do. He spent a while working down the coal mine. Those six months were some of the unhappiest in his life. He got up early in the darkness, to descend into the stinking, noisy darkness, only to rise back into the darkness of the cold, gloomy afternoon. He wasn't sorry when the pit closed down several months later. He spent a while on the dole, then a period in which his mother made it her job to fret about the lack of his.

"Honestly. I sometimes wish I'd never sold the business. If I hadn't, at least you'd have a trade."

It was through his old school friend Richard that he found one. Over a couple of pints in the Hope and Anchor, he told Stephen all about the coming revolution in home computing. Richard had begun to sell hardware and, as his business was expanding, he was looking to take on more staff. Stephen got in on the ground floor and quickly rose to become Senior Partner. The revolution was all that Richard had promised it would be. The hunger for home computing was immense. Stephen always had the latest model at home. Several of them promised *the arcade experience in your living room*, though he had yet to encounter a game as good as those he'd played at Xenos'.

When his mother fell ill, his considerable income meant that he could afford the best in private healthcare. Not that it did anything to slow the progression of her cancer; it replicated and spread as quickly as any computer virus, until there was almost nothing left.

The evening after her funeral, Stephen found himself with the cupboards bare and an urge to eat something comforting. He wandered around town until he found a fish and chip shop. When he entered, he looked not at the menu but the cabinet sitting in the corner, wedged between a table and the counter.

"Help you mate?" said the main standing at the fryer.

Stephen stood at the controls of the arcade game. The screen was blank and covered in a layer of dust. Someone had stubbed a cigarette out on one of the buttons. He looked down the side of the cabinet and saw that it wasn't plugged in, though there wasn't enough room for him to squeeze his arm into the gap so that he could turn it on.

"How long have you had this?" he said.

"Dunno. Ages. Not sure when it was last played to be honest with you. Was thinking of getting rid of it."

"Would you consider selling it to me?"

"What? You want it?"

"Very much, yes."

"Heh. Not sure it works, so I'll let you have it for a couple of hundred."

"Let's say two fifty and you agree to deliver it to my house tomorrow."

"Done."

Stephen shook the man's moist hand and ordered a large portion of soggy chips, which he threw in the bin on the way home. He couldn't eat; he was too excited, because he was sure that he had just brought the very same arcade game, the very same cabinet, he had played the day his father had died.

THE MAN IN the fish and chip shop was right. It didn't work. When he took the back off the cabinet it was perfectly clear why. The years spent in the takeaway had deposited a layer of grease over most of the components, and some of the wiring looked like it had been chewed on. After a few phone calls, Stephen was able to replace the damaged parts, and some cleaning and soldering saw to the rest.

When he turned the machine on, there was a part of him that expected to see his name on the score board but, of course, the scores were blank.

It felt odd playing the game in his living room, as though he needed to be surrounded by the booms and beeps of other machines and shrouded in a fog of cigarette smoke for the experience to be genuine.

Stephen had beaten this machine all those years ago, but it hadn't brought back his father; he still wasn't sure why he had expected it to in the first place. The things that had happened to him in his childhood hadn't always been pleasant, and he'd had his fair share of tragedy a little earlier than most, but he had been foolish to believe that he could change things. A game was just a game. Death didn't have to happen for a reason.

He wondered whether he could beat the machine again. It was already late, and Stephen had a meeting with a major supplier early the next morning; even so, he had done it before and he would do it again. Without the pressure exerted by spectators, and without Xenos in his booth, his vigilant eye sweeping the arcade, Stephen approached the game calmly. There was no stake here, other than the satisfaction of his own curiosity; the game gave itself to him easily.

Around the time that he should have been getting ready to go to work – the sun already lightening the curtains – he found the digital alien landscape once again unravelling, his ship flying over nothing. This time, however, he wasn't surrounded by enemy ships flickering in and out of existence, the score counter wasn't strobing as it reached its limit; instead, his ship faded, swallowed by darkness.

Stephen thought that the game had broken, and he shook the cabinet in frustration. When he looked at the screen, it wasn't the black-grey of a dead monitor, it was the black of nothing – the void.

A chill prickled the backs of Stephen's arms. He could hear the distant sound of a milk float doing its rounds, the twitter of birds in the tree outside his window.

There was something swimming up from the darkness of the cabinet. It had travelled a great distance, coming from far beyond the confines of the game.

Stephen's father looked out at him from the screen, no recognition or warmth in his eyes. His chill hands reached forward and closed themselves over Stephen's, where they rested on the controls. Stephen's breath misted in front of his face.

He looked at his father, and then at the blinking green text hanging before him – *Ready Player One?* – before reaching for another coin.

TURN

THE RAIN HAD driven us into the museum early. I had been about to take Josie to feed the ducks but instead we ran, dripping, into the hall of antiquities. Immediately we had unzipped our raincoats, Josie started in with "Daddy what's that?"

"It's a statue of a Roman noble."

"Daddy what's that?"

"A totem of a blue cat. Pretty isn't it?"

"Daddy what's that?"

She was pointing at an ancient penis sheath scored by tribal markings.

"A sort of wallet."

"Why?"

"To keep something in."

"Why?"

"Erm... because it is. Come on, let's see what else they have. Then, later, you can tell Mummy all about it."

Of course Josie didn't want to take the lift and of course she insisted on taking the stairs one at a time, counting as she went.

"One. Two…"

"Josie, shall Daddy carry you?"

"No, Josie do it. Three…"

There was a sigh of impatience from behind me and I had to stop myself from turning and shouting, "She's three for fuck's sake!"

On the first level, Josie spent a while pressing buttons on a case, lighting up the model of a Saxon village within. We spent a happy few minutes counting the links on a chainmail vest, though any number above ten was eleven to my daughter. A sign nearby promised face painting but the thought of spending time amongst rowdy toddlers with messy faces had me leading Josie deeper into the museum.

In a dimly lit room with a high ceiling we found a small sandstone building, which – according to the museum information booklet – had been discovered on an asteroid orbiting Jupiter. It had been transported here and reconstructed based on the best-available theories as to what it had once looked like.

"Daddy what's that?"

"I don't know. It looks like a sort of temple."

"What's that?"

"A kind of church."

"Why?"

But before I could fully explain Josie had run inside.

"Josie, no! You're not allowed in there."

"Actually, sir, we do encourage people to take a look," one of the museum staff said.

"Oh, okay."

I had to crouch to fit below the lintel. A narrow passage forced me to tuck my arms into my sides as I pushed my way within. I could hear Josie up ahead, singing the theme to *Postman Pat* – hardly a fitting hymn to whichever ancient alien god the temple had originally been raised. The main chamber at least allowed me to stand, though even with just myself and Josie inside, I could feel the onset of claustrophobia. The walls were engraved with indecipherable symbols and the floor was inset with seven circles of dark stone, evenly spaced. Josie stood on one of these and began to turn, her arms raised.

"So, what do you think?"

But Josie ignored me as she continued to turn.

"Come on, honey. Shall we get some lunch?"

Giggling filled the chamber a second before five toddlers did. They raced around us, their cries and exclamations almost deafening in the close confines. Josie didn't react to their presence, locked as she was in her own game. The children stopped suddenly to watch her and then they too each stood on a circle of stone and began to spin.

"Come on Josie. Let's go and do something else, eh?"

It wasn't just the children turning; the room began to sway, the symbols on the walls flowing into dark lines. Panicked, I stumbled for the exit, but the passage wouldn't stay still long enough for me to enter it. A pressure on my chest forced me back into the chamber until I was standing at the centre of the spinning children. My nausea abated. A sense of calm descended on me. The walls flickered past but I was now the one still point. The vague forms of the children elongated into shimmering columns. When they touched the ceiling, I felt the sudden lurch of acceleration. As I too began to turn, spinning with increasing velocity, I saw images of myself spiralling away – a seemingly endless procession of selves turning into the darkness. I closed my eyes, trying to draw those selves back into me, but this only meant that I was unprepared for the sudden halt and the floor rising to meet me.

I AWOKE AN indefinable time later. A hot wind blasted my face and I coughed as sand stung the back of my throat. I had no idea what had happened – perhaps an aneurism, or even a stroke? – but my first thought wasn't for myself.

"Josie?"

I looked up and found that I was alone.

I stumbled into the passage and out of the temple, ready to corner the nearest member of staff and demand that they call the police, but I stepped not onto the marble of the museum floor but the cracked paving of a dusty square surrounded by high walls. Directly across from me was a tall wooden doorway, like the entrance to a cathedral and, beside it, a small bell bolted to the wall at head height. The handle for the door was so far above me that I had no hope of turning it and so I rang the bell. It emitted a curiously flat sound and even pulling harder on the chain attached to it did not entice it to ring any louder. Even so, the summons was swiftly answered. A small inset door opened and a man stepped out.

"Where's my daughter? What's going on?"

He looked at me with a mixture of boredom and disappointment. The man glanced around the square, as though he had been expecting, or hoping for, someone else. Sighing deeply and shaking his head, he gestured me inside.

THE PART OF him that had hoped that this time they would find her had stopped hoping at least fifty or so bells back.

Every day was the same: the bell would ring shortly after the sun reached its zenith; he would answer the summons only to open the door to same man; his daughter would not be with him. As much as he wished that he could then just close the door and walk away, it was his job to escort the man through the corridors of the complex. He would protest all the way – "Where is Josie?" – and when the man was lead into the room at the heart of the complex and was stood before the master, his fearful gaze blinking up at his own face, the exact same question would be fired back at him.

"Where is Josie?"

And of course, he wouldn't know. No matter how many times he appeared, no matter how fervently the master hoped, his daughter would not be with him.

So the man was taken away and dealt with. This used to cause the master great physical pain, for the one being dispatched was himself, though the emotional pain he had once suffered had long since passed.

Behind the complex there was a pit containing the one thousand, eight hundred and twenty-five bodies of the master. No matter how many times he was killed, he would not give up looking for her.

THE BOY HAD everything he wanted – toys, nice food, his own room. He realised that he should have liked it here, but it smelled funny, a bit like a doctor's surgery. There were other children, five of them. They were friendly enough, though one of the girls wouldn't stop crying. That morning, after breakfast, a grown-up had gathered them together and had shown them several pictures, all of them seemingly of the same thing – a dark circle. The grown-up had told them that each circle had its own sound, and they had practiced the strange words he had asked them to repeat. Then they were taught the dance. It was easy. All they had to do was spin around and around, singing the strange words.

One of the boys had spun so fast he'd disappeared.

The grown-up had watched the place where the boy had been, as though waiting for him to reappear, but he never did.

Some of the children were upset at that, but the grown-up merely frowned and made a mark on a sheet of paper before picking up the phone.

"New male subject required. Inform the parents."

"AND YOU ARE aware of everything that every one of yourselves experiences?"

"Yes. Everything I'm doing. Every action I take. Every death I suffer or inflict upon myself, or others."

"I see. Well, it's my belief that these fantasies of your other selves are a way of imagining a scenario in which you may not be so helpless, in which you are doing something in order to get your daughter back. It is not an uncommon response among people in your position."

"But that's just it... nobody has been in my position. My daughter wasn't kidnapped. She wasn't murdered. She disappeared and I was split into many different versions of myself, each creating their own separate reality."

The doctor contemplates him from across the room, his expression one of sympathetic concern. The window is open. Outside, he can hear the coo of a wood pigeon; the sound of someone's radio. He hates these silences between them. It feels like he has stopped moving.

"Yes," the doctor finally says. "Now, what I'm going to do is prescribe..."

He stops listening then, and holds out his hand for the piece of paper.

THE ROBOT IS slowly scraping away the last few millimetres of earth. The floor has been revealed almost in its entirety, six inset disks of dark stone have been revealed and the machine is working on a seventh. It takes all of Christopher's self-restraint not to get down into the trench with the robot, but such delicate work as is required is all but impossible while encased in a survival suit. There are only a few hours of daylight left. Soon they will have to return to the habitat or risk freezing to death.

A sudden screech of static on the communications network has Christopher gripping his helmet, as though that will somehow block out the sound. He closes his eyes as the fillings in his teeth vibrate; sharp jags of pain lancing through his skull. It passes quickly and when he opens his eyes there is someone down in the trench. The sight of a man dressed in jeans and a T-shirt is so incongruous that Christopher thinks that he must be hallucinating. But when the atmosphere goes to work on the man, he knows that this is real.

The man only has a moment to mouth one word before the blood froths from between his lips and his eyes burst – Christopher isn't sure, but he thinks that it is a name.

* * *

"JOSIE, KEEP YOUR wellies on please we're about to go out. Carol...
Carol... *Carol!* You forgot your keys!"

But she had already gone.

"Mummy, come back!"

"Don't worry, Josie. We'll probably be back home before Mummy
anyway. Now we're going to have a nice time in town together, aren't
we? We'll go and feed the ducks and then, after lunch, we'll go to the
museum. Would you like that?"

Josie clapped her hands and nodded.

The doorbell rang and he opened the door to find a man standing
there, holding a knife. The man must have been wearing some sort
of clever mask, because the face looking back at him was his own.

"But—"

He got no further. With a swift, practiced blow the man drove
the knife up, under his ribs and into his heart.

Josie stood frozen in the hallway, her eyes wide with horror. The
man who had just killed her Daddy, who looked exactly like her
Daddy, held out his hand.

"Josie, please. I don't want to have to do this yet again. Please,
Josie, please don't run."

But she always did.

CAROL WATCHES HIM, trying not to cry.

Ever since their trip to museum, ever since Josie had been taken,
Richard has gone somewhere and nothing she says will bring him back.

He's taken all the books and shelving off the study walls. The wallpaper has been torn down in long ragged strips, and he's written something on the exposed plaster – strange symbols that make no sense. On the floor he's drawn seven dark circles onto the varnished wood, and it is in one of these that he now turns, spinning round and round, humming a tuneless dirge.

"Richard, please. Please come away from there. This isn't doing you any good."

She knows full well that he hasn't taken his medication, that he stopped going to therapy weeks ago. Carol has tried everything she can to break through to him, but she only has so much mental energy to spare and, anyway, this grief isn't Richard's alone.

Only when she crosses the threshold does Richard stop.

He rushes over to her and grabs her by the arms, screaming into her face, "What are you doing? Don't you want her to come back?"

"Of course I do, Richard. But it's not going to happen like this."

"God, Carol! I don't think you realise what could have happened. You could have disappeared too."

"Just… come to bed. We can talk more in the morning."

"You have to let me do this."

"Please, Richard."

But he doesn't say anything. As Carol closes the door she can hear the thud of his feet on the floorboards as he begins to turn again.

EVERYBODY TURNS.

He has long since lost count of the number of people before him, but it isn't his job to pay attention to the numbers. As long as everybody keeps turning then there is a chance. Those who flag are beaten until they pick up their pace and find the rhythm again; should they flag a second time they are immediately replaced. Most turn as though their lives depend on it, and they do. Some are so determined to show him that they care, that they want to please him, they spin themselves apart.

At first he had chosen just adults to turn before him, but when they failed to produce the result he so yearned for, he began to introduce children. What they lacked in stamina they made up for with enthusiasm, though they never turned for long.

From where he stood, he poured into them all of his desire, all of his will to find her. There were times that he thought that he could feel the universe shift, and then there would be a faint shimmering in the centre of the room – a soft light that was gradually clothed in flesh. The things that came through, however, were never her; the things that came through were never human, and they didn't live for long.

He would stand here through every revolution and it didn't matter what it took, it didn't matter how many perished – he would have her back; he would find her.

NO MUSEUM GUARD will give the temple more than a glimpse; a quick shine of the torch – *yup still there, not like it's going anywhere –*

and on with their rounds. Any more than a cursory glance and the voices begin – a confused susurrus, a million whispers in as many tongues. But it's that one voice that drives even the hardiest guard hurrying away. It's the voice of the little girl. There's such despair, such yearning in it that even to listen for more than a moment tears at one's heart.

For a time, the alien temple had drawn psychic investigators, hoping for a spooky thrill. But such people are only interested in historical phantoms, whose distance in time makes them seem tame, even comforting. None of them were prepared for the anguish that has taken up residence here. They were not prepared for the despair that came with being unable to say, *Yes, here I am. Don't worry. Everything will be fine. I'll find you.*

HIS JOY AT finding her safe and well had, for a while, occluded her true nature.

"Doesn't she seem different to you?" he had asked Carol.

"She's bound to be after what she went through."

"No, that's not what I mean. I mean that Josie doesn't seem, well… like Josie."

Carol had looked at him, her face blank, but the intent in her glare was hard to ignore.

"Okay…" he said finally. "Okay. I'm sure she's fine. Really."

But each day that passed, Josie seemed like and less like his daughter.

This morning, he had made up his mind. When he told Carol, she had seemed pleased – relieved, even.

"I think that's a great idea."

"And you're happy to have the day to yourself?"

"Of course. And I think the time together will do you both a world of good. It will help you get over... well, whatever this is."

He'd managed to smile and kiss his wife on the cheek.

When he mentioned where they were going, Josie had put on a good show of being excited, but he could see through her performance.

Why couldn't Carol?

Two hours into their journey, Josie fell asleep. She didn't stir as he pulled over onto the verge, didn't even wake as he lifted her out of the car. The weight of her in his arms, the smell of her, the warmth of her cheek on his shoulder – for just a moment they convinced him that he must be wrong. He saw through the deception, however. The fact that this imposter had got everything so exactly right revealed her for what she was.

He walked several metres from the car and laid her down in the long grass. She stirred in her sleep but did not wake. He didn't give his doubt any time to set in. Instead, he walked quickly back to the car and drove away.

When he got home and heard the happy sounds coming from the kitchen, his heart sank. He thought it had been too easy.

"Daddy! We're making cookies!" Josie called.

"Are you, darling?" Richard called back. "That's great. Just give me a moment, I think I left something in the car."

He drove away with little regard for the speed limit. He just wanted to put as much distance between himself and Josie as he could.

Almost an hour away from home a movement made him glace in the rearview mirror: Josie was sitting in the back.

"Daddy?"

He closed his eyes and opened them again but she was still there.

"Daddy?"

His foot pressed down on the accelerator. The road whipped beneath his wheels, writhing like an enraged serpent. Maybe he'd be going too fast to make the next turn. He didn't care.

"Daddy, where are we going?"

"THERE IS A way."

"One that will work?"

"This time, yes."

"I'm sensing a 'but'."

"Well, here's the rub. Each of the realities that were created when you fractured are just that – *realities*. In each, there is not just yourself – and sometimes an iteration of Josie – but billions of other living, sentient beings, oblivious to the circumstances that created them. Do you understand?"

"Not entirely, no."

"What I'm saying is that if we bring your multiple selves back together, we end those realities and everything in them."

"But it's not like I'll have killed them, not like they'll be dead in the true sense of the term. They just won't have existed."

"Not existing sounds very much like death to me, Richard. Listen, I'm just trying to make you aware of the possibilities."

"Will I get Josie back? Not some... iteration but my actual daughter?"

"We think so."

"Then do it."

"But you'll have considered the—"

"I said do it!"

IT WOULD HAVE been all too easy to turn and turn; all too easy to just let myself spiral away into the darkness, to lose myself completely. A part of me wanted that, it really did. But this time, as I felt myself begin to fracture again, I held on tight, keeping myself intact, whole.

The room continued to turn when I stopped and, for a terrifying moment, I thought that it hadn't worked. But then I saw Josie, and the room was still.

"I'm here," I said, as my eyes filled with tears and I fell to my knees before her.

THE LAST OF the children had run from the strange old temple in the museum, giggling, and there was just her and Daddy now. Josie had enjoyed the spinning game at first, but then Daddy had begun to turn faster and faster, making a strange sound, and she had stopped, frightened.

Daddy must have known she was afraid, because he stopped too. But then he began to scare her all over again, because he fell on his knees, crying, and gathered her into his arms in a fierce embrace. Had she done something wrong? Had she been naughty?

Daddy was being strange, but more than that, Daddy *felt* different.

When he wiped away his tears and smiled, Josie saw it in his eyes – like he was old but not old; like he had gone away and the part of him that mattered most hadn't come back.

"Oh, Josie. Don't be sad," he said. "Everything is going to be alright now."

He lead her from the temple and even his hand felt different: colder, less there. She knew then that this man was a stranger who only looked like her Daddy. In his eyes she could see that he had done some very bad things.

"Let's get some lunch." The stranger said. "What would you like to eat, Josie?"

Maybe she had left her real Daddy back in the temple. She vaguely recalled seeing lots of men who looked just like him as they were playing their spinning game.

Josie let go of the stranger's hand and ran back inside. There was no one in the temple now but she knew what she had to do.

Ignoring the stranger's cries she stood on the dark circle of stone at the centre of the room and began to turn. For a time, all she could hear was her own breathing and the soft shuffling of her feet, but then the stone began to sing. The dance came back to her in a rush and she gave herself to its discordant rhythms.

When the temple began to spiral apart around her – and Josie with it – she promised herself that she would find her Daddy, no matter what it took.

THE HORROR WRITER

EMERGING ONTO THE pavement from Leicester Square Tube, Simon swore softly as he once again found himself on the wrong side of the road. Taking slow, steady, calming breaths, he waited for a break in the traffic before crossing. If he were to be honest, Simon would have to admit that Charing Cross Road was the only part of London he knew relatively well. The rest of the city was something of a mystery, accessible only to those adept at deciphering the arcane tangle of multi-coloured lines that made up the Tube map. He knew that it was considered a classic of design; a complex system rendered in supposedly simple terms. It was just that every time he looked at it, a strange, buzzing itch would start to build in the centre of his skull, and the lines would blur. Getting around London was not something Simon was very good at, and he very much hated being lost; hated the panic that arose as he felt control slipping away.

Charing Cross Road was a sanctuary, with its easy access to theatres, cinemas and, most importantly, bookshops. Sadly there weren't as many of the latter as there had once been. Of late they had been closing down with depressing regularity. The last time Simon had ventured into the city, he'd found that one of his favourite literary haunts had been turned into a Subway. He was somewhat surprised, therefore, to find a second-hand bookshop where he was almost certain there hadn't been one before. At first glance, the store seemed rather minimal, so narrow it was almost as though the buildings that flanked it had been pushed aside to accommodate it, rather like a paperback being squeezed in between two hardbacks on a tightly packed shelf. Behind a window fogged with condensation, a display held a few tatty Dan Browns, a mildewed stack of Catherine Cooksons, and a couple of Stephen Kings that looked as though they had been chewed upon. What Simon could see of the shelves to either side of the cluttered counter seemed no more promising. However, he had a rule about bookshops, and that was never to walk past one with which he was unfamiliar.

He opened the door onto an almost tropical heat and a fug of tobacco smoke. Behind a desk piled high not just with stacks of books, but also half-empty take-away cartons and endless cigarette butts – and flanked on both sides by two furiously buzzing two-bar heaters – sat an unkempt man, rolling a cigarette and glaring down at a paperback with a broken spine.

"What is it, squire?" said the man, without looking up.

"Yes, I wonder if you have a particular volume of short stories. It's very rare and the title—"

"If we do, it will be through the back."

The man gestured to a darkened doorway at the rear of the shop.

"The back?"

"Here," the man rose to his feet, and placed his cigarette behind his ear. "Let me get the lights for you."

He waddled over to the doorway, reached within and flicked a switch.

A series of lights in metal shades blinked and stuttered into life, illuminating the corridor beyond. Lining the passage from floor to ceiling, as far as Simon could see, were row after row of bookshelves.

"This do you, squire?"

"Oh yes," Simon said. "This will do nicely."

"Just don't go getting lost."

Simon chuckled at that, but when he looked up, he saw that the man wasn't smiling.

SIMON'S DELIGHT AT finding such a wealth of literature was dampened when he realised that there had been no attempt to place the titles in any kind of order. Several hardback collections of Elizabeth Barret Browning's poetry sat next to a manual for a Ford Focus. A long line of Gabriel García Márquez novels was broken by four well-thumbed copies of *The Joy of Sex*. However, Simon found that a great deal of pleasure could be derived from the thrill of the hunt – the search for hidden treasures – and so he continued on, undaunted, into the stacks.

As he got to his knees to pry out a promising looking paperback from a low shelf, he noticed that a book had been inserted into the stack the wrong way round, and pulled it out with a view to correcting the oversight. The copy of *Dracula* began to crumble in his hand almost immediately, spilling gritty dust into his palm. Before it fell to bits, a single page drifted out intact and fell at Simon's feet. He was about to leave it where it was, shaking his head that a book could be so poorly looked after, when he noticed that something had been written onto the margin of the text.

Find me. Help me.

Simon had found all sorts of things within the pages of second-hand books – train tickets, faded family photographs, a single condom still sealed within its packet – but this was the first time he'd ever found a cry for help. He looked up at what sounded like the distant howling of wolves coming from somewhere near the front of the shop, only to find the doorway he'd come through shrouded in darkness. Had the owner shut up for the day and forgotten all about him?

"I say, excuse me!" Simon said, as he starting heading back between the shelves. His footsteps were halted by an icy blast of wind and the renewed howling of wolves. He was certain, then, that something was moving within the darkness beyond the doorway. Simon turned and ran, his hurried flight given impetus by the scrabble of claws on floorboards behind him. A sharp left-hand turn brought him into an almost identical corridor and Simon was halfway down it before he realised that he could no longer hear the sounds of pursuit.

Surely someone was playing a trick on him? This was clearly some elaborate practical joke. Perhaps a camera has been cleverly secreted within the binding of one of the books.

"Very good," Simon said loudly. "Very convincing, and certainly a little frightening. You got me."

When he was answered only by silence, Simon made his way back down the corridor and turned the corner, to find an avalanche of books completely blocking the passage. He was certain that he hadn't heard the books fall. Maybe whatever had been chasing him had upset them. The mound of books reached almost to the ceiling. It was clear that dismantling the barrier would take some time, and so Simon decided to head deeper into the shop, hoping to locate an alternative exit.

A short while later he breathed a sigh of relief when he came to a door, stencilled across which were the words *Fire Exit*. He pushed the metal bar, but instead of being greeted by a gust of damp air and the sounds of traffic, he was faced with yet another book-lined passage.

For much of Simon's life books had been a source of comfort and inspiration. A house wasn't properly furnished unless it contained at least a few bookshelves, and Simon's house had perhaps more than most, along with precariously stacked piles of paperbacks yet to be read or filed away. He loved to be surrounded by books, yet now he found the smell of old paper almost cloying; the aroma faintly reminiscent of an ossuary he had once visited while holidaying in Florence.

The corridor in front of him was a little lower than the one that preceded it and as Simon stepped down, the floorboards creaked ominously, as though there was a vast, hollow space beneath. The shelves that marched away into the distance were uneven; some bowed out into the passage, while others shrank back, hiding their titles in shadow. Simon reasoned that if he were trapped here for the time being – he tried not to think of it as being lost, anything but that – he may as well take an interest in the books. Perhaps he'd come out of this with a rare treasure to show to his fellow enthusiasts.

There were no words on the spine of the hardback he took down from a shelf and the cover was blank, giving no indication as to its contents. Inside, there was no title or copyright page. Instead, the text began right away and Simon began to read:

What a strange book. What was this anyway? He considered that it may be fiction, though of some experimental sort. Ordinarily, he would have little patience with such a thing, but Simon found himself curiously drawn into the text. As he read, he was distantly aware of the darkness rising around him, of the absolute silence that had closed upon him, like two soft, warm hands clamped firmly over his ears. No matter, *he thought, because the words had him now and it* was only by focussing on the smell of books and the vaguest thread of panic that had begun to worm its way up his chest, that Simon tore himself free and threw the tome to the floor. It landed on its spine, its blank pages brazenly open.

"What... what is this?" Simon said, backing away.

The pages started to turn, slowly at first, but they soon sped up, moving faster and faster with a hiss that sounded like dry, malicious laughter.

Simon turned to find the fire door firmly shut. With no way of opening it from this side, he had no option but to flee. He didn't care where his footsteps took him, as long as it was away from that damnable book.

He jerked to a sudden halt as he came to the top of a precipitous flight of steps. Looking down, he saw that the stairs were made not of wood, but tottering stacks of books. Each step was uneven, some deeper than others, making his stomach churn at the prospect of descent. But he could still feel those terrible blank pages at his back; still feel the influence of that wicked book as it sought to draw him in, and so he started down. The stacks shifted alarmingly beneath him and Simon grabbed the shelves to either side for support, only for his flailing left hand to punch deep into the guts of a rotten book. Steadying himself, he grimaced as he wiped his hand on his sleeve, shuddering as something with more legs than he was comfortable with skittered across his arm. He looked at the book he had destroyed and could just make out the words on the broken cover – *Metamorphosis, Kafka*.

From somewhere far above him came a chittering sound and a noise like a vast spider slowly picking its way across the ceiling.

Simon hurriedly resumed his descent, praying that whatever had emerged from the book wouldn't find him. The depth of the book steps became such that he had to get to his knees before lowering himself down each one. As Simon was negotiating a particularly deep stack, he felt the tower of over-sized hardbacks shift beneath him. The step settled with an exhalation of dust and a mouldering stench of rot before thousands upon thousands of pages suddenly crumbled and he found himself falling. Simon's cry was quickly absorbed by the tide of paper that carried him down into the depths.

SIMON'S WATCH HAD become detached in the fall, so he had no idea of the time. There were no windows down here; the only light was provided by the ubiquitous bulbs in their metal shades.

He had fought to the surface of the book pile, to find himself in the middle of a corridor, broken floorboards forming the edge of the pool he floundered in. Once he had climbed out, he sat with his back to a shelf, wondering why he should even bother continuing deeper into the maze. The most compelling reason, he soon realised, was to escape whatever was swiftly heading his way. On a breath of foetid wind he could hear the sounds of claws on wood and the skittering of huge insects.

As he ran – his breath burning in his lungs, his limbs heavy – Simon considered that whoever had trapped him here was using books against him, or rather the things to be found within their pages. He had never been a fan of scary stories, preferring instead works of a whimsical or pastoral nature. Perhaps, then, if he found some books with more pleasing content, his progression through this maze of literature would be less fraught. No sooner had Simon thought this then he came to a brightly decorated area, equipped with small plastic chairs surrounding low plastic tables, scattered with crayons and paper. Low bookshelves held a selection of brightly coloured titles and Simon was relieved to see a somewhat more friendly selection than he had so far encountered. He picked an annual from a shelf and smiled.

"Good old, Rupert. Perhaps you'll see me through the maze."

Only when he opened the book did he realise his mistake, and his blood ran cold as something snuffled and wheezed its way towards him.

SIMON HAD BEEN five, perhaps six, and it had rained all summer. His misery at not being able to go outside was intensified by being stuck in-doors with his Aunt Erin. Erin clearly didn't understand little boys and her palpable discomfort around him had only added to his misery. One afternoon, as the rain had thundered against the windows and Simon had listlessly flicked through a comic he'd already read five times, Erin leapt to her feet with an exclamation of, "Of course! Toys!" His elderly aunt had hurried up the stairs to return several minutes later with a water-stained cardboard box.

"I must have been given him when I was about your age," she'd said, lifting the flaps of the box. "I loved Rupert the Bear when I was a child."

The manky stuffed toy that Erin handed Simon had reeked of damp. Its checked trousers had long since fallen prey to moths and when he took the toy in his hands one of its button eyes fell out, a torrent of sawdust spilling from the ragged hole.

NOW SIMON'S SCREAMS as the wheezing, threadbare creature stumbled towards him were much the same as they had been on that rainy day all those years ago. Sawdust trickled from Rupert's empty eyes as it pawed weakly at his legs, the red stitches of its makeshift smile snapping open as it attempted to talk. And other things had followed the bear, childhood terrors that Simon had forgotten or suppressed; things that had been created to bring simple joy but which had, for whatever reason, filled him with fear.

Simon overturned bookcases as he backed away, throwing crayons and toys as though that would deter the horrors that pursued him. Exhorting him to play, asking him for cuddles as they held out their threadbare, moth-eaten arms.

In the end it wasn't difficult to outpace the childhood nightmares, most of them were falling to bits or struggling to run on legs that were little more than stumps. Simon only stopped running when a painful nausea gripped his stomach, reminding him that he wasn't as fit as he used to be. He leaned against a shelf as he caught his breath, making sure not to catch sight any of the words on the spines of the books that towered over him. How had he gotten himself into this terrible mess? He'd had an awful week at work and he'd thought that a Saturday spent shopping for books would have cheered him up. Even so, when he'd woken this morning he'd found it difficult to get out of bed. It had taken most of his energy to shove a meagre breakfast into his mouth and shamble down to the station. On the train into the city, Simon had found it hard to concentrate on the book he'd taken with him, nodding off over the same paragraph time and again. In fact, later, on the Tube, he'd only awoken just in time for his stop. And there had been someone—

Simon frowned, as a memory surfaced.

There had been that strange man beside him on the Tube. Simon had heard him whispering to himself as he sat down, and the man had leaned against him, slumping in his seat as though he were drunk. Simon had attempted to ignore the man, burying himself in his book, only to begin drowsing over the same paragraph. There had been a brief moment of darkness as the carriage's lights flickered; a sudden lurch as the train took a sharp corner. At first Simon thought he had just dreamed it, but now he remembered the man next to him carefully taking the book out of his hands and replacing it with another.

Was it possible, then, that he had somehow become trapped within the pages of this new book? Had the man on the train ensnared him with words? If this were the case – and after everything he had faced within the maze, it was no stranger an idea than any other – then Simon had to break out of the book.

Could he write a book of his own, perhaps? Simon quickly dismissed this idea when he realised that he didn't have anything to write with. Also, the sounds coming from further down the corridor suggested that he didn't have time for such a response. What, though, could pull him out of the book? Simon looked frantically about himself, and he was just beginning to succumb to panic when a misspelled word on the spine of a nearby novel gave him an answer.

Of course: typos.

Nothing ruined a story more than badly edited text. Simon was a stickler for correct grammar – his brother had once drunkenly referred to him as a Grammar Nazi, at a particularly unpleasant family gathering – and he detested seeing the English language misused. However, more often than not, a novel would contain at least one typo. But which one should he pick from the many texts that surrounded him?

As he was pulling books from the shelves, Simon saw the shadow of an elongated and many-jointed leg creep up the wall further down the corridor. He could smell an animal stench that reminded him of visits to the zoo, and hear someone weeping. He didn't have long, but every book he opened appeared to be perfectly in order. Simon refined his search, and chose the cheapest and most lurid looking paperback he could see. And there, fifteen pages in, he found a particularly egregious passage. Simon focused on the broken words and

when, would this train get tere? He was already to late for his
meeting. There had been reports of rats' in the tunnels on the news. But
this didn't panic him. Simon closed his eyes for a moment

and then snapped them open as the Tube screeched around a
tight corner. Beyond the windows a cascade of sparks lit up the
tunnel. Simon looked down at the open book in his lap, and the
blank pages almost drew him back in. He fought their pull and
closed the book with a snap. The noise seemed unnaturally loud, but
it wasn't loud enough to wake any of his fellow passengers.

Hunched over open books, swaying with the movement of the
train, sat six men and seven women, their closed eyes oblivious to the
text moving across the pages before them. None of them awoke to
his pleas or rough handling, and when he tried to wrench the books
from their grasps, he found them to be as immovable as statues.

With a squeal of brakes, the train came to a sudden stop as it
emerged into a station. The doors hissed open and Simon flinched as
a squall of pages blew into the carriage. Making sure not to catch a
glimpse of anything written upon the leaves swirling around his
ankles, he stepped onto the platform. He tried to ascertain where he
was but the words on the battered blue and red sign would not stay
still long enough for him to read them. There was only one exit from
the platform and Simon took it as the train hissed out of the station,
taking its cargo of insensate readers with it.

Rather than finding an escalator leading to the surface, as he had desperately hoped, Simon came to a stairway leading down. He supposed that he should have been thankful that the flight wasn't composed of mouldering books, but even so, he felt the ice-cold burn of fear as he descended. The bottom of the steps led into a short passage, which led to a vast circular chamber lined with books to an impossible height. As dismayed as Simon was to be surrounded once more by books, it was not the millions of pages that dried his mouth in an instant and set his heart racing – and he could hear the whispering of the text within each tome, calling to him – it was instead the column of formless darkness that sat at the heart of the library.

Before this seething mass of nothingness stood a desk upon which lay a book, its blank pages open. Simon stepped forward and a chair slid from the side of the room, its legs scraping noisily over the rough stone floor, before coming to a halt in front of the desk. The invitation was clear enough and though he really didn't want to, he didn't see that he had any choice other than to sit.

There was nothing written on the pages of the book, but the anticipation the volume projected was palpable.

"Who are you?" Simon said.

Words began to form on the paper, wet ink slowly drying as the text unfurled.

One who needs to be read.

"I don't understand."

In being read, I become.

"All those things in the bookshop, was that you?"

No, Simon. All those things were you. I merely make real what is within you.

"But why me? What have I ever done?"

Simon was all too aware that the note of hysteria that had entered his voice made him sound like a whining child, but he was painfully aware that he was talking to a book. Perhaps he would wake to find himself in a secure unit, babbling to the padded walls. The words before him were still and Simon was about to get up from the desk when the text began to write itself once more.

Because you used your imagination. You used words against me. Nobody has done that before. You are more than just a mere reader.

"What do you want from me?"

I want you to write a book, Simon.

"And if I refuse?"

Then you will be as those you saw on the train, captured by the story, possessed by the text.

"But why would you want a book? You're surrounded by books!"

The story that we'll tell together will be unlike any other. And each one who reads the tale will bring me closer to being. And then, Simon, we can control every story. Together, Simon, we can tell the world what it truly should be.

Simon thought about the dreadful free-fall his life was in – slipping from one mediocre job to the next, each month barely having enough to pay the rent. He thought about the despair he felt as he watched the news each night, the anger that things never turned out the way they should. His parents had told him that he could be anything he wanted to be, but the world seemed to have a very different idea. Simon had always wished that he could tell the world to just stop. Stop and do things *properly*. He didn't want to be trapped by his petty and meaningless fears. He didn't want to be like those cattle on the train that had brought him here, swaying uncomprehendingly over the words that had caught them.

"Okay," Simon said. "Okay, I will be your writer."

AND IN THE end it was all so very easy. There was no staring blankly at the page and waiting for inspiration to strike. Simon sat at his laptop, in his tiny bedsit, and the words just poured out of him. And though this was essentially a collaboration – although he was constantly aware of the whisper of the words spoken to him as he dreamed onto the page – Simon felt that he owned at least some of this tale. When he sent the manuscript out, he had to admit that there was a part of him that wished that that was that, that he was done with the story now and it would perhaps leave him alone. A month later when the first offer came, he was so shocked by the proposed advance that he almost accepted it right away. But no, his collaborator said, more will come.

And they did. And soon Simon was a very wealthy man.

In what seemed to be no time at all, he was sat behind a desk at Foyles on Charing Cross Road before a pile of paperbacks, pen in hand. The queue snaked out of the bookshop and stretched as far down as the National Gallery. A pretty young woman smiled shyly at him as she handed over her book to be signed. As a crimson pall rose from her neck and across her cheeks, she mumbled something.

"I'm sorry," Simon said. "I didn't quite catch that."

"I said… where do you get your ideas?"

And Simon grinned, and glanced towards the shadow that stood just behind his right shoulder.

He couldn't wait for the reviews.

BABY 17

THROUGH THE WINDOW, in the stark white room, Saul could see the child stirring. He turned to the screen on his right, checking the multi-coloured lines and numbers that flowed there – all of them agreed that the infant was in the best of health. His thin cry must be because he was hungry.

Saul pressed a button on the intercom.

"Nurse Simmons? Baby 17."

A moment later a young woman wearing a white uniform entered, carrying a bottle of milk. She didn't acknowledge Saul as she proceeded to the door on the far side, there to tap four digits into a number pad. He watched as she entered the room beyond, picked up Baby 17 and gave him his bottle. She didn't coo over him or rock him as he fed; instead she looked intently at her watch. When the last of the milk had been drained, she looked up and said, "Three minutes and twenty-seven seconds."

Saul nodded before entering this data onto the system.

"Thank you, Nurse Simmons," he said as she left.

Baby 17 lay in his cot, burbling to himself and opening and closing his tiny hands. Saul zoomed in with the camera, boosted the sound and observed the activity for a moment before satisfying himself that these were the normal actions of an infant. Even so, he made a note of the activity and recorded its duration. Just as Baby 17's gurgles became cries of frustration once more, the monitor in front of Saul chimed to let him know that he was free to take his lunch break. Sure enough, the door behind him opened and Peter entered, taking off the peaked cap that was part of his uniform.

"Go, be free," he said, his right hand idly toying with the rosary beads he always carried.

Saul nodded and headed for the canteen.

"AND THEN I'M gripped by something, and I can't move. And, you know, for a moment, I'm utterly terrified. But then this feeling comes over me, these great crashing waves of... of *love*. That's the only way I can think to describe it. And I know that this love is unconditional and that this love is bigger than anything. *Anything*. Right?"

"What are you guys talking about?" Saul said, placing his tray on the table and taking a seat. The men that surrounded him all wore the same uniform – black trousers, pale blue shirt, black tie, an identity badge just above the breast pocket.

"Richard was telling us about his encounter with God. You know, the one that cured his malignant tumour?"

Saul knew the story well. They all had them, every guard who worked on the project, these encounters with the divine. He lifted his coffee cup and drank, fixing his gaze on the far wall.

"I heard that Yannis saw an angel," Richard said. "An actual honest to God angel."

"Oh really?" Saul said, relieved that he hadn't been asked about his own encounter.

"Yeah, wings of flame, voice of thunder..."

Saul drifted away from the conversation, his thoughts turning to the child he had been tasked to observe. He knew that he really shouldn't let Baby 17 get to him; it wasn't for him to get involved. But he couldn't help it. Each time the baby cried, each time it squealed in hunger or pain, he felt that tug, deep in his chest. He'd thought he'd be okay. He'd thought he'd be able to maintain the level of detachment required. Saul looked around at his colleagues, wondering whether they too had begun to feel this sense of attachment to their charges. But of course they hadn't. They were professionals. Saul realised that he was gripping his coffee cup so hard that his hand was shaking. He made himself take a deep breath. He couldn't eat but, even so, he sat dutifully through the rest of his lunch hour, trying to maintain some semblance of workplace camaraderie. At 2pm three chimes sounded followed by the daily prayer, to which they all listened dutifully before saying, "Amen."

When Saul returned to his workstation, Baby 17 was asleep, and he turned the volume up until the sound of the infant's breathing filled his booth. He closed his eyes and listened. Somewhere between one breath and the next, a small cool hand lightly brushed against his and he started awake. He looked at the clock – it had just been a couple of minutes but if his employers had seen…

Saul turned the coffee maker on, rubbed his cheeks and yawned. He was a professional. He could do this. He owed it to Marian.

When 5pm came, Saul only gave Baby 17 the briefest of glances as he left the booth and the relief guard took over.

Outside the facility, he tried not to kick over any of the thousands of votive candles that littered the pavement. There were the usual hundred or so hardcore pilgrims out tonight and Saul acknowledged the few he recognised with a smile or a wave. A stall had been set up, selling T-shirts and posters, each showing a photo montage of all twenty-seven miraculous infants and the date and hour of their births. Beneath this were the words – *Praying for a Revelation*.

Saul ducked past the man waving a T-shirt at him – "Forty-three pounds! Special price, yeah?" – and took the most indirect route home he could; he wasn't ready to return to Marian. When it started to rain, however, he hailed a taxi.

WHEN THE LIFT doors opened and he saw the state of the floor outside their apartment, Saul cursed under his breath. Candles in red plastic holders; photos of the facility infants; badly printed images of Christ and pound shop plastic Virgin Marys, one of which broke under his heel as he stepped into the hall. For an absurd moment he felt guilty and his right hand dithered in front of his chest, as though unsure whether to make the sign of the cross or not. Instead, Saul settled for a quick prayer before he turned the key in the door.

He could already hear the sound of the television as he stepped into their apartment. Marian was in the lounge as usual, glued to the news. Saul couldn't stand it, this constant litany of despair, and didn't understand why his wife subjected herself to this barrage of daily misery. This thing that had happened, it had happened to them both, but they had learned to deal with it in their own separate ways; each unable to help the other come to terms with what they had been through.

"Anything?" Marian said, turning briefly from the screen.

"Just the usual."

He saw one of the posters they had been selling outside of the facility tacked to the wall beside the television.

"Been out?"

"What? Oh… no. No, that was a gift from Mrs Prendergast across the way. She says that it must be very exciting to be married to someone who works at the facility."

"I've got some things I need to do. Will you be alright for half an hour?"

"I imagine so."

In the bedroom Saul booted up the laptop. He slotted the memory stick into the side of the machine, downloading the data before wiping the storage device. He realised that what he was doing was strictly forbidden, but he had to know, and so he opened the first photo. The resemblance was uncanny: the dark, wispy hair, the way his brow furrowed in that comic little frown, even the way his hands were clenched into tight fists as he slept – Baby 17 was the spitting image of George. To confirm to himself that this was no coincidence, Saul opened a picture of their son as he had been at four days old, when both he and Marian had been exhausted from living somewhere between hope and despair. There was no doubt about it. Baby 17 could have been George's twin.

Saul's heart raced. That he had been assigned to *this* child, out of all the possible infants that could have been given into his care, and that this child should so clearly resemble their dead son. Well... it was nothing short of a miracle.

BEFORE MARIAN AND George, before the birth of the twenty-seven infants upon whom much of the world's hopes rested...

Saul hadn't been long out of the army and already he missed it like crazy. In the desert everything had been black and white. He felt lost now that there was no one to tell him what to do; home seemed just as foreign as any theatre of war. Unlike many of his comrades, he didn't have a wife or a kid to come back to, and Saul didn't have the first idea how to slot back into civilian life. There had been the opportunity to take officer training, but the thought of commanding men in the field and being relied on to make the right decision at the crucial time filled him with fear. And so, he simply drifted. He spent much of his time in bars. There were a few old faces he recognised amongst the drinkers, though he didn't think that any of them recognised him. In the afternoon he'd read the job ads over the first couple of pints, but there were no jobs, or at least none that he could do. After a while it became something of a ritual: two pints of lager, pretend to scan the paper, perhaps a quick trip to the bookies, then back to the pub to get properly settled in.

"You look like a man who could use a job."

He'd seen the thin-faced man every day for the last month or so. He always seemed to be nursing the one pint; Saul had never seen him buy his own. This afternoon he was sitting at what Saul had come to think of as *his* table, as though he had been waiting for him to arrive.

"Who doesn't?" Saul said.

His name was Kev. He was the sort of petty criminal Saul had seen the army beat into shape time and again; just a kid really.

Saul shook his head. He wasn't a soldier. He had to stop thinking like one.

"Cash in hand. Mostly small jobs to start with, but do well and there may be more in it."

Kev held out his hand; the first and index fingers had been stained brown by nicotine. Without really thinking about it, Saul took Kev's hand in his.

Kev smiled and returned to the bar to nurse his pint. "I'll be in touch, okay?"

Saul doubted it, but two days later, not long after lunch, his phone rang. The screen said 'Number Withheld' and when he answered it was Kev.

The first job was simple enough. All Saul had to do was offload some tobacco in the local pubs. The old alkies he sold to were more than happy to part with eight quid for an ounce of their favourite smoke, and Saul got to spend most of the day drinking, which worked for him. Kev was clearly impressed and soon Saul was selling more tobacco into more pubs. From cigarettes he moved onto liquor and that was when Saul first got a sense of the true scale of operations. For five weeks he worked at a rundown warehouse, bottling fake spirits. The labels looked just like the real thing, but when Saul tried to take a swig of the product, a heavy hand fell on his shoulder.

"I'm sorry," he said, ashamed to have been caught.

"No mate, it's not a problem. I just wouldn't do that if I were you. There's things in that 'vodka' I wouldn't want in my system."

A few days later the illegal distillery was shut down. Saul avoided arrest purely by accident, having overslept when he should have been working. He thought that was the end of it, but Kev called him later that day.

"Close one, my friend. But we're still in business. You good to roll? We've got a few more jobs we need doing, and I've got someone I want you to meet."

The man they met that night at the pub was clearly the head of operations. He exuded a certain sense of authority and menace, reminding Saul of a warlord he had once met while on manoeuvres. The man paid Saul for his time at the distillery and told him what he wanted him to do next. And despite the nature of the task, Saul agreed, because if there was one thing he was good at it was taking orders.

He found himself working harder than he ever had in his life; he didn't even get weekends off. But the money was good, and for the first time since leaving the army the world was beginning to resolve into that old black and white. He settled comfortably into his criminal career, and it was perhaps because of the complacency that comfort can bring that Saul didn't give a second glance to the man in the hooded tracksuit who stumbled into him outside the pub one night. What did make him stop in his tracks, however, was the pain that bloomed in his side following the collision. Saul touched his waist and his fingers came away wet. He looked around but the hooded man was nowhere to be seen.

Saul fumbled his phone out of his pocket but stopped short of calling for an ambulance. A visit to the hospital would mean questions. No, there was a man Kev had introduced him to. He'd see him right. After all, the wound wasn't that bad.

Saul headed down the alley. The streetlight at the far end made a strange fizzing sound as it burned its sodium glow into the night. There was the faint smell of cigarette smoke as he passed a shadowed alcove, and a line of fire drew itself across his left hip. Though it hurt like hell, Saul ran. Fear propelled him from the mouth of the alleyway like a bullet from a gun. His attackers raced after him – faces hidden by hoods; knives flashing.

The darkness encroaching on Saul's vision had little to do with the night, and he realised that if he didn't find sanctuary soon, he may as well stop running. He looked around but didn't recognise any of the streets. Shops hid behind steel shutters; houses stood in darkness with curtains drawn. The only source of illumination was a neon cross tethered to the wall of a house above an open door. Holding his hands firmly against his sides, Saul stumbled across the road and into the church.

Church was perhaps too grand a word for a room that had clearly once served as a lounge. A trestle table covered in a blue cloth in front of a boarded-up fireplace stood as an altar. Two rows of chairs numbered the congregation at not much more than twenty. Above a stereo that was playing a vaguely churchy sounding muzak, a poster depicted Christ surrounded by laughing children. The illustration was crudely executed but for the eyes of the Messiah; the eyes exuded a kindness and understanding that Saul had never seen before on a human face.

"Wherever you are in life, Saul," an army chaplain had once said to him, "no matter how low you have sunk, He will never turn you away."

A good long time had passed since Saul had last prayed. If he had been raised as anything it was as a Methodist, though neither of his parents had been particularly observant. Even so, Saul had never lost that belief in… something. And it was to this something that he now opened his heart, acknowledging that he had done many bad things, seeking forgiveness. This life that he was living was no life. He had no idea how many people he had harmed.

The eyes of Christ seemed to swim in his vision, and then Saul realised that there were tears trickling from the image's eyes. He felt a warmth spread through his wounds and when he lifted his shirt, his flesh was unmarked.

The stereo fell silent. Saul could hear his attackers arguing in the street outside but he had no fear that they would penetrate this place of sanctuary.

A sudden tiredness washed over him then and he lay before the altar and slept.

SAUL HAD PLENTY of money to fund a relocation. Even in a new flat and a new town, however, he expected retribution, but neither Kev nor his master sought him out.

The bars that Saul drank in now were no longer populated by embittered drunks, and he found himself beginning to make a few genuine friends. No longer did he see in that old black and white. The blessings of the miracle had brought not only a renewal of faith, but a renewal of confidence. It took him a while, things being what they were, but Saul eventually found gainful employment, and not long after that Marian came into his life. He hadn't been expecting, or looking for, an office romance, but when it happened he'd fallen for her hard. Within weeks it seemed like they had known each other for most of their lives, and within months they were engaged to be married. Two days before the big day, Marian announced that she was pregnant.

On honeymoon, after the sun had gone down and the crickets and cats sang to the night, Saul would lie with his head pressed gently against her stomach and would speak to their child, imagining their future together. Part of him couldn't believe that this was happening and he felt something like fear at the thought of the responsibility that was soon to be theirs. Even so, he daily gave thanks to the god that had so blessed him with this new life.

On the day their son was born, Saul couldn't find the words to pray. George was early and underweight. He didn't entirely understand why; the doctor's explanations were lost in a haze of anger that stole all rational thought. Under the harsh lights of the hospital everything seemed so fake, so staged. When the doctor told them he was truly sorry, Saul didn't believe him for a moment.

They had four days with George, and then he was gone. This gift that had been given to them wasn't theirs to keep.

And it wasn't just their world that had fallen apart. In the weeks following their son's death, Marian and Saul watched as a parade of atrocities unfolded on the news – images that could have come straight from a disaster movie. A dirty bomb had made Manhattan virtually uninhabitable; Pakistan had been all but wiped from the map by the latest in a series of catastrophic floods; rioting became a regular occurrence in the major English cities, and in Europe citizens were queuing for food. Saul could no longer think straight. He barely slept and sometimes he'd find whole days had gone by without him being aware of their passing. With so many wars underway, he felt like he should sign up, get back into the black and white. But there was Marian. She found refuge in the horrors that were unfolding, as though in the world's suffering she could find an explanation for her own. She'd have sat before the television round the clock if Saul hadn't reminded her to eat and sleep. He'd have taken her to a doctor, but they could no longer afford it.

With everything finely balanced on the edge of the abyss, another miracle occurred.

TWENTY-SEVEN BABIES were born to twenty-seven women at twenty-seven minutes past midnight on September the twenty-seventh – statistically not vastly improbable. What was unusual was that each of the women claimed to be a virgin, and subsequent scientific investigation confirmed this claim. For the protection of these immaculate children, it was decided that they would be looked after by the church, all housed in one ultra-modern facility dedicated to the welfare of the potential messiahs. As to their guardians, it was deemed that only those with direct experience of the divine would be suitable. When Saul heard this, he didn't hesitate to apply for the position. Many were the false applicants of course, and it took a good long while for the church to separate the wheat from the chaff, but with

Saul, their biometric and psychological tests – not to mention hours of prayer – confirmed that he had indeed been touched by God.

For a while, the world turned its back on war and wanton destruction, desperate for news of a new messiah and the message of hope he or she would bring. But after two months of the babies showing no signs of being anything other than babies, the world returned to its old ways.

On the west coast of America a massive earthquake flattened L.A. In the Middle East the use of nuclear weapons lead to the annihilation of two countries and millions of citizens. And every night, when Saul returned from the facility, Marian would be sat watching the endless parade of horrors, blankly accepting yet another atrocity as though the suffering of so many people touched her not one bit. She had stopped talking to him. There had been no warning, no row that lead to her silence. Marian's words just became fewer and fewer, and then there were no words at all. Watching the television with her that night, Saul thought that perhaps the world didn't deserve a saviour; nobody could lead them out of this darkness.

With Marian asleep, Saul returned to his laptop and opened a picture of Baby 17. The child had no name, just a designation. For a time, Saul had accepted this, but now it seemed ludicrous. Whatever else Baby 17 may be, he was a human being. He deserved the dignity of being treated like one. And so, Saul gave him a name.

"Goodnight, George," he said, touching the screen.

THE SMELL OF burning hit him as soon as he walked out of their apartment. The end of their street was barricaded by a wreck of blazing vehicles, beyond which he could just make out the swell and heave of a crowd. The sounds of police cars were converging. Saul hurried along the street in the opposite direction.

The riots had been getting closer. While they had been confined to the television it was easy to deny their reality. When the sound of clashes from the neighbouring borough had begun to keep them awake at night, Saul had stocked up on tinned goods and bottled water. He had told Marian not to leave the apartment for anything, but then realised how stupid that sounded – these days she rarely bothered to make it as far as the bathroom.

There was the thud of a detonation and Saul felt a burst of intense heat scorch his back as something lit up the sky.

After hurrying more than two miles out of his way, Saul thought that he had left the last of the rioters behind, but as he turned a corner – his shoes crunching on broken glass – he saw a masked man standing in his path.

Saul didn't pause. He put his head down and hurried by. He thought he had gotten away with it but then there was a shout and a bottle smashed at his feet. He looked behind him but the man was gone. Saul breathed a sigh of relief. All things considered, he had gotten away lightly. He wasn't even particularly worried by the small shard of glass buried in his left hand or the thin trickle of blood running through his fingers. Some part of him realised that he shouldn't be relieved, that the fact this was how things were now should make him as angry as the rioters. But he was in one piece and as he swiped himself into the facility, he even allowed himself a smile at the thought of the infant waiting for him.

Baby 17 – *George*, Saul reminded himself – lay in his white cot, swaddled in white cotton, looking up at the white ceiling.

This isn't right, Saul thought, and then immediately looked guiltily at the camera observing his booth.

Beyond the glass, the infant hiccupped and Saul laughed. Couldn't someone at least play with him? He realised that he was looking at the potential saviour of humankind, but would it really offend the dignity of the church to let him play with the boy? Saul had never had the chance with George. *Their* George. The closest he had ever got to his son was lightly stroking a hand through a hole in the incubation unit. George hadn't opened his eyes. Saul had been a father and he had no idea what it felt like to hold a child.

Crouching beneath the camera while balancing on a chair, Saul managed to angle it so that it was facing the wall. He wasn't supposed to know the code for Baby 17's room, but he had watched Nurse Simmons come and go enough times to memorise the pattern of her fingers on the keypad.

"Seven-One-Nine-Eight," he whispered as he tapped in the digits.

Saul ducked into George's room, crouching low beneath the camera; rising to his feet beside it, he carefully draped his jacket over the lens. He realised that he wouldn't have long, and they would soon send someone up to check on the fault, but he just had to do this.

He lifted George out of his cot.

"Hello. Hey there fellah, how are you, eh?"

George looked up at Saul with his large brown eyes, and – for the briefest of moments – the corner of his mouth twitched into something like a smile. Saul pressed his cheek against the top of the child's head, marvelling at how warm he was and breathing in the wonderful smell of him. This was what had been denied them; this miracle should have been theirs. For years now it felt to Saul that he had been saved only to be re-born into pain and loss. He held George tight as his breath caught in his throat and tears rolled down his face. The infant didn't once protest as the strange man came apart.

Reality only began to creep back in when the gash on Saul's left hand began to sting. George looked up at him intently as he closed a tiny hand around Saul's thumb. There was a familiar warmth deep in the wound and, as Saul watched, the cut closed up, faded and disappeared.

In a moment of frightening clarity, Saul realised exactly who he was holding.

Baby 17 was the *one*. The miracle the world had been hoping and praying for. The word made flesh.

In Saul's contract it stated very clearly what he was expected to do in just such a circumstance.

George nuzzled his head against Saul's chest, no doubt looking for milk he was unable to supply. Instead of cries of hungry frustration, however, George fell asleep. Saul could feel the infant's heartbeat against his chest, and that was what decided him. Baby 17 may well be the future saviour of the world, but right now he was a child and that was exactly what Saul was going to allow him to be. If the church were allowed to raise the infant, he would become nothing more than a pet messiah, repeating whatever doctrine was fed to him. George didn't deserve that and, right now, Saul wasn't even sure that the world deserved a saviour. But he and Marian, they deserved relief from their pain.

Saul removed his jacket from the camera and draped it over George. As he exited his booth he could hear footsteps coming up the stairs. He didn't hurry; he walked calmly down through the facility. He reached the exit and swiped himself out. Outside, the pilgrims looked at him curiously as he held his bundle to his chest. The vendor was now selling cheap-looking keyrings alongside his posters and T-shirts.

"Five pounds. Five pounds, my friend. Special offer."

"Look, just fuck off, okay?" he growled. He realised then that his nerves were beginning to get to him and he flagged down a taxi.

As the cab pulled away, Saul began to relax, though he didn't unwrap his bundle yet.

He was relieved to see that the tide of rioting had withdrawn from their street, leaving behind the detritus of unrest. Some enterprising soul had draped fairy lights around the edges of a shattered window. In the foyer of their building a fake fir tree twinkled at him as he passed.

Marian was where he had left her, bathed in the light of the television. She didn't even acknowledge him as he entered but the look of rage she turned on him when he switched the television off chilled him to the core.

"Marian… Marian, look. I have something better."

And Saul lifted his jacket to reveal the sleeping infant.

"It's George. He's come back."

His wife held out her arms and Saul handed over the child as she began to cry.

Outside, in the corridor, he could hear several voices raised in song, coming closer.

"Happy Christmas, Marian," Saul said.

THE RIVER

THERE ARE ABOUT two hundred of us living in this place, girded by precipitous cliffs no one has the ability, or the inclination, to scale. In our stone bowl, as Thomas jokingly calls it, we can only look at the distant mountains and wonder what lies beyond. When the sun reaches us it is never too hot; at night it is never too cold. The seasons are as predictable as the passage of time. Each of us, barring accidents, lives for exactly fifty years.

We want for nothing. The river provides for all our needs.

The river enters the village through the mouth of a cave that lies to the north and leaves by another cave that sits directly opposite some two miles to the south. The river runs straight and sits within well defined banks which it has never breached. The river gives us fresh drinking water and food. The river clothes us in the reeds that grow on its banks. The river takes away our waste and our dead, and it always runs deep and clear.

MY BROTHER THOMAS and I are fishing at our favourite spot, halfway between the two caves and sitting in the shade of the tallest oak. The fishing is no challenge, it never is. The trout are as hungry for our hooks as they are for the freshly hatched midges that cloud the surface. Already, a large mound of fish sits between us, and our rods can't have been over the water for more than ten minutes. Still, it passes the time, which is really all there is to do here.

As the sun crests the most easterly of the cliffs, my tummy rumbles. Thomas hears and puts down his rod. He begins to prepare a fire and gestures to me to gut one of the fish. The dead fish's eyes are bright and deep. Part of me wishes I were a fish. Not this fish, obviously, but I envy their ability to just swim on, never staying in one place for long. This fish will have seen more in its lifetime than I ever will in mine.

"If you're going to stare at it like that, you should at least do it the courtesy of giving it a kiss."

"What?" Thomas is grinning at me as the smoke rises before him. "Sorry."

I notice that the fish feels heavier than it should and I when I slit open its belly with my knife, a small square of bark slithers out of its guts.

"Is that—?" Thomas begins.

"A prayer? Yes."

Once a month everybody in the village – well, those that can write – write their prayer onto a square of bark before giving it to the river. It's inevitable that one of them should end up in the guts of a fish. But as I turn the bark over and read what is written there, my long silence – and no doubt shocked expression – cause Thomas to ask, "Are you alright?"

Oh, but I am, for sitting in my hands is *my* prayer, and it has been answered.

FATHER PETERS IS not difficult to find. All we have to do is look to the south to see him squatting over the river before the mouth of the cave.

Before I can open my mouth to hail the holy man, Thomas has snatched the prayer from my hands and is running. Father Peters has barely time to wipe himself and hoist his trousers by the time I catch up.

"Thomas, what is it? Why would you disturb me in my excretions? It's not proper, you know."

"It's a prayer." Thomas says, holding out the bark.

"Yes, I can see that. And you can wait for the correct time before giving it to the river."

"It's Michael's prayer, and it has been answered. We found it in a fish."

"Michael?"

"It's true, Father." I say.

Father Peters washes his hands thoroughly before taking the prayer and reading what is written there.

Into the bark, I had scratched:

Where does the river come from? What is its source?

And beneath this, in writing quite different from my own:

The source is the destination.

The holy man nods and mumbles to himself, as though he understands, but it is clear to us that he doesn't.

"The words of the river require much reflection," Father Peters says. "Tonight there shall be a gathering of the holy. In the morning we will share the voice of the river with the rest of the village."

I hold my hand out for my prayer, but Father Peters tucks it into a pocket before walking away, still mumbling to himself.

Thomas and I watch him go, neither of us saying anything. I look up and see that the sun has not yet begun to drop back below the cliffs.

"Fishing?" I say

"Fishing," says Thomas.

WE CAN HEAR the holy men chanting; we can barely sleep for their litany. It is often the way with matters of deep spiritual import. I remember the time my sister, Christine, said that she had dreamed the river would run red. The holy men had spent an entire week on that one: chanting, playing their discordant music, arguing loudly and volubly, deep into the night. All this, only to then pronounce that Christine's dream had been naught but a nightmare.

Now that the river has apparently spoken, who knows how long their deliberations will take?

"What do you think the river meant by 'The source is the destination'?" Thomas says.

"I don't know. The holy men will."

"They'll certainly take their sweet time over it."

I think again of the fish; the dead one that had been in my hands and its living fellows in the river – always moving, never staying in one place for long.

Suddenly, I have what seems to be a radical idea, and I genuinely can't think why nobody has thought of it before.

"Why don't *we* find the source, Thomas? Why don't we swim into the north cave and try and find the source ourselves?"

"Can… can we do that?"

"Why not?"

"Nobody has ever ventured into either of the caves."

"And why is that?"

"Well the river falls into a great chasm beyond the south cave. You can hear the roar of the water if you stand close."

"And what's beyond the north cave? What's to prevent us from entering?"

Thomas doesn't say anything to that, but he follows as I leave our house.

Outside, the moon has crested the lip of our stone bowl, but its light has yet to reach the north cave. There the river streams out of a darkness so absolute that one glace at it turns Thomas around and sends him jogging for the safety and comfort of home. I have to go back for him twice before he will finally stand beside me on the riverbank. When I lead him into the water he begins to shiver, even though it is not cold and the current is gentle. For a while we tread water and stare into the darkness. A soft wind breathes from the mouth of the cave, bringing with it the whisper of the river and the smell of wet stone.

"I don't know, Michael."

"And that's precisely why we have to do this, Thomas. Be a fish."

"A—?"

I strike out, knowing that he will follow.

Inside the cave the current grows stronger and for a time it's hard to know whether I am making any progress at all. And then the river takes me. I know that my brother is with me because Thomas's limbs become entangled with mine as we are swept along, careening from one bank to another. My hands and arms are slashed by sharp rocks. Thomas cries out and then coughs as he struggles for breath. Somehow I find his hand, and I don't let go.

The river finally releases us and we tumble up against a pebbly shore. Beside me, Thomas is sick as he gets to his hands and knees. The river roars past us and I am shocked by its fierceness, the loudness of its voice. I have never heard the river like this before and

it scares me. I don't want to go back into the water. As my eyes
adjust to the darkness, I see that the shore runs most of the length of
the tunnel, finishing just before a cave mouth to the north, through
which bright sunshine is pouring. I laugh with relief and Thomas
joins me, once he has stopped shivering. We have done what nobody
has done before. The source of the river must surely lie before us. I
take Thomas's hand as I lead him towards the light.

Several metres before the mouth of the cave, the shore slopes
gently down into the water. The river is considerably calmer here and
as we step into it, I glance down to see a shoal of fish parting around
us. I wonder if any of them carry more answers to the villagers'
prayers. Sunlight lays across the mouth of the cave like a skein of the
lightest cloth; it bejewels the water, dazzling me and making me
throw up a hand as we swim cautiously onwards. There is a moment
of dizziness, a feeling in my stomach as though we are falling. But
we are still in the river, carried by its gentle current out into the light.

This is wrong. Shouldn't we be swimming against the flow? A
cloud covers the sun and the scene before us resolves as we leave the
tunnel behind.

We have come not to the river's source but have returned to our
village. In the darkness of the cave and the sudden pull of the river
we must have somehow become turned around. Thomas curses and
slaps at the water with both hands, sending up great plumes of
spray. His gesture is futile; the river can no more feel his anger than
we can swim against its flow. Best just to live out our allotted fifty

years in comfort and boredom before the river takes us on that final journey.

It takes me a moment to realise that Thomas has climbed out of the river and is sitting on the bank watching me as I struggle with these fresh revelations.

"There is a mystery here, Michael," he says, holding out his hand and helping me out.

"Oh, and what is that dear brother?"

"Well, it was night when we entered the north cave, not ten minutes ago, and now it is day."

In my confusion I hadn't paused to take in this oddity, but he is right. The sun is almost at its peak. Through the trees the village is going about its business as usual. A thread of smoke is snaking its way from the chimney of our house. I race Thomas to our doorway, there to stand and watch Mother as she cooks on the range, singing to herself as she stirs something in a pan.

"Smells good," I say.

Mother gasps and drops the spoon. "Oh Lord, Michael! You gave me a fright. Is that Thomas with you? Where have you two been? The chores are stacking up and me with a world of laundry to do."

"We've been..."

"Fishing." Thomas says. "What of the announcement, Mother? Did the holy men decide on the meaning of the answer to Michael's prayer."

"Prayer?"

"Yes, the prayer that was found in the guts of a fish," I say.

"I think that you two have been out in the sun long enough; the heat has clearly addled your brains. Now get in here and finish cooking while I prepare the table."

Thomas shrugs when I look over at him, open mouthed. Did we fall asleep while fishing and imagine all that had gone before? Maybe we both received a knock on the head in our struggle with the river.

Nothing makes sense, but with food in our belly we at least begin to feel a little more positive. After all, it isn't for us to question the river; it will surely reveal its wisdom in the fullness of time.

THAT NIGHT MY dreams dart out of the darkness like fish – brilliant flashes that are gone before they can be understood. When I awake I find myself repeating the words "The source is the destination" in a dull mantra that reminds me of the chanting of the holy men, and it is to these so-called men of wisdom that I decide I must address the questions that crowd my brain.

The church sits in the centre of the village, the houses radiating away from it like the spokes of a wheel. Inside the air is heavy with incense and the reek of body-odour. The holy men are kneeling with their heads to the ground, whispering, as though telling their secrets to the stones. I clear my throat and tap my foot but not one of them turns around. I have to wait until they are done with their prayers before they deign to speak to me.

"I need to see Father Peters."

"I believe you will find him by the south cave."

And there he is again, though this time he is not squatting over the water with his dignity compromised. Instead, he is staring into the darkness of the cave, an absent look on his face.

"There is where we all go," he says.

This is hardly a profound statement. Not when all of us know precisely the day and the hour of our death. I begin to realise then that I don't actually know what the holy men are for. After all, where does their wisdom actually lead us?

"Father Peters, what did you discover about my prayer?"

"Prayer?"

"Yes, the prayer that was answered by the river."

"It was? Oh, but this is wonderful news! *Wonderful*. The river speaks! We must tell everybody."

That this is a revelation to him dismays me, but before Father Peters can race back to the village and share the good news, he is stilled by the sound of voices raised in song. For a moment I think that it is the holy men, singing some hymn to the river, but then I realise that the voices are coming not from the church but the north cave.

From out of the darkness the river carries our dead. They float on their backs, their voices raised in song, as full of life as they ever were before they were taken. I recognise my father as he pulls himself onto the riverbank. He is dead – I know this because we were all there at his Death Day – yet he looks so alive. He sees me watching him and smiles before heading for home. Others are drifting up against the banks and rising, dripping, from the river. Father Peters' own father drifts gently to a halt by his feet and raises his hand. The holy man is crying as he lifts him from the water and they embrace.

"The river has spoken," he whispers into the older man's shoulder. "The river has spoken."

I AM DISTURBED by the lack of fear in the village. Nobody seems perturbed by the dead amongst us.

My mother cheerfully lays extra places at the table, for not only has my father returned, but his father and his father's father, and mother and mother's mother… and so on. All our dead are here.

I stare open-mouthed at my father as we sit to eat – a little afraid of the healthy, vibrant flush of his cheeks – and it takes me a moment to register that my mother is asking me to pass him the potatoes.

Thomas and I eat little and we find the small-talk stifling. Nobody is asking the question which we must surely all be thinking – so I pluck up the courage and finally say it.

"What's it like being dead?"

And so the dead tell us, and that is when we find out the main problem with the dead – when they start talking, they don't stop.

"FOR THE LOVE of all that is holy, when will they stop?" Thomas cries, burying his head beneath his pillow.

Even after the living have retired for the evening, the dead continue to talk. Dawn is already paling the mountains and all we can hear are the murmur of voices from below. When we finally reconcile ourselves with sleeplessness, giving up our beds as a bad job, and descend the stairs, the dead are there. They don't turn to greet us and there's no break in their conversation; they just carry on, telling each other – and anybody who will listen – all and nothing.

After a while their chatter becomes little more than background noise. Once the mystery of death has been revealed to us, the fascination is dispelled and the dead become just another mouth to feed. The only people who truly listen are the holy men and even they, after a while, realise that the dead have nothing much to say. And when the dead run out of words, that doesn't stop them; instead they stand around making idiot, infantile sounds or singing tuneless nonsense songs.

The miracle of the river giving up our dead quickly pales, and once there is no distinction between the dead and the living, death ceases to be.

When one of our uncles is on the verge of reaching his fiftieth birthday, we gather around him expectantly, ready to say our goodbyes before we send him into the darkness. But the day of his birthday comes and goes without his passing. Perhaps, we reason, we have got our dates wrong. But no, a quick consultation of the almanac confirms that Uncle James is the first person in the village to ever go beyond fifty years of age. Naturally, my uncle is thrilled at this occurrence, but with the absence of death we all soon realise that we have a very big problem indeed.

It would seem that with death comes no diminishment in appetite. We are pulling more fish out of the river than ever and because the dead don't sleep, they eat far more than the living. Father Peters suggests that we give the dead back to the river, but nobody wants to be the first to put this plan into action. "After all," one of the holy men reasons, "the river clearly returned our dead to us for a purpose."

No one is particularly convinced of this, not even the other holy men.

We pray to the river, sending our fragments of bark into the darkness, but the river is either not listening or deigns not to answer.

"You do realise, don't you," Thomas says one afternoon, an afternoon in which our rods have hovered over the water for hours with not one bite, "that this is entirely our fault. We should never have tried to find the source."

So twice more we venture into the north cave, hoping that by doing so we will somehow reverse what has befallen our village. But each time we drift out of the darkness, the dead are there to greet us.

"Maybe," Thomas says, "we can ask the dead what to do about the dead."

And, of course, it is obvious now that he says it.

* * *

MY FATHER IS sitting by the chicken coop, making a sound like "awooawooawooawoo" and scooping up handfuls of dirt before letting them trickle through his fingers. He looks up as we approach. "Awoo?" he says, and smiles.

"Father... *father!* Listen to me, please." I say. "What are we going to do now that nobody dies? What does the river want us to do?"

He stops making his idiot sounds and, for a moment, just stares at us.

"The source is the destination," he finally says, and I almost scream in exhausted frustration.

IT IS THE fourth week since the return of the dead and the river itself has died. There are no more fish and the water no longer runs clear. In desperation we have started to eat the reeds that grow on the banks, but they provide little sustenance. Our food stocks have dwindled rapidly and now the only clean water we have to drink is that provided by the infrequent rains. We can't live like this. I'd take my own life but for the fear of becoming one of the idiot dead. I don't know what to do and I have grown sick and tired of listening to the desperate prophecies and portents of the holy – all of which are, of course, utter nonsense.

At night I barely sleep; instead I go and kneel by the south cave and listen to the roar of the now poisoned water as it tumbles into the unseen depths. And it is as I watch the water rush against the banks one evening that I finally realise what we have to do.

THE RIVER, *OUR* river, has died, so I have decided that it is time to make a new one.

Thomas looks sick, paler than I have ever seen him, and I'm afraid that he won't be up to the task. When he hears what I have to say, however, a big grin splits his face and, even so soon, his health appears to improve.

"It is the only way, Thomas."

He nods and reaches out a hand so that I can help him out of his bed.

Nobody tries to stop us – not our family, not even the holy men – and nobody seems at all interested as we retrieve the pick-axes from the old opencast mine on the edge of the village and bring them to the south cave. As our axes bite into the rock, however, the dead begin to gather. Their strange murmurings and breathy, wordless songs make a bizarre counterpoint to the rhythmic bite of our tools. My father is amongst them and he watches intently as a mound of rocks begin to pile up at the base of the wall on which we work. Looking from the stones to the sluggish passage of the river, something like realisation crosses his face.

My father picks up a rock, wades out into the river and places it just before the mouth of the south cave. Another of the dead, seeing what he has done, likewise picks up a rock and places it beside the first. The dead fall silent then and Thomas and I fear that something terrible is about to happen, but as we watch they fall into line, each one shuffling forward to pick up a rock and add it to the wall. Seeing what is happening – and not quite being able to believe that it is – we work with renewed vigour. The labour is exhausting but by the evening, the dam covers the whole of the south cave.

After that it doesn't take long for the river to break its banks, spilling murky, stinking water into the village. Looking up, I can just see the edge of the moon as it begins to rise over our stone bowl, and I take Thomas by the hand to lead him to the oak beneath which we used to fish.

Father Peters finds us there. He has seen the dead trailing us, and the dam.

"Michael, Thomas – why would you do this?"

"It's time to leave, Father," I say.

"And where is it we are supposed to go?"

"Up."

Homes are flooded and possessions are ruined. The majority of the villagers are understandably angry with us, but what choice did we have? The river is dead to us. After generations of silence it has answered a prayer and returned those we thought long gone. It is clear to Thomas and I that the river wants us to leave, to make our own way. Who are we to question the will of the river?

It doesn't take long for our stone bowl to start filling up. The village is somewhere beneath us now, maybe twenty feet down. As we rise with the water more of the distant mountains become visible; I can see trees on the slopes, more trees than I have ever seen. Out there, there is so much space.

Our mother swims towards us, Michelle, our youngest sister, grimly clinging to her shoulders, her hair plastered to her brow.

"Michael, what have you done? Have you not thought how many people have drowned because of you?"

I gesture for her to look around and she smiles as she understands. Of course, she realises, we are all here. Death has lost its meaning, its finality.

The lip of our stone bowl grows ever closer. I find myself already feeling nostalgia for the village but, no, this is not what the river wanted. We are to move on, we are to allow ourselves to be carried by the current into whatever lies beyond.

The rim of the bowl is level with the top of my head, now my eyes, and oh… what sights! I squeeze Thomas's hand as the water crests the lip of rock, and together we ride the new river down to the plain.

THE SEA BETWEEN THE STARS

I'M ON THE edge of the ocean. Beyond my toes, the land falls away in a sheer wall. If I lean out a little, I can just make out the occasional lit window, behind most of which sit people staring blankly at screens, completely unaware that they are under water.

I can't see all the way to the bottom. My view is occluded by the multitude of creatures that swim beneath me. Most are small – tiny aluminium fish darting here and there, their lights barely penetrating the gloom – but occasionally something vast disturbs these waters; iron leviathans that look far too heavy to swim. For the most they stay their course, but from time to time their jaws open, scooping up the fish that aren't quick enough to get away. The leviathan that drifts just a few metres below pauses to read me. It will scan me as a cleaning droid, rather than flesh and blood, thanks to an illegal download that I recently purchased. The tech will expire within the next ten minutes, however, and there is nothing to stop human eyes on the other side of the canyon from registering my presence, and so I raise my arms and take the plunge.

WHEN I AWAKE, it is to see a digital shark swimming around the tiny cubicle in which I lie.

"Good morning, patient," it says. "We advise that you would benefit from a further day in recovery, however your credit limit has been reached. How would you like to pay for your continued treatment?"

"What?" I blink open my account and see that the shark is right; I've been completely cleaned out. "How is that even possible?"

"Suicide attempts are charged at a premium. Would you like me to show you the relevant section of your contract?"

"It was not a suicide attempt."

"With respect, patient, what then were you trying to do?"

"Swim."

I DISCHARGE MYSELF, though it is all I can do to get out of bed and get dressed. As I hobble through the hospital, the shark swims alongside me.

"On a scale of one to five, how satisfied would you say you were with your treatment? One being not at all satisfied, and five being very satisfied."

"Go fuck yourself," I grind out as the exit swishes open and I step into the din of the street.

Fortunately the shark does not follow me over the threshold of the hospital; even so, I am surrounded by sharks. The mascot of the corporation that owns and manages all of Grace is everywhere. A happy shark family eating sushi tries to entice me into a nearby restaurant; a news screen shows a sombre basking shark reporting on yet another mine collapse, and the great white graces the uniforms of the security patrols that keep our streets safe and clean – so many sharks and not one ocean to be found anywhere on the planet.

Grace used to be almost entirely covered by ocean, a couple of hundred years ago, before it was terraformed by the corporation. They waited until the planet was at its closest position to the sun, and the ocean was free of the ice that bound it for much of its orbit, before the ships descended and sucked up all that lovely water; an entire world drained so that the corporation could move in and harvest the planet's mineral wealth. Now Grace is a labyrinthine world of deep canyons broken by the scars of the corporation's rapacious greed.

A nearby bar erupts with joyous yells and a mob of drunken young men barrel into the street to dance and chant. They are all wearing shark masks, their hands held palm-to-palm on the tops of their heads in lieu of fins. I force my way through the press of sweaty bodies only to be accosted by yet another digital shark – this one enquiring about my health insurance.

Really, I shouldn't find these interruptions so aggravating – at least half the sharks I will encounter on my way home will have been programmed by me – but I'm just not in the mood, and I need to get to my apartment before the air again turns to water and I drown.

I CAME TO Grace to make a lot of money very quickly. Back then, the corporation was recruiting every able-bodied human it could and it was relatively easy to get picked for the team. Mining was no more dangerous than any other work I had done and Grace had the added advantage of a breathable atmosphere. I wouldn't have to commute from orbit or spend every night packed into the stifling atmosphere of a bunkroom far beneath the surface.

Whether the corporation had been lax in their safety procedures, or whether I was simply in the wrong place at the wrong time, there was an incident.

I probably shouldn't have headed that far from my team, but I had a gut instinct about the depth of a mineral vein, and I didn't think I'd be out of radio contact for long. While taking some samples, I broke through into an unexpected cavity – the mineral deposit not nearly as deep as I had hoped – and the next thing I knew, my suit's warning indicators were screaming and there was a strange smell that reminded me of the sea. I came to in the hospital, almost penniless. The profit I had made working in the mine had been eaten up by medical bills, and it turned out that the health insurance package I had been sold wasn't quite as flexible or generous as I'd been promised. I left the hospital determined to start again, get back below ground and earn enough to be able to leave Grace behind and try my hand at something else, but it turned out that the corporation had placed the blame for the accident squarely on my shoulders, and I was no longer welcome in the mines. I tried to appeal against the ruling but the corporation won, though they did throw me a bone. In a previous life I'd been a programmer, specialising in basic AI, and the corporation needed someone to work in their advertising department, amongst the sharks. It didn't pay half as well as mining, but it was better than begging.

This would all have been fairly tolerable were it not for the hallucinations.

The first time it happened I was at work. I'd been three weeks above ground and in the new job, and I'd just leant back in my chair and was looking across the office when suddenly we were underwater. No one else seemed to notice; my colleague in the adjacent cubicle was staring blankly at his terminal as a school of tiny fish flittered before his eyes; some sort of crustacean had crawled out of my trash basket and was climbing up the leg of my chair. I closed my eyes, but I could feel the sharp chill of the deep ocean and a suffocating sense of panic rose in my chest.

I opened my eyes and I was dry and breathing air. The ocean had gone, though I thought I heard the whisper of a wave retreating from shore.

I returned to the hospital and spent most of a week's pay on getting a scan. A cheerful shark informed me that there were some signs of brain damage, but it was minor enough that it shouldn't affect my life on a day-to-day basis, and anyway my insurance and current credit rating wouldn't cover any further treatment which – the shark was pleased to say – I probably wouldn't need.

Probably. Great.

It would seem that whatever I had inadvertently inhaled far below Grace's surface had scrambled my brains.

At first the hallucinations weren't a big issue. Three second bursts of the life aquatic could be ignored if I simply closed my eyes, but over the last few months things have gotten a lot worse. It may be work stress exacerbating the problem; I'm still a long way off being able to afford a shuttle ticket, and the chance of promotion looks to be slim to none. A week ago I awoke to find myself floating a foot above my bed, my duvet drifting lazily over me like a manta ray. I struggled into my clothes and swam from my apartment to the elevator, to be disgorged into the lobby in a flood of salt water and a tangle of kelp. Of course, when I said good morning to the desk clerk I was fresh and dry, as was the lobby and the elevator behind me. I downloaded some music to keep me distracted on my way to work and tried to ignore, as best I could, the fronds of the sea anemones that surrounded my terminal, and the calls of the vast creatures that boomed throughout the office, shaking the windows.

Yesterday evening was the worst, though. I could have died.

I CAN'T AFFORD medication. My next pay cheque isn't due for another two weeks. I don't know what I'm going to do. I don't want to have to swim to work every day and I certainly don't want to attempt diving again. (I was lucky to survive that; apparently I landed on the roof of a passing security dirigible.) I don't have any friends I can talk to, not in a system close enough that conversation won't be made practically impossible by communication delays.

I trail the network for online psychological advice, but strangely enough *symptoms of inhaling an unidentified alien gas* doesn't bring up any useful hits. I remember the catchphrase of one of the advertising sharks I'd been working on: "Here to help."

Of course, the shark doesn't have what you would call *true intelligence*, but it's a hell of a lot brighter than most humans I know, so I access my home terminal and ask it to project the shark into the centre of the room. Surefix Shark is an AI that customers who spend over a certain amount at any of Grace's Surefix stores can access for free. Usually the shark is required to do little more than dispense advice on putting up shelves or mounting a door, so I'm not entirely convinced it will suffice as a rudimentary therapist.

"Hello Robert, I'm here to help," it says as it circles my sofa. I strip away the DIY routine and open it up to general conversation.

"I'm not well," I say.

"I'm sorry to hear that. As you know the corporation has a variety of therapies available—"

None of which I can afford. I shut down automatic linking.

"Look, I just want to talk. I need some perspective."

"I'm here to help, Robert."

How do I put this in terms a digital shark will understand? Surefix has a basic level of empathy, but I'm not sure how far that extends beyond flatpack problems and tiling solutions. I tell the shark about the incident in the mine, my exposure to the gas and the subsequent hallucinations.

Surefix glitches and reappears above me, looking down with its black, lifeless eyes.

"Do you know what a shark is, Robert?"

"Well, sure. I work with them every day."

"I'm not talking about the corporation's mascot. I'm talking about real sharks."

"I've seen videos."

"Sharks have been extinct for almost a thousand years, Robert; killed by human greed and the destruction of their natural habitat. Do you not find it strange that the corporation chose the symbol of an extinct animal only to enact an even greater extinction when they changed Grace?"

"There was very little life on Grace, just some single cell organisms – nothing we haven't come across on many other worlds. Nothing worth conserving, anyway."

"Are you sure about that, Robert?"

I don't like where this is going. Surefix is supposed to be helping me and this is starting to feel like an interrogation.

"The shark was one of Earth's greatest predators, Robert. Some would say the perfect predator."

Surefix glitches again, and now we are nose-to-nose. I know it's only a projection, but I swear I can feel its breath on my face.

"Even as the corporation destroyed this world's oceans, something spoke to it. Just as, Robert, it is speaking to you now."

"I'm sorry?"

The shark is over by the kitchen unit. It swims through the refrigerator and drifts back towards me.

"Just as I am speaking to you," it says.

Surefix is beginning to scare me, so I shut it down. This was a stupid idea, expecting free therapy from an advertising AI. Even so, I pull up another digital shark. If my tech knowledge were a touch more advanced, I'd take a shot at hacking a Doc Shark, but those things are surrounded by complex security 'ware, and I wouldn't have the faintest idea where to begin.

Nanny Shark is jolly, cloyingly so. I find her a shade more biddable than Surefix, however, so we chat.

"My child is suffering from hallucinations," I say. "Says he keeps thinking he's underwater, like in the sea. What do I do? I think it could be stress related but he did recently have an accident." I realise what I have just said, and throw up a block on the message the shark was about to ping to Social Services. "Not that sort of accident," I stress. "I wasn't there at the time. Though I do look after him... naturally."

This doesn't feel like it's going any better.

"How old is the child?"

Thirty-eight. "Erm... thirteen? I mean, is that a bit young for stress-induced hallucinations?"

"Why are you afraid of the ocean, Robert?"

"Oh God," I sigh. "You're just as much use as Surefix."

As though summoned, Surefix pops into existence just behind my right shoulder. I jump a foot off the couch and tumble straight through Nanny Shark.

Both sharks turn as one to face me, hovering side-by-side.

"Yes, Robert," they say, "why are you afraid? Why are you not hearing what we say?"

I try to dismiss the sharks, but they stay in place, even when I turn off the projector. I'm going mad, absolutely insane, and there's no one on Grace – or even in this solar system – that can help me.

"We can help you," the sharks say.

"Shut up."

"We can help you, as you can help us. Is that not what you want?"

"Shut up. Shut up. *Shut up!*"

"The incident in the mine was no accident, Robert."

"You found us. You made first contact."

"There's nothing to fear," Nanny Shark says in a soothing voice, right next to my ear. I feel the brush of a fin against my cheek. "You have been chosen. You are special."

I could end it properly this time. A hot bath and a sharp razor are all I need.

Instead, I brush the tears from my cheeks, sit down and listen to the sharks.

"DO THE SHARKS ever speak to you?" I ask the man who works at the terminal beside mine. I think his name is Dave; he looks like a Dave.

"Well, yeah. That's what they are for."

"I mean *really* speak to you. Tell you things."

"I think that's probably just you."

"I told you you're special," says the angel shark under my desk.

Of course, Dave has no idea of the beauty of Grace. He can only see Grace as it is now. He can't see the world that was.

I've applied for a day's leave and my manager has cheerfully given it to me. After all, it means that a portion of my wage will be returned to the corporation; they own everything on Grace.

"Not quite everything, Robert," Surefix Shark reminds me as I step into the elevator.

There are a number of things I could be doing with my leisure time; Grace has a thriving nightlife catering to all tastes and proclivities, and if I really wanted to push the boat out I could book passage to a suborbital casino, where my money will be taken steadily from me as I am plied with 'free' booze.

I smile. "A fool and his money, eh Surefix?"

"I don't follow, Robert."

"Don't worry about it. It's just an expression."

No, I'm not about to spend a night on the town so much as beneath it; five thousand and thirty eight metres beneath it, or thereabouts. It's not even the deepest or largest mine on Grace. Perhaps that's why the safety measures were lax enough to lead to the accident; though, as the sharks are so keen to assure me, there was no accident.

Security is tight, so getting on site requires clever timing and a stroke of good luck. As I approach the mine, the sky turns to sea. Everybody around me is slowed, but I can walk through water as easily as air, and I'm hidden by the striated flank of a behemoth that chooses that moment to drift past. Once I make it into the staff area and pull on a pressure suit, I no longer have to hide my presence; the suit does that for me. Now I look just like any other miner, my face barely visible behind the thick visor and my form lost within the folds of the heavy suit. Access to the explosives locker is likely to be more difficult, but I'm delighted to find that they haven't changed the code and my name is still on the list of authorised users. Things really have gone downhill.

Talking of down. The elevator now descends two thousands metres deeper than it did when I worked here, and I have to put in a special request to be let off at the level where I was working on the day of the incident.

"Maintenance, are you?" The operator says. I just nod. "Not sure you're going to need all that then." He gestures to the mining tool belt cinched around my waist, but I merely give him the thumbs-up and hope he will leave me alone.

"That was close, Robert," Surefix says as the elevator begins its descent.

I'm the only one to step out when the elevator stops at my level, and I try and shake off the sensation of suspicious stares burning into my back as I walk down the tunnel. It's eerily quiet; in the distance I can hear the *clink clink* of a solitary hammer as one of the maintenance crew tinker with something. There's no roar of drills, crunch of stone or the grinding juddering of conveyors that used to fill my days in the deeps.

"Not far now," Surefix says.

There's been no attempt to shore up the site of the incident. A dusty hazard notice is pasted to the wall beside the cave-in, but that's it. I check the toxicity readings before taking off the suit. It's as hot as hell without the benefit of its cooling units, but the air is at least breathable. I continue to disrobe until I am completely naked, and then stand at the site of the collapse. There's a faint damp breeze coming through the rubble, mineral rich and fresher than anything I've ever inhaled on Grace.

Surefix is no longer by my side, but I can feel a larger presence beyond the tumbled stone.

I don't have to be particularly fussy with how I place the explosives; quantity is the key here rather than trying to carefully direct the blast. I spare a thought for the thousands of miners toiling below, unaware of how their world is about to change. I should feel guilty, I suppose.

I retreat down the tunnel and around the corner before I take the cap off the detonator. When I press the button, the explosion is only slightly louder than the roar of the ocean as it pours into the mine.

THIS TIME IT feels like I really am about to drown. The water is bitterly cold and pitch black. A freezing tide grabs me and shoves me into a wall, shards of stone opening my flesh as I am dragged along, salt water flooding down my throat, rich with the taste of my own blood. The cold lessens and a sluggish warmth spreads through me. There's a deeper darkness in the black and I reach out towards it, ready to give myself over to that endless night, but just as my senses start to fade, something else finds me. My jaws are prised open and a noisome, fleshy presence pushes into me; it fills my chest and my lungs burn as they are emptied of water. Almost against my will, I take a breath, or something takes a breath for me.

Open your eyes, Robert.

I'm expecting total darkness, but instead there's a soft, amber glow. Threads of scarlet light, pulsing to the beat of my heart, criss-cross a ceiling that lies only a few inches above my face. I am anchored to this strange canopy by the thick root of flesh that has entered my mouth. I panic and try to pull the invading presence from between my lips, but as soon as I touch it, a searing pain grips my chest and the darkness threatens to rush in again.

Robert, don't. I am keeping you alive.

Who are you?

We are the ones who called you.

The sharks?

The sharks were a useful analogy. To understand what we are, you must see us.

My vision fades, but I am not losing consciousness. Instead, it is as though I have been dropped into the middle of a virtual world entertainment, but this is utterly unlike any game I have played.

I'm floating in a vast cavern. The water is alive with millions of tiny creatures, their glittering lights a myriad stars. There's a sudden flurry of movement and the phytoplankton swirl aside as something vast pushes through them. It is larger than one of Grace's security dirigibles, far larger. I've seen videos of whales, the huge creatures that once swam Earth's oceans, but these are on a different scale entirely, and they are alien. Oh, I've seen alien life on other worlds, but none I've witnessed until now have been so obviously *sentient*.

The glimmering jewels of tiny creatures are scattered once again as another of the enormous beings drifts into view.

We are the ones who called, Robert.

I realise that I'm seeing through the eyes of one of these leviathans, am within it, as a deep boom travels through me, and is answered.

There's so few of you.

We used to be more, many more. Let me show you.

GRACE TURNS BENEATH me, but this is no world of dry, jagged ravines, dust and smoking pits; this is a world of water, a brilliant blue ocean planet turning through the void.

A shadow crosses Grace's sun, and then another, and soon a vast fleet of ships has turned day to night, except they are not ships. They have been travelling for thousands of years, their enormous bodies fuelled by the light from distant suns, sustained by reserves that have now dwindled to almost nothing. As they descend through Grace's atmosphere, they shed outer skins hardened by the merciless climes of space, scarred by the impacts of millions of cosmic fragments. The wave thrown up by their impact is catastrophic, encircling the planet in a matter of hours, churning up and killing a billion marine creatures. The slaughter, however, is far from over. War has come to Grace; the invaders are outnumbered a hundred to one, but they have determination on their side – they have been preparing for this conflict for millennia, and this is a planet that has never known war. Soon the invaders have taken control of the ocean, and the waters are permanently stained with the blood of the dead.

Grace continues to turn through the void, just as it has done before, but now it is moving further and further from its sun. The seas are cooling, but the process is not registered by the planet's new masters until it is too late. As a crust of ice begins to cover the world, they retreat to the darkest depths, barely surviving on the sparse flora and fauna they find there. They consider an attempt to flee back into the void, but they have long since shed the skins that made travel between the stars possible, and they would never break through the ice now. They didn't count on how far Grace would travel from its sun, how long this winter will last. Over thousands of years they barely survive beneath the ice; the story of their exodus through space and the invasion of Grace passed on through the generations until it becomes a myth, a comforting fantasy. As the centuries pass, the black chill waters change the invaders until the magnificent biological systems that had enabled their long-ago cosmic diaspora become little more than a faint memory buried deep in their DNA.

All things change, all things come to pass, and as Grace passes its aphelion and begins its journey back towards its sun, the seas once more began to warm. The ice takes a long time to melt. Once it has gone, and the children of the original invaders begin to enjoy an ocean rich with life and abundant with light, a different sort of invader turns their eyes upon Grace.

With the human invasion, the slaughter is on an unprecedented scale. The former masters of Grace are butchered; their corpses rendered and shipped off-world to be used as fuel or food. Resistance is impossible against the ships that hang like mountains in the sky. Not only do the invaders bring death to the inhabitants of Grace, but they take away the oceans, draining the seas and exposing the bones of the planet, glittering with the mineral wealth within.

Yet the ocean is not entirely dead, nor is the genocide of its former masters complete. A small pocket of sea remains, far underground, populated by the last survivors of this once fearsome interstellar species. The invasion has ignited a memory buried deep within the survivors, of a time long before Grace, when they had swum the sea between the stars. The yearning for the limitless ocean returns, and with it a desire to leave this world behind.

WHEN WE TOUCHED your mind, when you encountered us for the first time, we knew that it was you who could help us, Robert.

I'm still stick from the history they have revealed to me. I knew that the corporation were ruthless – how could one work for them for any length of time and not know? – but I had no idea of the scale of their corruption. Grace is a dead world, they said, waiting to be reborn. Come and be a part of that resurrection.

Now you will be the agent of ours, Robert.

How?

We can change you. The corporation chose the shark as their mascot, without really knowing what a shark was. We can turn you into a shark amongst men. In return, you will help us leave this world.

Take me with you.

There is a pause long enough to make me feel as though I have offended them. As I wait, I become aware of the creature's heart beating in time with my own.

You will come with us, it says.

Relief turns to panic as the fleshy canopy descends, tightening around me like a second skin. The pain begins as my heart stops.

I DRAG MYSELF from the ruins of the flooded mine, barely able to stand on legs that feel inadequate to support my weight in the thick, smoky air. The first step is the hardest and I have moved little more than a metre when I am surrounded by the corporation's guards. I smile with a mouth that feels too full of teeth when I see the horror in their eyes. I can only imagine what I look like in my new form. They don't have time to shout a warning, let alone twitch their trigger fingers, before I lay them low. I barely have to think for the ventricles running along my flanks to dilate open. There is a sharp, mineral smell and the guards are on the floor, drowning in an atmosphere suddenly rendered toxic.

The going is easier after that. My new body may be unwieldy, heavy in the alien atmosphere of Grace, but no one can stand against me. I don't want to have to kill my way to the top, but if that is what it takes, I will. I will command control of the ships that drained this planet. We will take Grace's last sea, and with it the creatures who were once its masters.

Earth is a long haul, but a lot can happen in that time, we can change. Together we will reclaim its oceans, and populate them with a new kind of perfect predator.

IN THESE ROOMS, THESE HOUSES

HE DIDN'T FEEL like reading. The press of bodies surrounding him, the muggy warmth of the bus, made it difficult to concentrate on the words, and so, having read the same sentence eight times, he closed the book and looked out of the window.

They were out of the city and into the suburbs. Rows of near identical houses scrolled past; the occasional pedestrian pushing their way through the weather, battling with flapping coats or battered umbrellas. The child in the pushchair a few rows in front of him began to grizzle, accompanied by the sighs and tuts of his fellow commuters, as though one so young should have a better handle on their emotions. He sympathised with the boy; he was tired and fed-up too. The bus slowed as the traffic bunched up, and he turned back to the window, the procession of houses. Some rooms had lit windows, the curtains open, and through these he could see snapshots of life.

The back of a head rising above a sofa, in front of a television playing something bright and fast; a woman reaching into a kitchen cupboard; a man gesturing emphatically, his glare directed at someone out of sight; a man standing at a kitchen counter, chopping vegetables.

The bus stopped as a traffic light turned red, and the man looked up and caught his eye. He looked away immediately, his face flushed with embarrassment. There was something shameful in these voyeuristic glances, these domestic peepshows. But even so, as the bus pulled away, he turned from his book back to the window.

The next time they stopped, the doors opened, passengers alighting as a blast of freezing air entered, whipping a stray newspaper along the aisle. It slapped against his leg and when he peeled it away, he saw that it was the property section – prices beyond the reach of most, *conveniently situated, robust character;* houses that would never be a home, at least not for him.

He scrunched the newspaper into a ball and dropped it at his feet.

The mother with the crying child alighted next and he was glad of the peace, though he felt for the woman now battling through the squalls with the pushchair. He remembered days like that with his own children.

As the bus pulled away he looked back out of the window. Across the way, a man was chopping vegetables in his kitchen. It was the same room he had seen earlier, it even looked like the same house, the same man – he urged him not to look up, though he couldn't stop watching; had no desire, or the will, to look away.

The bus took the house from sight, and replaced it with another that looked just like it, and another. Slightly breathless and feeling dizzy, he returned to his book, hopeful that the words would anchor him, the story sever him from this floating feeling of dread. Again, the same sentence slipped through his mind, and no matter how many times he returned to it, its meaning was lost.

He looked back out of the window and wished he hadn't.

The same man, the same room – but, of course, how could that be? This time the man turned from the kitchen and entered the adjacent living room. (He wished that people would keep their curtains closed. Why display such intimate scenes?) The man kissed a woman seated at a table and ruffled the hair of a child sat beside her. He just had time to look up and catch his eye again before the bus passed.

THE FIRST THING he did when he got home was close all of their curtains. They didn't get much traffic on their narrow private road, but he didn't want to put their lives on show.

There was the sound of a key in the lock. The front door opened.

"Brian?"

"In here."

"God! The traffic was murderous," his wife said, entering the kitchen. "How was your day?"

"Yeah, you know…"

"Uh-huh. Darling, would you be a love and chop some vegetables for dinner, seeing as you're here? I just have a quick call to make."

Most evenings were like this; just the two of them. The boys rarely joined them for dinner. He wasn't even sure where they were.

He went through the vegetable drawer in the fridge and found two carrots that looked almost identical. He sliced the first one into eight approximately equal pieces before applying the knife to the second. He remembered the man looking at him through the kitchen window – the illicit glance that made the connection. He pressed down with the knife until a sudden sharp pain in his thumb made him look at the chopping board.

There was a fat scarlet disc next to the orange coin of the sliced carrot. He looked at the blood trickling down into his palm as he held up his hand, and a voice at his shoulder said, "Oh Brian love, you need to be more careful."

"Sorry," he said. "I was miles away."

IT DIDN'T MATTER how long he left it. Each time he stepped from the door, his neighbour would be stepping from his own home, briefcase in hand, his greeting always a jovial, "Off to work are we?" which he smiled and silently nodded at. He had no desire to engage him further.

The bus was overcrowded as usual that morning, and as usual he found something comforting in being part of the mass, losing his identity in the crush of swaying bodies. He couldn't see the windows from where he stood in the centre of the aisle, and so could not observe the houses that swept by.

The phone in his jacket pocket vibrated.

Dad. Am at Jases tonight. Ok?

He texted back *fine* before realising that he didn't know which of his teenage sons he was responding to.

When he got to work, he'd barely sat down before his colleague at the adjacent desk leaned over and said, "You'll never guess what's happened." How on earth was he supposed to respond to that? Regardless, it didn't seem to matter as Charles ploughed straight on. "Charlotte is preggers, and I think we all know who the father is, don't we, Brian?"

But he didn't know who Charlotte was let alone the father of her unborn child.

"Honestly, Charles. I have to get on."

He turned on his computer and glanced around the office as it booted up. All the way down at the other end of the large open-plan room he could see his manager moving behind the window of his private domain. Was he dancing?

After he had entered his password and logged onto the server, he opened the task list for the week only for an explosion of windows to erupt onto his screen. They kept multiplying, layer upon layer of nonsensical data, broken web-links and blank rectangles. No matter what he did, he couldn't shut them down; they appeared far more quickly than he could get to them.

"Ah, it's happened on your machine too," Charles said, leaning over his shoulder. He shrank away, aware of the warmth of his colleague's bulk so close to his back; the slightly stale odour of his deodorant. "Yeah, it's the whole office. One of the temps working late last night thought he'd try and download a naughty movie. Bye bye firewall. Anyway, IT are on it but it could take a while. It's sort of hypnotic isn't it?" Charles gestured at the endlessly spawning windows. "I dunno, what would you call it… An infinity of windows?"

His stomach lurched as he gazed into the screen, and he had to turn away. When he opened his eyes, the room was still spinning, swaying in time with his manager in his room, turning, his arms outstretched.

LIKE THE COMPUTERS in the office, the traffic was jammed. It took over an hour for the bus to turn up, and it then crawled sluggishly through the city. The bad tempers of his fellow commuters were barely contained by their dark muttering as they jostled against him. It was well past seven o' clock when they reached the outskirts of the town where he lived. One man standing towards the front of the bus had lost his patience, and was berating the driver for being lazy and blaming the bus company for running a shitty service.

The driver responded by stopping the bus and opening the doors.

"I'm going to have to ask you to remove yourself from the vehicle, please, sir."

"Is this a joke?"

"No. And unless you want to delay your fellow travellers further, and want me to call the police, then I suggest you step down."

"Are you fucking kidding me?"

One woman sighed deeply and shouted, "Look, just get off the bus. We're all going to be even later because of you."

"Yeah, you fucking wanker!" Another passenger called out. "Fuck off out of it so we can all get the fuck home."

He swallowed, dry-mouthed, feeling the tension rapidly rising. Squeezed as he was between many other bodies, he was acutely aware of his own vulnerability.

The driver was barely managing to contain himself now, as he shouted, "Get off the bus, or I will call the police. Get off the bus, or I will call the police."

"I ain't moving, mate."

But *he* was, thankful for his slim build as he made his way through the press of bodies – not caring about the muttered profanities his egress elicited as he forced his way into the night.

He quickly outpaced the flow of traffic. Had he stayed on the bus it would have taken an hour or more to get home, but on foot he could make the journey in half the time.

The houses he passed sat mostly in darkness, as though their inhabitants were stuck in the sluggish stream of vehicles that flowed beside him. The few lit windows he saw, he couldn't help but glance into. Most of the rooms were uninhabited – television sets playing to themselves, kitchens where pans bubbled with no one to attend them. A lot of the houses were larger than his, and he felt a pang of jealousy as he wondered how much they were worth.

He came to a house fronted by a glass porch, looking out onto a broad, newly-paved drive. He slowed his pace as he gazed into the enormous living room – warmly lit and tastefully furnished. He could imagine himself there, sitting on the plush sofa, reading a book as he sipped a glass of excellent red, waiting for his sons to join them for dinner, perhaps bringing along their girlfriends, introducing them to the family for the first time with shy smiles and coy hand holding. Yes, this looked like a place a family could live and be happy.

He'd taken two steps up the driveway before he realised what he'd done. He backed away, shame and embarrassment making him hurry towards the pavement; the sound of the front door opening and a voice calling out quickening his pace.

It was only when his name was called a second time that he turned.

"Brian, I thought that it must be you. Really, you should have parked the car on the drive. After all, we have more than enough space."

"I-I don't have a car."

"Written off the beemer, eh? Don't tell me that you took public transport. Not on a day like this."

"Well—"

"Tell you what, let's get a G&T in you and then you can tell me all about it."

As he stepped into the warmth of their home, not even the sound of the door closing behind him gave him pause for thought. Once over the threshold, he knew that he belonged.

The man left him in the lounge as he hurried away to prepare his drink, and as he sat on the sofa, the cushions settled to his form – not too soft, not too hard.

"Just right," he sighed.

A woman entered, her face lighting up at the sight of him. "Darling," she said, opening her arms. "Brian. So good to see you. I didn't notice your car in the drive."

"Yes, well, managed to write off the beemer, unfortunately."

She appeared to be a little older than his wife, though she was taller and more shapely. He could feel the push of her considerable bosom as they embraced.

"So sorry to hear that," she said. "How on earth did you manage to get here? Not public transport, I hope. Not on a day like this."

The woman gestured towards the window, but there was not a whisper of traffic on the road.

"There you go, old chap," the man said, returning and putting a drink into his hand.

He wasn't accustomed to drinking at home. He wife took the odd glass of wine with a meal, but he had never really developed the taste himself. As he took his first tentative sip, the man and woman watched him expectantly. The tonic did little to disguise the burn of the gin and he had to suppress a cough as he swallowed.

"Nice and strong, eh?" The man said. "Just the way you like it."

He noticed that neither the man nor woman had a drink in their hand.

"Now," the woman said, "I've promised a certain someone that if he's very good, he can come down and say hello before he goes to bed." The woman leaned out of the lounge door. "Sweetie?" she called.

There was the thunder of small footsteps descending the stairs and then a young boy ran into the room, crying, "Uncle Brian! Uncle Brian!"

Without thinking, he embraced the boy, looking down at the curly strawberry-blonde hair as the child threw his arms around his waist.

He pulled away and looked at the child, his breath catching in his throat as he saw the boy's face properly. It was as though he were looking at his own son, Stephen, at five years old. However, where Stephen had been an unusually surly toddler, seemingly full of contempt for his own father, this boy was clearly delighted to see him.

"Can we play, Uncle Brian?"

He looked up at the boy's parents, who were smiling.

"Okay, but five minutes and then bed, young man," the woman said. "I should be getting on with dinner. My love, can you give me a hand in the kitchen?"

The man and woman left.

On the thick-pile carpet of the cosy lounge, he and the boy constructed skyscrapers from colourful bricks, before knocking them down with savage glee. He lost himself in a playful, constructed Eden, adding to the boy's stories, delighting in their invention. He sat back on his heels as a thought came unbidden, as vicious as a lance: Barbara saying, *But you never play with them, Brian. They miss you terribly when you're not here.*

"I had to work. I did it for you all."

"Uncle Brian?"

He came back to himself, to the scatter of plastic bricks and the innocent eyes of the child. "Yes, erm…"

"I need a wee."

"Oh, well. Do you need my help?"

"No, thank you."

The boy scampered off, and he looked down at the house they had been building together. It was an elaborate construction, they had even gone so far as to place a family within: a plastic mum and dad with their plastic boys, each identically happy. He listened for the flush of the toilet. The boy must have been in there for at least ten minutes now. How long did it take to go for a piss, anyway? There were no sounds from the rest of the house, either. He would have expected a clatter of pans from the kitchen; the smells of cooking. It was so quiet he could hear the ticking of his wristwatch.

Outside, the soft whisper of traffic built to a steady roar. The phone in his breast pocket vibrated and he took it out to see that he had missed several calls and there was a text message from his wife.

I'm not angry, I just want to know where you are. That you're safe.

He looked down at the plastic house, a feeling of claustrophobia driving him towards panic.

He left the house, his stride just short of a run. He flagged down a cab and then sat frozen as his mind refused to deliver his address. Eventually, it came to him and the car made the short journey home.

There were lights on in the upstairs window when he alighted, but when he stepped through the front door and called out no one answered. In the kitchen he made himself a sandwich and listened to the sounds of footsteps crossing the ceiling. He waited for his wife to descend the stairs, but the footsteps retraced their path and then there was the creak of the bed settling. When he got into it a short time later, it was cold and she wasn't there. There was no light on in the bathroom and the boys' rooms were silent. He just had the energy to text his wife – *Home now xx* – before sleep took him.

THERE WAS NO one in the house when he awoke, though the lingering smell of toast in the kitchen reassured him that his wife must have set off early for the day.

As he stepped out of his front door, he turned to the right, expecting to be greeted by his neighbour, but the adjacent door was closed. It wasn't the weekend already, surely? He looked at his watch and saw that it was Wednesday; that felt about right. Even so, there was a strange atmosphere on the bus into work. His fellow commuters were as blank as ever, the bus driver, as usual, almost aggressively disinterested – he just felt that he was out of place somehow. In the office the sense of disconnect continued. He spent much of the morning wondering where he had left himself, feeling like a ghost as he sat on the same chair he had inhabited for twenty or so years.

Charles, for the first time since they had been working together, had dispensed with his usual false bonhomie. He swung his chair fractionally to the right. "Boss wants to see you."

"About what?"

"Not a clue. Computers are working again, by the way."

His manager had rarely been pleased to see him; in fact he was lucky if he ever got more than a slightly raised eyebrow in lieu of a greeting, so when he entered the office and was welcomed with a smile, he felt himself to be on the back-foot.

"Brian, good morning. Do have a seat. Scotch?"

"I… Scotch?"

"I don't usually advocate drinking during working hours, but a little pick-me-up, I find, helps to ease one into the day."

"I…"

"Excellent. On the rocks, isn't it?"

"I must admit, erm… Neil, that I'm not a big drinker."

But the Scotch was surprisingly smooth and went down a lot easier than last night's gin and tonic.

"Sorry to hear about the beemer, by the way. Stan told me you totalled it and had to get a bus, of all things, to his and Kit's place. Dreadful way to travel. I would have caught a cab myself."

Stan and Kit? He must have meant the couple from last night. The fact that his boss knew them went some way to easing his creeping sense of dread. It was possible, he supposed, that they had been introduced at some point and he had just forgotten.

Then he remembered the boy and, "Uncle Brian! Uncle Brian!"

"Anyway, Brian, two bits of good news. First, you'll be getting a company car, so you don't have to worry about that beemer. Secondly, you've been way below your paygrade for a while now, so how do you feel about a ten kay raise and a promotion to regional manager?"

Ten thousand pounds? He realised then that they would finally be able to afford that extension, and they deserved a holiday, the boys too.

"That sounds wonderful. How about we seal the deal over another Scotch?" he said, raising his glass.

HE DROVE HOME, a small part of him wondering why he hadn't had to sign anything before taking the car, but his worries were soon allayed by the smooth workings of the vehicle, the smell of new leather, the sense of whispering through traffic, rather than pushing against the homeward-bound exodus. As he drove onto the motorway, he began to overtake his usual bus, and slowed, wanting to see the faces of the passengers, wanting them to acknowledge, with an envious glance, that he was no longer part of the herd. All he could see through the heavily-misted windows, however, were pale ovals hunched above seatbacks, or swaying below wrist straps. Usually there would be more traffic at this time of the day, but his journey was effortless, and he listened with pleasure to the crunch of gravel under his tyres as he parked on their drive; a part of their house that hadn't seen a car for a good decade or more.

He was brought up short as his key refused to turn in the lock. He knew things hadn't exactly been amicable between him and his wife, but surely she wouldn't have gone so far as to change the locks? He rang the bell, and was disturbed not to hear the usual electronic tinkle – two tones, one high, one low.

Ding-dong.

His neighbour answered the door in a stained apron, a knife in his right hand. "Brian? Can I help you?" He looked past his shoulder. "Of course, if you need the space you're welcome to park here, but can I ask what is wrong with your drive?"

"Oh, I'm... this isn't..."

"Your house? No. Listen, I can see you've been overdoing it at work again, and really it shouldn't be our place to say this, but shouldn't you be thinking of spending more time at home with the family?"

"Of course, sorry. Sorry again to disturb you."

He moved the car to the adjacent driveway, and this time his key fitted the door just fine.

The door opened grudgingly, pushing a slew of unread mail before it. The house was cold and dark. He thought he heard footsteps descending the stairs, but when he looked up there was nobody there. He walked from room to room, always with the feeling that each time he entered, somebody had just left. The house felt wrong, and was this actually their lounge? He couldn't remember the sofa being that colour, and he certainly wouldn't have permitted that wallpaper with the bunches of tropical fruit and the parakeets. However, when he looked at the mantelpiece, the photo that stood there clearly showed him and his wife, and their two smiling boys; he wondered where that had been taken, they looked happy.

He took off his tie and sat for a moment in silence, looking at the blank screen of the television and his dim, distorted reflection. He wished he could recall having lived in this house, but he didn't have any recollection of the place at all. Clearly they had created a home together; the pencil marks on the wall by the door showed the boys' heights, year by year; the photos on the bookshelves of beach holidays they had apparently taken together – he supposed he must have been in love, the happy smile on his face in the pictures was testament to that.

He and his wife should be celebrating, toasting his promotion with champagne and an excellent meal, but there was nobody here to acknowledge his success

As he sat and waited, dawn rose. He couldn't remember sleeping, though he supposed he must have, as he didn't feel tired. He half expected to find the company car gone when he looked out the window – if anything, that really *had* felt like a dream – but it was still there.

He drove to work. He had his own office now, adjacent to his boss's and almost identical. He opened up a spreadsheet on his computer and stared at it blankly for a few moments before he realised that he actually had no idea what he did. The phone rang and he picked it up to be told that his first meeting of the day was here. The door opened and a large man blustered into the room, gripping his hand in a handshake that bordered on the aggressive.

"Great to see you finally being given the recognition you deserve, Brian. Long overdue. Long overdue."

For the whole of the hour that the man was in his office, he had little idea what he was talking about, though the interjections that he made were greeted with enthusiasm and emphatic agreement. By the end of the meeting he had come to the realisation that he *did* deserve his promotion and, really, what had taken them so long? He clearly was one of the most efficient and incisive members of staff. Buoyed by his new sense of success, that evening it felt as though his car drove him, rather than the other way around. He sat back and relaxed as the streets scrolled past the windows; the glass and metal towers of the business district stepping down to make way for the grimy terraces at the edge of the city, these, mercifully, giving way to the greenbelt that, in turn, was soon threaded with streets of neat semi-detached houses and soulless bungalows. Once he would have stopped here, but such a vehicle as he rode in didn't belong on any of the driveways he passed. Such a man as he would not be at home in any of these houses.

The properties he passed became more widely-spaced and larger;

grand gardens giving each house the illusion of privacy, the residents the lords and ladies of their own exclusive estates.

The car slowed and indicated, turning into a long, gravelled driveway that lead to a three-storey Georgian house. As soon as he saw it, he knew that this was what he had always envisioned. There really was no other place for him, or those he loved. The porch was lit by the soft glow of a carriage lamp. The door opened onto a large hallway and reception room. Everything was tastefully furnished, beautifully appointed, nothing like the house he had set off from that morning. That, after all, hadn't been his home.

Whatever was cooking in the kitchen smelled delicious. As he sat on the sofa in the vast living room, a drink was put into his hand, a kiss placed gently, and warmly, on his cheek. He smiled as her subtle perfume lingered. The solemn-faced boy that was ushered before him, just before seven o'clock, told him all about his day at school, and then beamed with delight at the praise he received, throwing his arms around him and saying, "I love you, Daddy," before scampering off to bed. There was soft music coming from somewhere. In the fireplace a log popped and the flames wavered. He looked at his glass and realised that it was empty. He waited for a while but no refill came. The lazy warmth emanating from the fire was making him sleepy and his head fell back against the cushions for a moment before he snapped awake. He looked at his still empty glass and got to his feet.

Beyond the living room, the corridor felt narrower than it had before. A chill breeze blowing under the front door cut across his ankles. The kitchen door was closed and there were no sounds issuing from the other side.

He knocked. "My love? Hello? Any chance of another drink?"

When no one answered, he opened the door and stepped through.

The woman who was kneeling beside a seated figure at the table looked up at him with accusing eyes. He had never before been looked at with such hatred, and it made him take a step back.

"And where," she shouted, "the fuck have you been?"

He recognised her, but, for the moment, couldn't place her face.

"Brian? Didn't you hear me?"

This was… Barbara. His wife? He wanted to take another step back, close the kitchen door, return to the well-appointed living room, gaze sleepily into the fireplace. But when he turned to look behind him, he found not a carpeted corridor, but a narrow flight of stairs.

"Brian! I'm talking to you."

"I'm… I'm sorry, my love." He took two steps into the shabby kitchen. There was that stain on the ceiling, put there one disastrous pancake day; those sun-faded curtains that they had always intended to replace but had never got round to. With a sinking feeling, a dread that filled the pit of his stomach, he knew for certain that this was his house. No, *their* house.

"Never mind where you've been, Brian," Barbara said. "The fact is that you're never here for the boys."

There was a sob from the young man sitting at the table and he moved round so that he could see him. It was his son... Jase? No, not Jase. That was who he had been going to stay with the... was it the other night? This was Steven, with this mousy brown hair, his perpetually slumped shoulders. He of the monosyllabic answers, sneers and contempt for his parents. He sat, his head in his hands, blood dripping from his nose, falling to the table; fat ruby coins.

He didn't know where their other son – Paul – was; Barbara probably didn't either.

"What happened?" He managed to say.

"He's been dealing again. I'm surprised he wasn't killed for his troubles this time."

He remembered playing with a child; their triumph and joy as they constructed plastic castles and houses, peopling them with happy plastic families. He remembered warm arms around him and, "I love you, Daddy." He remembered houses that should have been theirs, lives that had been lived, but not by them. He remembered looking into passing rooms with yearning and envy.

He supposed he could tell them about his promotion and the company car, but he didn't think that they would believe him.

He went over to the kitchen door, closed it and opened it, again and again – closed, open, closed, open. Each time, however, the scene beyond stayed the same: the same short hallway, the same narrow flight of stairs.

"We don't have to stay here," he said, turning back to the kitchen.

"This is our home," Barbara said.

"Trust, me, I'd rather be anywhere else than this fucking dump," said Steven.

He looked at them looking back at him, hurt and confusion in their eyes. It *would* work, he just had to trust his own instincts, believe in what he wanted for all of them.

He took Barbara's hand, put his other hand on Steven's shoulder.

"Come outside. I can fix this."

Barbara looked at him and he thought she might be afraid. "What do you mean?"

"We deserve better than this."

Reluctantly, his wife and son followed him outside.

"Come on," he said, opening the car's passenger door, "in you get."

"Brian, just tell us where we are going." Barbara said.

"Just trust me on this. Please."

Barbara's features softened a little. "You've got a lot to make up for."

He got into the driver's seat and turned the ignition key. It took a few tries to get the car started, as though it has sat unused for the best part of a week, but finally, with a sound somewhere between a cough and a groan, the engine spluttered into life.

He looked to either end of their road. He could see nothing beyond the weak glow of the streetlights but the night.

Though there was nobody to see, he indicated left and turned out of their drive.

None of the windows were lit in the houses they passed, and once past the last streetlight, the headlights illuminated only the road before them.

"Dad, where the fuck are we going?" Steven said.

He shifted into fourth gear and tried to ignore the darkness that surrounded them. He pictured the miles of road before them, the night giving way to broad swathes of countryside – rolling hills, distant mountains, a far lake catching the moonlight. He pictured the road narrowing, trees crowding in on either side, a canopy far overhead through which soft starlight filtered down. He pictured coming to iron gates that swung silently open at their approach, revealing a long, broad driveway, running straight to a large house. He pictured the warm glow coming from the windows, the soft crunch of gravel under their wheels as they came to a stop.

He pictured all of this as he willed the darkness to give way.

"Brian, where on earth are we going?"

"Home," he said, shifted into fifth gear, and put his foot down.

THE LANGUAGE OF BEASTS

I'D BEEN WORKING at the abattoir for almost four years before I discovered that I could read animal entrails. I was passing through the area where cattle carcasses are slit open when the tumbling of a cow's organs spoke to me. Those dark, glistening jewels – stomach, kidneys, liver – whispered as they fell. I only caught a few words, but what they conveyed... well, it was profound. When you tell people that you are a slaughter man... actually, you don't tend to, because folks have opinions, don't they? They'll imagine you wading through blood, up to your elbows in guts, but that's far from the truth. The abattoir is kept cleaner than my kitchen. Everything is regulated and accounted for. Anyway, when people find out that you are a slaughter man, inevitably, the first question they ask is, "What's it like, seeing an animal die?"

It isn't like anything. One jolt and they're out. Quick and dull.

And then there's, "I bet working there has made you a vegetarian."

No. Not me. I love meat. I just never expected it to talk to me.

ENTRAILS ONLY SPEAK if they are fresh. It's no good buying a packet of chicken livers from the supermarket, dumping them on the kitchen counter and expecting them to sing. They've already told their story, and likely to one who wasn't listening. Thousands of chickens are processed at the plant every day, and not every slaughter man has the gift. There are others, though.

One afternoon, heading out from the killing floor to go for a smoke, I paused to watch the evisceration of a pig. The man who was working on the hog removed its heart and lungs and hung them on a hook, ready to be processed for pet food. The heart was unusually large for a pig of that size, and there was just enough left in it that I could make out a few words before the organ fell silent. These I quickly wrote down in a small notebook. When I looked up, I caught the eyes of the pig butcher and he nodded, as though to acknowledge the truth of what I had just written. I quickly looked away, feeling momentarily guilty, caught in the act.

Later, in the canteen, the butcher sat opposite me and pushed a used scratch card across the table.

"What this?" I said.

"Five hundred pound win, that."

"Okay, so?"

"Want to know how I did it?"

"It's luck. Nothing more."

"No, mate. I won that because a pig's insides told me the numbers."

I blinked at the winning card. "Bollocks."

"Come on, I know that you're a hepatomancer."

"A... what?"

"One who can read what is inside. I saw you writing in your little book. But you're going to have to be a bit more subtle about it if you don't want to get into trouble. Start hanging around, gawking like that, and you'll have people thinking that there's something wrong with you, that you're some kind of pervert."

"So, what do I do?"

"There's a group of us. We get together every Wednesday and swop stories over a pint or three. Fancy coming along?"

IT WAS A fair walk from my place to the Brewery Tap, and when I saw that it was one of those estate pubs with a flat roof, I almost turned back. Such boozers may serve cheap drinks but they're pressure cooker environments; violence barely held in check. One of the windows had been boarded over; a chalkboard out front announced that Wednesday night was Meat Raffle Night. How appropriate.

I smelled our group before I saw them. No matter how many showers you take, something of the abattoir will always cling to you. It's not an unpleasant smell, but it is distinctive, *raw*.

There were three men sitting in a booth. The pig butcher – Markus – was the only one I recognised. I saw that their drinks were low, so I offered to get a round in.

"No need," Markus said. "Lloyd's at the bar already. What you drinking?"

"Scotch."

"Lloyd? Add a Scotch to that, yeah?"

The drinks arrived and Markus made the introductions. Lloyd I'd met before. The other two were Sean, who worked in admin, and Dave – isn't there always a Dave? – who'd recently started at the abattoir, but apparently showed "great promise."

"Chaps, this is Alex," said Markus, gesturing to me. "Needless to say, he's one of us."

Nobody used the word 'magic', though that's what we talked about. The other men in the group referred to themselves as Readers. Only Markus referred to himself as a hepatomancer, the pretentious twat. Aside from Markus's lottery win, Lloyd had backed a winning horse, twice, Sean had bet on the right dog, and Dave had helped his Nan to a victory streak on the bingo. All thanks to their gift for reading entrails.

"So, how come you're all still working down the abattoir?" I asked.

"How do you mean?" said Dave.

"Well, if you can just read the offal and pick a winner, can't you keep yourselves in readies that way?"

"The biggest win we've had was the five hundred on that scratch card," Markus said. "And the wins are few and far between. Dave got lucky. It look Sean and Lloyd considerably longer. Anyway, at the moment we're investing our winnings."

"Investing them in what?"

"The big one," Lloyd said.

"The problem with trying to get a proper read at the abattoir," Sean said, "is that everything is processed so quickly. You usually only get, well... bits and pieces."

"You get the best read if you take your time," Markus said. "Hepatomancy is an art. It shouldn't be rushed."

"Ideally, you should read an animal you've slaughtered yourself," Lloyd added. "That way your bond with the meat is that much greater. You get the time to properly see what's there."

"Speaking of which, gentlemen..." Markus said, necking the rest of his pint. "Shall we?"

"Are we going somewhere?"

"We need to see how you do it, Alex. Get a read on your read."

"And I have a chicken," Dave said.

WE ALL CRAMMED into the back of a cab. I sat sandwiched between Dave and Sean. The driver had turned up the heater way too high, and by the time we got to Dave's place, I was feeling more than a little sick. The blast of cold air as I got out of the car provided a welcome respite.

Dave's house was part of a non-descript terrace. From the level of squalor in his lounge, he clearly lived alone. In the small backyard – beyond a kitchen with a peeling lino floor – a tatty chicken scuttled up and down a narrow cage. It would be a mercy to put this bird out of its misery.

Dave opened the top of the cage and lifted out the hen. "Hey there, Masie. Come on now. Nice and calm."

The chicken was passed over and I took it. It looked at me with its stupid beady eyes, head cocked. I didn't have a great deal of hope that it would give up any significant secrets.

"Right you are then, Alex." Markus said. "You do the business and we'll see what's what."

"You want me to kill it?"

"Of course. You're a slaughter man, aren't you?"

But there's a world of difference between firing a bolt through the skull of an animal that's already been restrained and stupefied, and slitting the throat of a live animal while holding it upside down over a kitchen sink. Blood sprayed across the sink, arced over the counter, and splattered the mugs of tea that Dave had just made for us.

"I asked for two sugars, not half a pint of blood, you cunt," Markus said, laughing.

I waited until the chicken stopped twitching before I pulled fistfuls of feathers from the breast, revealing just enough of its flesh to give me an in.

"Can I get a bowl?" I said.

Markus and the others crowded round as I eviscerated the chicken and put its organs into the bowl that Dave had provided.

"Do you see the way the lungs are resting against the heart there?" Sean said, leaning in for a closer look.

"Easy, mate," Dave said. "This is supposed to be Alex's read."

I took the organs out of the bowl and placed them on the kitchen counter.

Those gathered around me were no doubt expecting numbers for that Saturday's lottery draw, or the name of a derby-winning horse.

But that's not what I saw.

"I'm not sure. There are things… but…"

"It's alright, Alex." Markus said. "It can take a while. We're not expecting you to be dead on first time round."

Dead. There was nothing wrong with the chicken's liver, but when I picked it up, I knew that there was something seriously wrong with Dave's.

"He's got something. You've got something, haven't you?" Dave said.

It was inevitable. It would come on swiftly, unexpectedly. Dave would be dead within three weeks.

Steadying my breathing, I put the liver down and said, "Yes, I've got something. Fetch me a pen and paper."

I wrote down six numbers at random. Dave took the paper and looked at it with a delighted expression, as though I had solved all our problems.

"Nice work," Lloyd said, patting me on the back.

Once I'd washed my hands and Dave had plucked the chicken and put it in the fridge, we sat in the living room, and I asked, "So, what's this 'big one' you were talking about in the pub?"

"Well," Markus said, "as we were saying earlier, you get tend to get more of a significant read on a bigger animal. So, we're saving up to buy our own cow."

They were all looking at me expectantly, as though I'd agree that this was a brilliant idea.

"Okay. So, once you've got this cow, where are you planning on slaughtering it? Surely not at the abattoir where they monitor everything?"

"There's a patch of ground near Tilsley Woods," Lloyd said.

"That's going to be tricky; not just transporting the animal," I said, "but killing it out in the open without the use of proper restraints."

"We'll manage," Markus said, dismissing my concern. "So, are you in?"

Perhaps I could think of it as a strange sort of social club, I reasoned. I'd been glad of the company that night. Sure, these men may not have been amongst my usual circle of friends, but as I had no circle at that time to speak of, who was I to be picky?

"I'm in."

Dave cheered and treated us all to the contents of his liquor cabinet.

BY PURE CHANCE, three of the numbers I had written down turned out to be spot on.

"That's twenty-five pounds towards the cow," Markus said, proudly. "What's wrong? You don't seem particularly happy."

"It's Dave," I said.

"Trust me, you're doing better than he did. It took Dave much longer than that to give us a halfway decent read."

"It's not that, Markus. The chicken entrails didn't give me those winning numbers – that was a fluke – but they did show me how and when Dave is going to die."

The colour drained from Markus's face and he put down his knife and fork. "Just Dave?"

I smiled. Trust Markus to think of himself first. "Yes, just Dave."

"Have you told him?"

"No. Of course, he might already know what he's got, but I doubt that he knows the exact time and date of his death."

"Well, we should tell him."

"I don't think that going in mob-handed is the answer. This should come from me."

I GAVE IT a couple of days before I approached Markus again; plenty of time in which to have spoken to Dave, though I neither intended to nor did.

"Fancy a pint?" I said, waiting until Markus had finished processing the pig carcass that was hanging before him.

"Sure. It's a bit short notice, like, but I'll let the lads know."

"No need, mate. I wanted a chance to chat with you in private. I think you'll want to hear what I have to say."

"Alex... *Alex!*" I was being glared at by the floor manager. "Can you and your boyfriend do this some other time? Those pigs aren't going to butcher themselves."

There were wolf whistles and cries of "Get a room!" Markus actually blushed.

"Meet me at The Grapes at seven-thirty."

IT BEING A Monday night, The Grapes was virtually empty.

Markus arrived twenty minutes late with alcohol on his breath. That had me worried that he'd been with the others beforehand, but more than likely he'd just had a nip of something before coming out.

"What's this about?" he said, sitting down without getting himself a drink.

It occurred to me then that Markus was scared of me.

"The results you're getting from animals, they're good, Markus, but you could be getting more."

"More what?"

"Knowledge, power."

"Money?"

"That too."

"I think we've got a pretty good thing going, Alex."

"Sure, but you don't want to be working at the abattoir forever, do you?"

Markus shrugged. "It's a job."

"But you could have a *lot* more."

"How so?"

"I know when Dave is going to die, to the exact minute; I've already read that, as you know. And you also know that with a bigger animal you get a better read."

"No. No no, mate. What that is is murder."

"For pity's sake, keep your voice down! No, Markus, it is not murder. In a matter of weeks Dave is going to be dead either way. There's nothing to be done about that. But we can make his death mean something."

"But what you're suggesting is wrong."

"Listen, Dave is okay with this. I've already talked to him."

"You have?"

"Yes," I lied.

Dave was stupid. Dave wasn't the sort of person to go to a doctor. He'd told me he didn't trust doctors. He'd pass away, lying in his grubby bedroom, pale as wax against the soiled sheets. A lot about Dave repulsed me, but it was his insides I was interested in.

"And what do we do about the body? Even if we put the organs back, someone is going to notice that he's been interfered with."

"Well, we'll have to dispose of it."

"Christ, I feel sick. I think I need a drink. You need another?"

"Double Scotch, ta."

Markus's hand shook as he placed the drink before me. The fact that he hadn't done a runner spoke highly of him. "We'll be careful won't we, Alex?"

"Of course we will."

"And it will be worth it?"

"Oh yes, trust me on that."

The good thing about Markus was that he was greedy. To be honest, I had no idea whether going through Dave's entrails would make us richer, not in the monetary sense. Whatever he would reveal, however, would be priceless.

BREAKING INTO A dead man's house proved trickier than I had anticipated. The first thing I checked for was a key under the plant pot out the front, but though Dave was stupid, he wasn't that stupid.

It was around two in the morning and the street was quiet but for a few yobs gathered around a car blaring drum and bass, or techno, or whatever the fuck it is that kids listen to these days. In any case, their music helped mask the crunch of splintering wood as Markus shouldered in the door as surreptitiously as he was able.

Dave's house stank. His cat looked like it had starved to death and then something had had a go at eating it. Markus gagged, but I pushed him quickly through the lounge before he had the urge to vomit.

Up the stairs we went, Markus treading as lightly as an inept cat burglar. I gestured him back as I turned the handle to Dave's bedroom. Inside, it smelt almost as bad as the lounge. I crept to the edge of the bed, and sure enough Dave was still breathing. It was no trouble helping him along with a pillow to the face. He didn't even struggle.

I leaned back out of the door. "It's alright, Markus. You can come in now."

The first thing we did was cover the room with plastic sheeting, like that chap from *Dexter*. Disposing of the body would be bad enough, but I didn't also want the hassle of having to clean the carpets and the furniture. This would be messy, and we could hardly hang the corpse upside down from the light fitting and bleed it. It took us an hour or two to get the room prepped and by the end of that we were sweating like bastards. We stopped for a smoke and a couple of tins.

"It's what he would have wanted," Markus said, looking over at Dave's corpse.

I very much doubted it. Then again, Dave struck me as the sort of man who didn't know what he wanted.

I belched and opened up my kit bag.

"Right, let's get on with this shall we?" I said, gesturing to the implements within.

"Where did you get that lot?"

"C.O.W. Courtesy of work. Don't worry, we'll clean and sterilise them and be in first thing Monday to return them. No one will be any the wiser."

I'd never eviscerated a human before. I went in through the front, carefully; I didn't want to rupture anything and be up to my elbows in shit and half-digested food. I pulled back Dave's skin and started to flense away the fat and the membrane sheathing the organs.

Markus watched silently, a look of fascinated horror on his face, as though he had never seen the insides of an animal before. With the layers of fat and other material cut away, the organs were revealed, and I gestured to the cavity I had excavated, turning to Markus with my eyebrows raised. He lit a cigarette and stared down at the cadaver. I could see where the loops and curls of the intestine formed a curious script, and I was just beginning to comprehend some of it when Markus gestured at the glistening coils. "Get that shit out of the way for starters."

Shit is exactly what we smelt as I removed Dave's intestines, and I too lit a cigarette, to mask the smell as I worked. I laid the intestines carefully beside the corpse, making sure they remained in roughly the same formation they had taken in the abdominal cavity.

"May I?" said Markus, reaching for the knife. I nodded and stepped back, standing by the open window, taking deep breaths of fresh air as he crouched over the corpse.

Markus removed Dave's liver. It was far darker than it should have been, nobbled with fat, looking as though it would burst in his hands.

"This is what killed him, so this is where we'll start." He pulled up a chair to the foot of the bed and sat with the organ in his lap, staring at it intently. I looked back at the intestines lying on top of the plastic sheeting. There was definitely something there, written in that strange curling script, a message in a mound of flesh, but the words faded as the organ cooled; the further away it got from being alive, the more fragile the meaning. I grabbed my notebook and scribbled down what I could before it entirely dissipated.

"Got something?" Markus said.

"I think so," and I showed him my notes.

"I don't get it."

"No." I hadn't expected him to. "What about you? Have you found something?"

"Oh yes," Markus said. "You were right, Alex. This is far bigger than anything you can get from an animal." And he squeezed the liver so hard that I stepped back, fearing that it would rupture.

After that we examined Dave's lungs, kidneys and stomach – we even prodded his bladder – but any insights the organs may have contained had now faded.

We put Dave's innards back roughly where we had found him and I stitched him up.

By the time we had tidied out the room and got the body into the boot of my car, the first light of dawn had touched the horizon.

"I'm knackered, mate," Markus said. "Mind dropping me back at mine? I'm in desperate need of some kip."

"You're joking aren't you? No. You're going to help me with the contents of my boot. There's no way I'm doing this solo."

It took us most of the rest of the day to dispose of the body, discretely and quietly. By the time we had finished, Markus looked as white as a sheet, near enough a corpse himself. I agreed to drop him off at his house, and as he climbed from the car, I reached over and grabbed his arm.

"Let's not tell the others about this right away, yeah? Let's keep this for us, just for the time being."

Markus nodded and stumbled towards his front door.

I watched him go and then headed for home.

TWO WEEKS AFTER we delved within Dave, Markus turned up at work in a brand-new sports car.

"Either you're having a mid-life crisis," Lloyd said, "or you've come into some money."

"Well, an aunt I never knew passed away and it seemed a shame not to do something with my new-found inheritance."

Markus was a bloody awful liar, but Lloyd just nodded, eyed the Toyota covetously and said, "Something to look forward to, come the big one, eh Sean?"

Sean was leaning against the wall, smoking and watching us all with a bemused expression.

Part of me wanted to tell them that we had gone even bigger than the 'big one', but I realised that they were not to be trusted with such knowledge. Each of them was only in this for monetary gain. I had shared something of a sacred moment with Markus as I had opened up Dave's corpse, and he had used the unique insights received on something as meaningless as a new car.

"Lads," he said, pointing the key fob at the bright red monstrosity and locking it, "after the big one, we'll all be driving these beasts. And who knows, maybe we won't have to work in this shithole for much longer."

DAVE'S DISAPPEARANCE WAS commented upon, but only in passing. It turned out that nobody in our group had much liked him. As far as most of them were concerned, the old piss-head had probably wondered off and gone for a nap in a bush and just not woken up. When I wasn't working, I poured over the words and fragmented phrases I had gleaned from his intestines. They were either verse from a strange poem, or weird religious rhetoric – I just couldn't get a handle on what I'd found. I could tell that the words were important, desperately important, but I had no idea what they meant.

I still went to the weekly meeting at the Brewery Tap, though I didn't really pay attention to what was said. I even agreed to cough up the £700 required from me for the buy-in on the cow. Having part-shares in a heifer didn't exactly fill me with joy, but it was all for show. If I changed tack now, I'd draw their suspicion. I hoped I wouldn't need Markus and crew for much longer. I had to keep the faith that at some point that which had been revealed by Dave's corpse would become clear.

The date for the evisceration of the cow was set for the middle of the following month. Lloyd would rent a van and he and Sean would drive the animal to Tilsley Woods around 3am. Markus and I would be there, ready to meet them and carry out the deed. Lloyd mentioned some nonsense about the positions of the constellations on that night, but it was clear that nobody put much credence in his words.

A couple of weeks before our date with the cow found me in a state of despair. Despite my ministrations, nothing that I had divined from Dave's guts had offered up a revelation. It was true that I could have probably put what I had already learned towards financial gain – as Markus had – but there was so much more to the words I had written down.

I was beginning to resign myself to the mostly thankless task of rooting around a cow's insides when an incident at work changed everything.

MARKUS HAD BECOME increasingly cocky since our evening of divination with Dave – messing about with others at work when he should have been attending to the animal in front of him; taking longer smoke breaks than usual; even answering the supervisor back.

One afternoon, he burst into song as he was in the process of cutting up a cow – I seem to remember it was *Money, Money, Money* by ABBA – and he swung around the electric saw as the animal's entrails fell, showing off. I don't know exactly what happened, maybe the blade of the saw glanced off a bone, or Markus fumbled his hold due to his gloves being covered in blood, but the next thing I heard was an awful screech as the saw swung into his torso.

He dropped to the floor, falling amongst the offal and off-cuts. His boiler suit was slashed open at his midriff and I could see the wound in his side: the flesh had been neatly parted and his organs were already squeezing through the rent in his body.

I should have raced across the room and hit the power-down button; I should have called for help.

Instead, I used the moment of confusion to hurry to Markus's side. I crouched over him, as though to comfort or reassure him, but really I wanted to hide what I was about to do. I knew Markus was going to die. I had heard the words – whispered at first, but rising to a shout only a select few could hear – as his organs were exposed to the air. I had no doubt he would have done the same were our positions reversed, so I felt no guilt about sliding my hand between the lips of the wound and running my fingers over the wet jewels that pulsed within.

Markus screeched even louder; his face awash with tears and snot. He was deathly pale. It was clear that he didn't realise what was happening as he looked at me with terror-filled eyes.

"Shh, mate. Shh. It won't take long, and you'll give me – *us* – so much."

My hand rested on Markus's liver and it immediately begun to speak, the words so powerful that they buffeted me like a shockwave; I closed my eyes as I focused on committing them to memory. The fragments and partial phrases that I had gleaned from Dave's viscera were here continued; the story was enriched. What had made little sense before started to become clear. Though I realised, as the whispers enfolded me, that there was still much to tell. It was a shame I didn't get longer with Markus, but with a spasm – blood spraying from his mouth in a final cough – he died. The words fragmented as the syntax distorted, meaning crumbled. The supervisor raced towards me, carrying the redundant medical kit. I bowed my head over Markus's corpse and jolted my shoulders in a feigned sob.

I looked up. "He's gone," I gasped. "It was so quick... so, horrible!"

I rose to my feet and ran from the room, scrabbling in my pocket for my notebook, desperate to write down the words that had been revealed.

WHAT HAD BEGUN in Dave's intestines had continued with Markus's liver. The phrases I had written down in the squalid bedroom over Dave's corpse were now given context, further meaning, but I still hadn't got the entire story. I felt that I was close to some revelation, something that would bring me so much more than a new car, or even a new house. Whatever was in these words would *mean* something. But the writing in my book still refused to yield to my scrutiny. I threw it across the room and shouted "fuck it" at the top of my lungs, which started off the neighbour banging on the connecting wall, again.

WE MET AT the Brewery Tap a few days after Markus's death, and sat awkwardly sipping our drinks, avoiding each others' gaze.

Sean was the first to break the silence.

"Cunt."

"What?" Lloyd said.

"Markus. He was a stupid cunt."

"Asked you to write his eulogy have they?"

"No, I mean it. He got cocky, complacent. So, let me state for the record right now, that whatever we find inside that cow won't change me like that."

"That's still on is it?" I asked.

"Of course. We're all paid up. I'm still ready to go."

"To be honest, mate," Lloyd said, "I'm not sure I've got the stomach for it anymore."

A part of me wanted to reply, "Neither has Markus," but I held my tongue.

"It's what Markus would have wanted." Sean said.

"Are you sure?" I said. "Only, a second ago you were calling him a cunt."

AT MARKUS'S FUNERAL it became clear that none of us had really known him. He had a wife and two children that he had never told us about, and the vicar doing the eulogy called him a valuable member of the church community. I was almost temped to take a peek in the coffin to check that we were honouring the right stiff.

Afterwards, in the nearby working men's club, over warm canapés and weak beer, Sean laid out the plans for the following night.

Lloyd was back in, which was just as well, as he was the only one of us with a valid driving license. He and Sean would drive the cow to the woods where I would be waiting with the equipment to stun and butcher it. Anything we divined from the entrails we agreed to share, and the same went for any money gained from our divinations.

Rain had been forecast, but in the event it was crisp and clear. This far away from the city's lights, the stars were brighter than I had ever seen them, and, looking up, I did wonder whether there was anything in what Lloyd had said about the auspicious positions of the constellations.

I heard the van long before I saw it. Along with the sound of an engine on its last legs, there was an irregular metallic booming, like someone beating on a garage door with a hammer.

Lloyd drove the van into the clearing, the balding tyres bouncing the vehicle over the uneven ground, kicking up divots of mud, pulling up just before the tree-line, the breaks squealing. When they got out of the van, I saw that Sean and Lloyd were drenched in sweat. As we looked at each other, the lowing and banging of the cow set the vehicle rocking.

"Please tell me that thing's restrained," I said.

"It is," Lloyd said, "but I don't think Sean tightened the ropes sufficiently."

"Oh that's a bit fucking rich that is," Sean said, turning on Lloyd.

"'I'm just the driver,' he kept saying. Well we'd have been here a bloody sight quicker if he'd helped me get the bastard cow into the van."

"Well, we're here now," I said. "So I'd appreciate it if you two could get the cow out of the van without getting trampled or gored in the process."

The cow was eventually unleashed, Sean and Lloyd hanging onto it like a couple of drunks at a county fair trying to take their prize bull to auction.

Bolt guns are not designed to be used on a moving target. Twice I lunged in, only to be shoved aside by a heaving, sweating flank. We were being pushed dangerously close to the road when I finally darted forward and discharged the weapon against the forehead of the cow. It wasn't as clean a shot as I would have liked; the bolt went in at an angle and pushed the cow's right eye most of the way out of its socket. Even so, it dropped instantly.

We stood over it, hands on our knees, panting for breath. Lloyd went to reach for his cigarettes but I stayed his hand.

"No," I said. "We have to do this *now*."

There's a world of difference between eviscerating a cow that has already been skinned and hung for you, and one that is slumped on the ground, its last breath misting in the night air. Still, this didn't have to be neat; there was no way this beast was going on to be choice cuts and beef burgers.

"So," Sean said, "who wants to be mother?"

"I reckon it should be Alex," Lloyd said. "Seeing as how he was so spot on with that chicken."

"You flatterer you," I replied and knelt to the cow.

We all gathered around, staring into the bulging opening I made like a group of art critics trying to read meaning in a surreal installation.

"Well, the stomach's giving me nothing," Sean said after a while, before turning to us. "Chaps?"

Lloyd shook his head. "Nada. Alex, get rid of the stomach and see where that takes us."

I hauled out the cow's guts, and as Lloyd and Sean had already observed, there was nothing to be read. Even so, I heard a muffled whispering coming from somewhere, though when I paused to listen, I couldn't be sure that it originated in the carcass.

"That's more like it," Lloyd said, lifting up the left foreleg and peering into the cavity. "Lungs and heart for sure. But you're going to have to move quickly, Alex. The fresher they are, the better the read."

Sean pressed forward. "You're right, Lloydy. No doubt about it. Alex, cut them out, sharpish like."

"If you fuckers step back and give me some room, I might actually be able to see what I'm doing."

Sean and Lloyd set to dispensing 'helpful' advice as I began to carefully remove the organs; that combined with the poor light and the urgency of the task made my hands less steady than they should have been. The blade slipped.

I was lucky. A couple more inches to the right and I would have been fountaining blood. Instead, I gave myself a nasty, deep gash just below my left thumb.

"Bastard!" I cried.

Lloyd was more concerned with the cow's entrails than with me. He took the knife from my hand and shoved me aside so that he could finish the job. I clutched my left hand in my right, blood welling up between my fingers, and as I bled, the whispering became clear.

The story that I had read the beginning of in the curls of Dave's intestines, which had continued in Markus's liver, would be finished within me.

"Mate, you have to see this," Sean said, holding the cow's lungs in front of my face, his arms streaked with blood and offal. But what did I care for the words pouring from that cooling organ? The meaning to be read there wasn't anything like as revelatory as that which was trickling from me now.

The bleeding slowed as the blood began to clot, and the words once more died down to a whisper.

"We're going to be rich, Alex," Sean said, shaking his grisly prize. "I just know it."

TO READ ONESELF – the revelations that the act would bring would change everything, but would I be able to open myself? I had experimented with merely bleeding, cutting deep but superficial wounds into my arms and legs, but though I had divined a few words

– a sense of the importance of that which lay within – it did not give me any viable results. I contemplated asking Lloyd and Sean to help me out, but this message wasn't for them, they wouldn't know what to do with such knowledge – wouldn't know how it could be used to change everything – and I didn't entirely trust either of them with a blade.

No. I had to do this myself.

A little internet research suggested the foolhardiness of such an undertaking. But true pioneers are not to be dissuaded by the threat of danger, and if I died in the process, at least I would have died trying.

I took an entire week off work, unsure as to how much time I would need to recover from the self-administered operation. Though I worried that they would blunt senses vital to the process, I realised that I wouldn't be able to tolerate the pain without some chemical intervention, and so I solicited the services of a friend of one of my work colleagues: a man who frequented the Brewery Tap and looked like he was probably responsible for the bar room brawls that often broke out there. "These will either sort you out, or fucking kill you," he said, surreptitiously palming a small packet into my hand. "Looking at you, though, mate. I'm not sure that bothers you."

Once the drugs had taken effect, it was all I could do to maintain a steady hand on the knife. I had thought to perform the operation while lying on my bed, but felt that such a prone position could be disadvantageous and, ultimately, more dangerous. Instead, I sat upright in a tatty old armchair in front of the television. I had prepared the lounge with plastic sheeting on the floor and furniture, and I had my mobile phone to hand should something go wrong and I needed to call for assistance.

The knife felt freezing cold as the blade sank into the flesh and began to part it; the pain almost made me stop, and it would have done if it weren't for the crowd of voices that filled the room with that first incision. They spoke of the treasure that lay within; the knowledge that could be gained from truly knowing oneself; the power that would come to me if only I could reach inside. What I had read within Dave and Markus – that had been only a fragment of the story.

Finally I was open. My screams had elicited the rage of my next-door-neighbour who started shouting and banging on the wall. I only hoped I had time to finish what I started before she made good on her threat to call the police. I reached inside myself and it was the most intimate thing I had ever experienced. I had to fight against the urge to eviscerate myself entirely, to pull out handfuls of organs and lay them on the ground before me. It would be pointless to gain this forbidden knowledge if I was unable to use it. My hand rested on the mound of my intestines, caressed the smooth curves of my liver. I would have gladly stayed like that for ever. Instead I withdrew my hand, wiped away the worst of the gore, and wrote down what I had learned, before carefully stitching myself back up. That done, I passed out.

I came to sometime later, relived that I hadn't died, and invigorated by what I had learned. I had to peel the plastic sheeting away from where it was stuck to me by dried blood. I looked over what I had written and immediately called the abattoir, telling them that I wouldn't be returning to work. I didn't need it, and with what I now knew I wouldn't need to work ever again.

MINE IS NOT the only story. The entrails of animals provide us with an inkling of the bigger picture, but that's all you get – the merest inkling, the merest whiff of power. It is within ourselves that the biggest stories are told. I am living proof that we can read those stories, live and share them with others, and in so doing change our world.

So, this is what I will do. I will bring the good news to others. All I need is a sharp knife, and a small amount of your time.

Jonathan Oliver is the British Fantasy Award winning editor of *House of Fear, Magic, End of the Line, The End of The Road, Dangerous Games, Five Stories High* and *World War Cthulhu*. For almost thirteen years he was the Editor-in-Chief of Abaddon Books and Solaris, and for five years served his time as a 2000 AD editorial droid. He lives in Oxfordshire with his family.

Lightning Source UK Ltd.
Milton Keynes UK
UKHW041118181120
373486UK00021B/82